FANTASY PLAY

HOTEL™

ATWOOD COLEMAN II

Fantasy Play Hotel™
Atwood Coleman II

Jodie Jamison

A Fantasy Play Series Book

To request permissions, contact the publisher at info@flyingbluemonkeypress

Paperback ISBN # 978-1-7366347-4-5

Library of Congress Number 2021907395

First edition

Edited by Brett Kinsey
Cover Art by MJCImageworks

You may additionally enjoy these titles published by
Flying Blue Monkey Press LLC

Fantasy Play 101 by Kattrina "Katt" Morgan
ISBN: 978-1-7366347-0-7

Lacey Unlocked: Atwood.Coleman I by Jodie Jamison
ISBN: 978-1-7366347-1-4

Printed in the USA

Flying Blue Monkey Press LLC
350 North Leavitt Road
Unit #1271
Amherst, Ohio 44001

www.flyingbluemonkeypress.com

Dedicated to those with passion discovered,
and the courage to follow after.
Lacey

CHAPTER 1

Nick nudged me, letting me know the plane was preparing to land. We made it! South Carolina! Two weeks of no work, which meant two weeks of Nick *and* Frankie to myself! I was surprised I had fallen asleep as my mind was all over the place due to the evening's long-overdue conversation, and Mr. Sandman had taken his time to arrive. Both Nick and I were less than thrilled by the increasing dangers of my job, and the latest incident with Jack Turner solidified that. I knew it was time to make some life changes; however, I wasn't sure which direction I wanted to pursue next.

Nick reminded me there would be one less bill to pay when I ultimately made a move into his place — our place — next month. Besides, Katt Morgan's generous compensation for the Fantasy Play Hotel™ photo deal was more than enough to keep me afloat during the time it would take to find a new venture to pursue. Still, walking away from social work was easier said than done. We agreed to shelve the conversation for the next fourteen days, and I was more than eager to shove everything "social work" to the back of my mind.

I gently lifted the hard plastic window shade and looked out the window. We were flying over the ocean, and I watched as the sun transformed the vast blueness into countless shimmering shards of brilliant liquid glass. An excited giddiness overtook me. According to the weather forecast, two full weeks of beautiful weather lay ahead. Nick was excited to introduce me to the city he loved, and we planned to keep an open schedule as much as possible. These two weeks were to be a stress-free time of recharging, and that was something we both deserved *and* needed.

Nick did have a meeting with a few Charleston gallery owners on Monday regarding a business proposition similar to "Cleveland in the Streets." Additionally, the hotel's grand opening was next Saturday, which meant I had exactly eight days to prepare mentally. Besides those two scheduled events, we wanted to spend some quality time with Mark and focus on spending the rest of the trip as typical southern tourists.

Thank God for Mark Santauri, Nick's best friend, who had pulled off some magic for our visit. Over the past few years, he had developed a vast network of friends, including some of Charleston's wealthier couples, the Morettis being one of them. The couple had "adopted" Mark as a pseudo-son when he first moved to Charleston, with Frank Moretti eagerly stepping into the role of fill-in father as well as having become a valuable business mentor. Fortunately, Nick and I now reaped the benefits of that relationship.

Quite coincidentally, the annual Moretti family trip to Italy landed on the same dates as our visit to Charleston. Buster, the family's St. Bernard, would *not* be going to Italy and would need a sitter. When Mark told Nick that the Moretti home was on Rainbow Row, his face lit up like a little boy on Christmas morning. I had no idea of the historical or financial implication of owning a house on the famed street until Nick told me. Now that I did, I was just as excited to see our home away from home for the next two weeks.

Mark was our welcoming committee as the Morettis had left for Italy early morning, and he was doing an excellent job of it already. Nick received a "***show this to Lacey***" text with an attached photo before departing Cleveland. The home's secluded ivy-covered and cobble-stoned back patio, complete with fountain, called my name, and I already pictured myself spending many an early morn or moonlit evening surrounded by those stone walls. Mark added that something was wrong with us if Nick and I could not relax and enjoy ourselves in that home. No worries there!

Twenty minutes later, our plane landed, and after grabbing our luggage and securing our rental car, we were on our way. The car's temperature gauge read in the low 70s, and it was only 9:30 a.m. The sky was as blue as a sky-blue crayon in a crayon box, and the bright sun sent warmth down on my thirsty northern skin. There was no way I was returning to Ohio without some southern sun having kissed my skin!

I looked over and smiled at Nick. No sooner had we started to drive from the airport, an infectious excitement had overtaken him as the vacation "vibe" settled over us. We left the weight of daily expectations and demands behind with the plane, and I sent the city of Cleveland, the Turner family, my job, and the field of social work in general, on the return flight to Ohio. Nick was my sole focus now!

During the drive to Rainbow Row, Nick talked about the places he wanted to show me: The City Market, Waterfront Park, Folly Beach, The Battery, Magnolia Plantation, and of course, he added, after I had relentlessly bugged him about it, a ghost tour was on the to-do list as well. I was determined to return with proof that the rumors of a haunted Charleston truly existed. I also planned on talking Nick into visiting Cypress Gardens. Maybe, just maybe, I could even convince him to join me in recreating *The Notebook's* iconic rowboat scene. I didn't want to press my luck, though, as he had relented on the Ghost Tour, but none of that mattered at the moment as Nick steered the car into our vacation home's driveway.

Mark was sitting on the steps and waved to us as we drove up the driveway to # 477772 East Bay Street, our southern home for "pretend." It was gorgeous, and that was just the exterior. The house, painted a pastel-yellow with black trim, sat at the end of the street, and I immediately fell in love with the projected quaintness. Rising three stories high, it featured a wrought-iron enclosed balcony that wrapped around the entire second floor. I didn't want to leave, and I had just arrived! There was now a genuine possibility Nick would have to return to Ohio without me!

Mark stood from the steps and walked toward the car. Upon reaching it, he wrapped his arms around Nick, giving him a few "brotherly" pats on the back before turning to me. He smiled, opening his arms for a hug, which preceded a welcoming kiss on the cheek.

"Welcome to Charleston, Lacey!"

Turning toward Nick, Mark motioned for us to follow him up the steps and through the front door, where we met Buster, the Moretti's St. Bernard, which just happened to be the most lovable dog I ever met. After the three of us showered Buster with some love, and he shared some of his drool, Mark waved us further into the home.

"Come on in. Let me give you the tour."

I was in love with the house before I crossed the threshold, and after venturing in a bit further, my love affair only intensified. The pastel-painted rooms were expansive, and southern charm flowed through each room we walked through. Mark related the home's history while leading us down the hallway into the kitchen, and once there, I became immediately mesmerized. The kitchen was a food lover's dream. I had drooled over similar kitchens in magazines but had yet to be fortunate enough to set foot in one until that moment. I walked around the kitchen, ogling all the amenities: the double oven, the marble-topped island and hanging pot rack above, the fully stocked, recessed refrigerator, and the built-in countertop grill. Nick had some competition — I was smitten with this home!

I sensed the rest of the house would be equally impressive, and I was right. We followed Mark up the dark-stained wooden staircase and then turned into a gorgeous main bedroom, complete with an attached bathroom and a sunken corner Jacuzzi. Nick and I exchanged looks, and there was no need to guess the X-rated thoughts behind those eyes! Three other bedrooms spread out down the hallways, all just as beautifully decorated. The main bedroom, and one of the additional bedrooms, had double doors that opened onto the wrap-around balcony where lounge and patio chairs were scattered, providing numerous views of the inviting Charleston Harbor. If all of that wasn't enough to impress me, balcony stairs led to a rooftop deck replete with a little bar set-up.

Making our way back downstairs, we resumed the main floor tour of the study, the living room, and a formal dining room. All the rooms were impressive and tastefully decorated in the welcoming southern-charm style, but my favorite place — my absolute favorite room — was the sunroom. Sunlight streamed through the floor-to-ceiling windows flanking the double, multi-paned glass doors, which stood open, leading outside onto the stone-walled, ivy-covered, cobblestone patio. Cozy-looking chaise lounges beckoned with anticipated relaxation, and the mermaid-splashing fountain promised a sharing of future conversations.

Nick's voice sounded from behind me, snapping me out of my hypnotized stupor. "Hmm, Lacey, I think we need to make it our mission to christen every one of these rooms over the next two weeks. What do you think?"

His hand drifted down my back until he reached my butt cheek, which he then gently squeezed. Yes, I had no difficulty envisioning us making love on the rooftop under the stars, and in the Jacuzzi, and within the walled garden to the sound of the mermaid splashing in the fountain, and in, okay, any of the rooms.

Tour complete, Mark walked outside with Nick to bring in the luggage while I made my way back out to the walled serenity. I walked over to one of the chaise lounges facing the fountain, sat on the chair's edge, and looked at the watery vision in front of me. The mermaid was copper-colored, and she wore a smile on her upturned, toward-the-sun, face. Her scaled tail was submerged halfway beneath the water, and her hands spread open so the water could flow down over them, splashing into the fountain's basin below. She was stunning, and I had to restrain pinching myself to confirm this as reality. Instead, I fished my phone from my purse and took a picture of it, immediately texting the image to co-worker Abbie, along with the text: **My home for the next two weeks! More pics to follow!**

Nick's voice came from behind me. "Hey, don't you go sharing our location, Ms. Coleman."

I turned and looked toward the patio door where Nick leaned against the wooden frame. I returned his smile as I arose from the chaise and walked toward him, wrapping my arms around his waist.

"Nobody's going to find us here. I promise."

Mark joined us, walking in through the door. "Geez, I swear you guys. Always hugging and loving on each other. It's enough to make a guy kind of jealous, ya know?"

We all laughed, and the three of us spent the next hour relaxing on lounge chairs as the mermaid eavesdropped. Well, it was relaxing until Mark shared some details about the upcoming, highly anticipated, and slightly anxiety-triggering event, the hotel's grand opening. Recently-forgotten nerves returned as Mark informed us that the Morgans were due back in town sometime later during the week. Katt had requested Mark extend an invitation to us for a treated dinner at his restaurant upon their return. I scolded the little butterflies threatening to flutter around in my belly. *Relax, Lacey.*

Nick looked over at me. I returned his look with a nod and a smile on my face. "Sounds good to me, babe. I'm looking forward to it!"

As the words left my lips, I willed some convincing confidence to follow with them. After all, I *did* still have several days to feed some mental Dramamine to the butterflies itching to take flight inside my gut. I needed to keep those fluttering flyaways in slumber while my inner diva prepared to pump some mental iron before meeting the one and only, Kattrina Morgan.

My thoughts drifted while the men talked about plans for the upcoming weeks. I caught bits of the conversation while I engaged the mermaid in some fancied sharing. According to the history lesson accompanying Mark's earlier tour, this house boasted an age well over two- hundred years, meaning that the bronze siren had undoubtedly overheard and bore witness to numerous scandal-laden conversations. Her mystery, as well as the projected promise of serenaded tranquility, already ensured I would be a frequent visitor to the patio.

Mark, rising from his chair, brought me back to the here and now. Nick was already confirming a 6 p.m. dinner reservation for the evening at Santauri's, which still allowed plenty of time to unpack our belongings and relax before dinner, and with the close of the door behind Mark, Nick and I officially started our vacation.

One hour later, our suitcases remained unpacked at the foot of the bed. After lugging them upstairs into the main bedroom, we had stepped outside onto the shaded balcony to check out our new vista before unpacking. Nick had positioned himself behind me, snaking his arms around my waist, his head leaning forward so our cheeks touched. The combination of the warm air, the bright sun shining down, and the ocean, brilliantly glistening with shards of sunshiny reflections, made it a picture-perfect postcard. However, Nick had more on his mind than the breathtaking postcard view. An unmistakable vibe rose from behind me along with the presence of something else arising, and as he led me back through the balcony doors, a thought drifted across my mind; *How many more of Katt Morgan's 101 ideas could I check off during this little vacation of ours?* I was eager to discover the answer to that question!

Approximately thirty minutes later, I mentally checked off the main bedroom's christening as we contentedly snuggled on the big four-poster bed. What had just happened was one of those heart-filling "love-making" sessions versus a stomp through *Fantasy Play 101*, and I was engulfed in that cozy, giddy, "I'm so in love" feeling. My thoughts drifted to the future with Nick, and I decided that, perhaps, the vacation would be the perfect time to figure out some wedding logistics. Before leaving Cleveland, Abbie jokingly warned me that I better not run off and elope, yet lying next to Nick in a state of pure bliss, it didn't seem like that bad of an idea at all!

A wisp of gentle, warm air drifted through the balcony doors and carried my thoughts away with it as it skimmed over naked bodies, lulling us both to sleep, until we awoke two hours later, completely relaxed and in full-hunger mode.

Santauris, here we come!

CHAPTER 2

I had heard about good ole' southern hospitality, and let me tell you, it's all true! I was sadly accustomed to down-turned heads and silent faces, a direct result of rampant apathy in a skeptical society, as well as the ever-present distrust frequently directed toward social workers in general. Charleston seemed to be in complete opposition to this. Granted, nobody here in the charming town knew I was one of "those social workers," but there was an unmistakable genuine sense of welcome. Walking from the parking lot to Mark's restaurant, every person we passed greeted us with a smile or a "hello." Charleston was winning me over, without even trying!

The southern charm and romantic elegance of Santauri's beckoned as we turned the corner and neared the restaurant. It immediately became apparent that a lot of thought and strategic planning had gone into Mark's dream, as the restaurant snuggled perfectly between the adjoining buildings; the building's exterior mimicking the cobblestone streets of old Charleston to a tee. Two arched, eight-count paned windows flanked each side of the double wooden doors and offered a view of the cozy, candle-kissed lighting from inside, beckoning lovers, and "want-to-be" lovers, to enter. Delightfully adding to the sensory tease, jazzy, bluesy music drifted outdoors toward the side patio, where white firefly-lights dangled overhead in the tree branches across and above the diners. Nicholas Ventricci's restaurant in Little Italy immediately came to mind.

A mouth-watering aroma joined the sultry notes and wafted out each time the doors opened. Mark previously boasted of his master chef's ability to perform feats of culinary magic with seafood and pasta, and the intoxicating, inhaled tease attested to that magic. Walking through the wooden doors, I felt wrapped in a blanket of romance and comfort, a pleasurable experience to which I was quickly becoming accustomed.

Candles adorned each table, and candlelit, chandelier-shaped wine bottles hung overhead. A wooden, open-spiral staircase to the hostess's right led affluent diners to a more intimate dining experience on the second floor. Mark had described the restaurant's upper level as if he was the proud daddy of a newborn baby. Intent on providing his guests the ultimate dining experience, Mark had teamed up with a visionary engineer to create a unique retractable double skylight. An outer layer of glass opened during the evening hours, while the inner layer allowed diners the opportunity to eat under the stars without direct exposure to the elements. From where I stood, I could glimpse the view from above.

Additionally, the restaurant's upper level offered cozy tables for two, hidden from view within intimate private rooms, each one having its little private terrace looking over the city. A door separated these *more intimate* dining experiences from the other diners. Mark recounted a story of the waiter who had rushed up to him, a guilty smile on his reddened face. It seems that the waiter had forgotten to knock before entering one of these intimate dining rooms and walked in to see a certain well-known actor on his knees in front of his date. Apparently, he had opted to order from his own "special" appetizer menu!

Nick provided his name to the tanned young lady standing behind the hostess stand, and Mark magically appeared as if summoned by a hidden button. After a round of hugs, he turned to me with a smile. "Welcome to Santauris, Lacey."

I opened my mouth to respond, but a voice summoned Mark from beyond, and he turned back to Nick. "I have to go play in the kitchen but will connect with you two a bit later." He winked at Nick, who returned a smile, along with a slight nod of his head. *What was that all about?*

Mark turned to the tanned hostess before walking off. "Put them in the Top Two, Marci."

Marci turned to smile at us. "Right this way, you two."

Top Two turned out to be one of those intimate secluded tables on the second floor, and my gaze drifted upward as I ascended the stairs. The skylight was open, and the beginning transformation from brilliant blue to the dusky pastel colors of the upcoming sunset was stunning. Reaching the second-floor landing, I looked around the room to see that the tables were full, which indicated Mark was doing something right, and all but two of the private dining room doors were closed.

Marci escorted us to one of the two open doors and stood to the side so that we could enter the cozy private room. Two upholstered, cushiony chairs faced each other across a cloth-covered square table, which sat next to an open-shuttered window, complete with its own tiny wrought-iron window balcony. On top of the little windowsill, a vase of beautiful roses emitted a heady floral aroma. A wooden cabinet nestled against one of the walls, and on that, an ice bucket held a chilled bottle of wine. Adjacent to the ice bucket, a small platter offered an assortment of cheese and crackers.

The pastel-painted sky appeared through the open window and, along with the room's atmosphere, made me feel part of an Impressionist painting. Another smiling face joined Marci at the door, and she introduced us to Nathaniel, who proceeded to inform us he would be our server for the evening, stating his goal was to "make this a dining experience to remember."

Nathaniel walked over to me and pulled out my chair. After waiting until I sat, Nick sat down across the table, and we both looked up at Nathaniel as he spoke. Informing us that Mark had requested the privilege of selecting the menu choices for our dining experience, he waited for our pending approval. Nick looked over at me with a questioning look, and I nodded that it was fine with me.

Nathaniel looked at Nick and grinned. "Thank you, sir. I was to respond to any answer other than an affirmative one with 'tough shit, Nick,' and I must say, I'm happy I won't have to do that."

Laughter erupted inside the little room, and after filling our glasses with chilled wine, Nathaniel excused himself, closing the door behind him. Nick reached across the table and took each of my hands in his. "Pretty damn impressive, don't you think?"

I nodded my head in agreement and took a sip of wine before replying. "I know. The attention to detail is amazing. Kind of reminds me of another certain guy I know."

Nick looked across the table with narrowed eyes. "Hmm. Well, so that you know, I intend to pay attention to every detailed inch of your body later this evening."

I opened my mouth to respond, but a knock at the door announced Nathaniel had returned, and after Nick gave the go-ahead, he walked in, bearing lobster bisque within two steamy oyster-cracker-filled bowls. He disappeared as quickly as he arrived.

The bisque was delicious, and Nick and I quickly devoured every spoonful as we began planning a tentative date for the trip to the Magnolia Plantation. Nick's excitement to share the historical site with me was contagious, and I listened with rapt attention as he provided a verbal visual. A repeat knock at the door soon signaled the arrival of our main course, and seconds later, Nathanial placed in front of me one of the most massive lobster tails I had ever seen! Seasoned fingerling potatoes and buttery garlic asparagus spears completed the plate. I had doubts I would succeed in joining the Clean Plate Club this evening!

Nathaniel noticed my widened eyes and smiled at me. "I'll leave you two alone now. Enjoy your private dining experience, and should you need anything or to signal when you've finished, just flip the switch by the door."

That switch ended up taking *quite* a while to be flipped.

The food was positively delicious, and as much as I convinced myself that I wouldn't be able to clean my plate, I quickly discovered there would be no trace of food left behind; the food was superb! Scooting my chair next to Nick's, we spent the next hour filling our bellies while laughing and talking about anything and everything, including some shared thoughts about the hotel's grand opening. Nick did his best to reassure me that I would love the Morgans, and we both admitted we were excited about seeing how the LEDs turned out.

Nick stopped talking during the conversation and looked at me, causing me to pause mid-sentence. I returned his look with a questioning expression, nervously giggling. "Uh, do I have food on my face or something? What are you looking at?"

He didn't break his gaze. "Sometimes, I just can't get over how drop-dead gorgeous you are, Lacey."

I pushed my chair back and motioned Nick to move his chair back a little bit as well. Scooting between the chair and the table, I positioned myself sideways on Nick's lap and wrapped my arms around his neck.

"You, sweet guy of mine, continue to make me feel as if I'm the luckiest woman in the world."

I leaned forward and kissed Nick and then returned for a replay; this one a lot more intense and a lot more effective. I surmised the "effectiveness" as I soon felt a familiar hardness from beneath my thigh. Nick and I looked at each other, and I noticed, much to my delight, familiar mischievous darkness replacing the twinkle in Nick's eyes. We were on the same wavelength, and Nick pushed the table back a bit more. I was concerned the noise of the moving table would invite an unwelcome invasion by the wait staff.

"Shh, Nick, I don't want Nathaniel to come barging in."

Nick instructed me to stand up and then reach down to lift my skirt to straddle him when I sat back down. With a heightened awareness of my surroundings, I glanced out the tableside window; no spectators were welcome to the events about to unfold! I could see people strolling on the street below under the now-glowing streetlights, and the gentle breeze brought my attention back with it as it flowed into the room.

I sat back down on Nick's lap, and his hands immediately settled upon my hips. He looked intently at me with a goofy-looking smile.

"Hmm, I saw the way Nathaniel was checking you out. I don't think he would be *too* disappointed by accidentally walking in." Nick's eyes darkened. "Lacey, what would you do if he walked in and saw us in the middle of messing around?"

I thought about it for a moment, the question throwing me off my game. There was an added sense of excitement catching me off guard, and unexpectedly, I experienced an adrenaline rush with the thought of being caught "in the act." The feeling took me back to my teenage years of having to sneak around in fear of being caught in the throes of adolescent passion.

I waited another second before responding to Nick's question. "Hmm, well, I would probably be just a *little* bit embarrassed."

He smiled, and I leaned forward again, bringing my face close to his. Taking Nick's bottom lip between my teeth and gently pulling back a bit, he immediately tensed. I smiled and put my arms around his neck, my hands mindlessly playing with his hair. "But then again, if something, or someone, was causing my attention to focus elsewhere, I wouldn't even know to care, right?"

I slowly slid off Nick's lap and knelt between his knees. Loosening his belt and unzipping his pants, I unleashed the monster inside as Nick's hands traveled to the back of my head to gently pull my mouth downward. Amid the moans drifting from above, I could tell that Nick was enjoying the same "special dessert" just as much as I was. Another moan escaped from his mouth.

I pulled back and looked up at him, shaking my head. "You aren't very quiet. Do I have to stop?"

Nick looked down at my upturned face with a "no-don't-stop" look. I didn't trust his ability to keep quiet, though. I stood up and looked down at him before walking toward the side shelf, where I picked up a clean cloth napkin before returning to the table. Reaching under my loose sundress, I tugged my panties down and climbed back on his lap. "I guess I'm going to have to make sure you stay quiet, huh?"

Instructing him to open his mouth and bite down on the cloth napkin, Nick offered no resistance, and as I lowered myself on his lap, he entered me, deep and hard.

Another muffled moan escaped from behind the napkin. I looked at Nick, shaking my head. "Shh!"

Beginning a slow grind with Nick deep inside me, his hands tightened on my hips, and the thrusts quickly intensified. Trying to remain as quiet as possible wasn't an easy endeavor, and I kept imagining a bunch of eaves-dropping ears right outside the door, or even worse, prying eyes from down below, outside the window.

I will admit, the thought of Nathaniel's unheard knocks, as well as the possibility of unknown entry, danced through my mind, and to be quite honest, I was fully aware that Nathaniel had been checking me out. *What would Nathaniel do? Would he just stand there continuing to watch? Would he walk away embarrassed? Would he say anything?* The imagined scene played through my mind, creating an increased intensity as Nick and I moved with primal urgency. His grip tightened on my hips, and I felt the familiar increase in size within me. Nick was close, which was okay, as I was on the brink as well, and the next time my butt hit his upper thigh, we climaxed as one.

I reached up and took the napkin from Nick's mouth, replacing it with a kiss, and we sat in silence for a minute, neither of us moving. I waited to hear steps walking away behind the door or a sound of movement, signaling someone standing right outside, but thankfully, I heard nothing. Arising from Nick's lap, I walked over to the cabinet and grabbed two more cloth napkins, one of which I offered to Nick, the other I kept for my use.

Now, I faced another dilemma. "Nick, there's *no* way I'm leaving these napkins in this room. Give me yours."

I folded the two napkins, so that the unused side faced out and stuck them inside my purse for discarding later. I hadn't exactly prepared for a post-rendezvous cleanup. Nick stood and zipped his pants, re-positioned the table, and sat back down, and after glancing around the room to make sure there were no tell-tale signs of after-dinner sex, I walked over to the door, flipped the switch requesting Nathaniel's presence, and rejoined Nick at the table.

The knock at the door happened almost too quickly. *Hmm. Had he heard anything? Had he heard **everything**?* The door opened, and Nathaniel entered. "How was your dining experience?"

Nick looked over with a smile on his face and then looked up toward Nathaniel. "The food was fantastic. Compliments to the chef. Will you please tell Mark we'll be down in a few minutes to drag him over to the bar so I can buy him a drink?"

Nathaniel looked at Nick and then at me. "I will certainly do that, sir. Would you and the lovely lady care to look over the dessert selection?"

Nick looked over at me and winked, a grin spreading over his face, before turning back to Nathaniel. *Uh Oh, I've seen that grin more than once.*

Before I could deliver a kick to Nick's shin under the table, he spoke. "No, but thank you, Nathaniel. We incorporated dessert into our meal already."

It took Nathaniel perhaps three seconds, at most, to register what Nick meant. Poor guy, his face probably mirrored mine, forty shades of red. I could have killed Nick. Hopefully, the gracious tip left by Nick helped ease any embarrassment Nathaniel felt!

Marci reappeared to lead us back down the staircase and over to the bar, where Mark soon joined us, and the three of us headed outside to the patio with drinks in hand. We spent the next hour sitting at one of the black, iron and wood tables near the fireplace, Nick and I showering Mark with praises over his restaurant success. Mark shared some ideas for a planned expansion, and I allowed the guys to do most of the talking while I leaned back and soaked in the fire's warmth, which delightfully mixed with the cooling night air. I proceeded to settle into cozy relaxation *until* I heard Mark mention the Fantasy Play Hotel™.

"They want to eventually open a few more hotels in some other major cities. It'll be interesting to see how things work out for them."

I felt Nick's hand on my leg under the table. "That makes sense, Mark. From everything I've been hearing and reading, the hotels are at full capacity almost every evening."

Mark looked at Nick and then over at me. "So, when are you two going to check it out?" You going to wait until the grand opening, or are you planning a visit before next weekend?"

A wave of apprehension coursed through me while waiting for Nick's response. I was under the impression we were meeting the Morgans the evening before the party, with our first visit to the hotel being the next night at the grand event, and I silently sighed in relief when Nick verified that same thing to Mark, who shook his head and laughed.

"I'm telling you, my man, there are some crazy things available over there. You'll see."

Nick sensed I was a little uneasy and quickly changed the subject by asking Mark about his upcoming schedule, which despite being quite busy, allowed us a couple of evenings for the three of us to connect.

The conversation continued to flow over the next twenty minutes, only to be cut short by a hostess's summoning with questions regarding next week's catering menu. Nick and I chose the opportunity to make our getaway, as we still wanted to drive over to Folly Beach for a bit, so after the hugs and another round of verbal applause for Mark's restaurant, we departed.

Forty minutes later, blanket in hand and our bare feet in the sand, we walked to the shoreline under the starlit sky. The full moon provided a contrast to the darkened sky, and the outlines of strolling couples walking hand-in-hand, deep in conversation, could be seen. A group of teenagers sat in a circle surrounding a strumming guitar player. Simultaneously, a few other couples shared the same idea we had and were either lying back on their blankets or sitting side-by-side, looking out over the calm water.

We located a spot and spread the blanket before walking over to the warm water, which gently rolled over our feet as we stood in the surf. Nick moved behind me, and his arms wrapped around my waist, gently pulling me back against him as we soaked in the ocean's vastness and listened to the lapping waves. Cleveland felt a million miles away at that moment. Nick leaned his head forward a bit, and I felt his lips near my ear, which caused the sprouting of goosebumps to appear on my arms. *Please never let me lose this feeling.*

"Maybe we should have a beach wedding right here by the ocean, barefoot in the sand. What do you think, Lacey?"

I looked at Nick's face to see if he was serious or just wanting a reaction. I think he was serious; well, his face *looked* serious. I turned to face him, snaking my arms around his waist, and looking up into his captivating eyes. "Like, are you meaning right here, right now, at this moment?"

Nick looked back at me with his "you know what I mean" expression. "No, soon-to-be-wife-of-mine. Not right at this exact moment." He looked around. "Unless somebody here is licensed to marry. Wait, let me ask."

Nick opened his mouth to yell, but I quickly covered his mouth with my hand. "Don't you dare!"

His eyes danced, and I felt a smile forming under my hand, followed by his tongue sneaking out to tease the palm of my hand. I looked at him, fake sternness filling my eyes. "You going to behave if I take my hand away, Nick?"

He shook his head no. I laughed and lifted my hand.

"Lacey, I'm kind of serious, though." Nick pulled me closer to him and bent his head down a bit, so our faces were thisclose to each other. "I want to start the rest of our lives together. I know you hate to talk about it, but I want to provide you the opportunity to quit your job and do whatever your heart desires. I want to wake up to your gorgeous face every morning and not have to say goodbye to it ever again."

I felt the conga drums warming up inside of my chest. *How can someone be the total perfect package? How was I the lucky one?*

Nick continued before I could reply. "And, no, this isn't the alcohol talking, Ms. Coleman."

I didn't know what to say, and I certainly hadn't expected Nick to say anything like this. We had talked about wedding stuff before but hadn't actually arrived at any concrete decisions. He was dead-ass serious right now, though, and I was pretty sure he could read the confusion on my face, as maintaining a poker face wasn't exactly one of my better attributes.

Nick reached up and put a hand on each side of my face, "Okay, Okay, I know, I know, you're a woman, and a woman who over-thinks. I'm no dummy, Lacey. I know women want to plan *the* perfect wedding. Babe, you just let me know when, and where, and what I need to do, and I will be there at the end of whatever aisle you're walking down."

I giggled. "You, Nick Atwood, definitely have a bit of a buzz going on because that's the only time you talk this much."

He removed his hands from my face and wrapped his arms back around me.

I continued. "And no, I don't need some perfect big wedding ceremony to begin my life with you. As a matter of fact, a beach wedding sounds beautiful, just you and me, but let's have this conversation again when you don't have any alcohol running through your veins and controlling your mouth."

Nick opened his mouth in a fake gasp, and the next thing I knew, I was being scooped up and carried further into the water. "That's it, Lacey, you're going in!"

I was laughing so hard while simultaneously yelling at him to put me down, which he eventually did, but not until I silently questioned whether he was really going to throw me to the sharks or not. Alas, the finned fish would have to go hungry. My love and I dried our feet, gathered up the blanket, and walked back to the car, the moon reflecting off the ocean surface behind us. It was time to head back home to christen another room!

CHAPTER 3

Oh, to have a magic wand that could halt time's progression. I wanted to slow down every single hour of every single day, and I was sure that, somehow, vacation time moved quicker than any other time. Nick met with the gallery owners, and the final details of next year's "Real Charleston" project were underway, and *that* meant another vacation trip to what had become my favorite city!

Mark came over one evening during that first week, and we cooked steaks on the grill, after which the three of us ventured into town to hear a jazz player at one of the downtown pubs. Nick and I spent one full day strolling through the outdoor City Market, where I was captivated by the sweetgrass basket makers, and successfully convinced Nick we needed a couple of baskets for the loft back in Cleveland.

We spent one full day at Folly Beach, where we both scored some sun-kissed skin; that's not to say we hadn't made sure to joyfully spread sunscreen over each other's bodies every second we could. "This is the life," quickly became our new, over-used phrase that day as we floated next to each other, hand-in-hand on the double raft. Later that afternoon, as I changed out of my bikini, Nick surprised me with tickets for a dinner cruise, during which I experienced my first encounter with the beauty of playful dolphins attempting to gain attention.

However, what truly captured my heart was our midweek venture to The Magnolia Plantation and Gardens, where we spent practically the entire day. Nick was in his element, camera in hand, capturing some incredible photos of the roaming wild peacocks and the beautiful garden, as I just tried to soak it all in. The inner social worker poked her head out and appeared when we came upon the manor and slave cabins. I closed my eyes, ultimately failing at even coming close to imagining some of that era's injustices.

The adjoining swamp tour was just as incredible, and I was more than thankful that the basking alligators remained content on the halfway-immersed swamp logs during the swamp visit. As much as I dreaded the thought of having to return home after vacation, I *did* want to do it as a complete body.

Days passed as quickly as it takes to turn the page on a calendar. Our late evenings, and many early mornings, were spent making love in all the different rooms. Yes, even in front of the lovely mermaid confidante — just another secret to hold deep within her bronze body. We watched the sunset and sunrise several times on the upper balcony, wrapped in our cozy robes, and delightfully fell into that lazy vacation mode. Time ceased to exist, and everyday life flowed at a relaxed pace, something to which I could quickly become accustomed. I kept my mind as occupied as the hours, or so I thought.

Silly me to think that all anxiety had somehow disappeared with vacation relaxation. I knew the big morning was imminent; as hard as I tried, I could not slow time at all, and Friday morning appeared before I had adequate time to prepare myself mentally. The Morgans were flying in sometime during the afternoon, and our dinner date was later in the evening. I was excited and *not* excited, at the same time, if that makes any sense. Waking up before Nick, I french-pressed a cup of coffee and walked outside to have my morning mental conversation with the laughing bronze mermaid. Call me crazy, but a calmness settled over me every time I watched the water cascading over her shiny copper body.

Leaning back in the comfy floral chaise, I took a sip of coffee and attempted to quiet my mind.

What are you so freaked out about, Lacey?

Now, that was a good question. *Is it because Nick was the photographer for Katt Morgan's book jacket cover?* I thought about it for a moment. No, I didn't think that was it at all. Any feelings about that had disappeared. I knew, without a doubt, Nick had no romantic interest in Katt.

Come on, lovely mermaid, help me figure this out.

The mermaid smiled back at me. She knew, and, at once, I did too. It was the hotel itself that was intimidating to me. I mean, I don't think I am naïve in any way, but, come on, a Fantasy Play Hotel™? What if Nick walked into the hotel and realized he wanted more adventure, more excitement in his life? His life *was* changing, and he *was* becoming exposed to the finer things in life, to more of the people most others *wished* they knew. Grr, these Jack-in-the-Box insecurities needed to go!

You need to get a grip on this, Lacey. Nick is in love with you. My Gosh, Lacey, he just said he wanted to be married on the beach a few days ago.

I looked back at my mermaid and smiled at her bronze face.

Okay, you're right.

I almost jumped out of my skin when I felt a hand on my shoulder. The bronze mermaid silently laughed as Nick bent down to plant a kiss on my forehead. "What are you doing up so early?"

I watched Nick walk around my chair and then sit in the chaise to the right. Not one to pass up some cuddle-time, I joined him on his chaise, sitting between his legs as we watched the mermaid playing in the water for a few seconds. Leaning back against his chest, I professed the catalyst for my early rising.

"I think I'm just dealing with some last-minute nerves before meeting the Morgans tonight *and* attending the grand opening tomorrow."

His arms tightened around me. "Lacey, you have nothing to worry about. There's no reason to be nervous."

I leaned my head back and looked up at Nick. "The Morgans are so freaking rich, and I believe this is the second or third Fantasy Play Hotel™, Nick. I'm going to be seeing my almost-nude body hanging from those walls tomorrow, *and* I'm going to see the reactions of a bunch of other people as they look at them." I laughed. "What about *any* of that doesn't equal nerves, Mr. Atwood?"

Nick turned to his side and scooted under me while at the same time pulling me on top of him so that I peered into the face of my future husband as he spoke. "Lacey Atwood to-be, listen to me. There is no woman; rich, poor, famous, unknown, tall, short, or anything else you can think of, who can compare to you."

He shook his head and looked into my eyes.

For the second time since I had known Nick, he surprised me. His eyes glistened with wetness, suddenly full of emotion threatening to tip over his bottom eyelid, and he made sure he was in control, just enough, to keep that from happening before he spoke again.

"You still just don't get it, do you?" I didn't have a chance to respond before he continued. "You are so fucking beautiful, you have a heart so full of love, your soul gives off warmth to every single person who meets you, you have made me see the world in an entirely different way, and you are the sexiest and hottest woman I have ever, and will ever, come across. *And* to top it all off, you have one hell of a kick-ass, rocking-fine body, Lacey Coleman!"

I was at a loss for words. All the insecurities and nerves, or whatever they were, vanished, and I was rendered speechless for a few seconds. Nick's vulnerability over the sharing of emotion filled me with an unexpected sentiment. I looked at him as I blinked back tears that threatened to topple over my bottom eyelids.

"You, Mr. Atwood, have one hell of a way with words, and you have no clue how much I love you." I kissed the tip of his nose. "And, by the way, I've been thinking about your suggestion from the other night."

He looked at me with puzzlement. I sighed and returned the same expression. "You know, the whole being married on the beach idea."

Nick maintained his stoic expression. "What in the world are you talking about, Lacey?"

My eyes widened. *Had it been just the wine? Did he not remember the conversation*?? I started to feel a wee bit embarrassed, and I was majorly confused.

I continued. "NICK!! Remember after dinner when we were on the beach? You suggested we exchange vows on the beach. I told you we should think about it, remember?"

Nick once again threw me a puzzled look and responded with an equally puzzled tone to his voice. "A wedding ceremony on a beach? With all that sand everywhere?"

The longer his face remained in its seriousness, the more the sense of confusion and concern began to flow through my veins. He continued again, but now I saw the twinkle of amusement in his eyes, and the tone of his voice started to betray him.

"What are you thinking, Lacey? I mean, come on, having to deal with colors dancing across the sky at sunset, having to hear waves hitting the shore, the warm air hitting us. And if that wouldn't be bad enough ...," Nick's grin began eroding the solemnity of his expression, as he continued, "... me having to look at the most incredible woman standing across from me with her beauty. What are you thinking?"

I shook my head, laughing at my brief gullible moment, and playfully poked him in the stomach. "You brat! You're so in trouble for making me feel I was losing my mind."

Nick just continued to smile at me.

"You wait, Mr. Atwood. Payback is going to bite that nice fine ass of yours!"

He pulled me even closer to him. "Hmm, biting and ass sound like a great combination to me." His thumb moved over the silk, tracing the crack.

Ahh, the forbidden treasure. Nick had been so patient with my desire to wait a while before having anal sex. As always, he never pressured me to do anything I didn't feel comfortable doing, but I was beginning to want it just as much as Nick, and the thought of completely giving myself to him had crossed my mind often over the past few weeks. I brought along our Fantasy Play spinner without Nick knowing; however, this time, also unbeknownst to him, all the spinner ideas were from the "AFLAME" section of *Fantasy Play 101.*

Nick pulled my face closer, and we had just started a passionate kissing session when the front door buzzer sounded. We exchanged looks. Nick stood and looked down at Frankie, now masquerading as a weathercock, ready to point in one of the four cardinal directions depending on which way he turned, and I giggled as the buzzer again sounded.

I looked at Nick, then the patio doorway. "You get Frankie under control. I'll answer the door."

Wrapping the thin robe around me, I padded my way to the front door as Nick went upstairs.

I opened the door to Mark Santauri's goofy grin. He stood there, juggling three large styrofoam cups of coffee and a bag of bagels, or donuts, or something, smelling deliciously fresh-baked. My stomach rumbled.

"Mark! Hi! What are you doing here so early in the morning?"

"Good morning, lovely Ms. Coleman. Umm, could you grab two of these cups before they all go crashing to the ground?"

I reached out and rescued two of the cups, saving them from imminent peril, and stepped back from the doorway, motioning Mark to come inside. He followed me to the kitchen, where we set the coffees on the marble island countertop. Mark opened the bag, allowing a sticky sweet, caramel-cinnamon aroma to infiltrate the kitchen. My stomach growled again, loudly, resulting in Mark's wide eyes and laughter.

Stepping toward the cabinet, Mark took down three small sea-blue plates and set them on the counter, then reached into the bag, removing three gigantic glazed-cinnamon buns, placing one on each plate as he spoke. "So, don't tell me that lazy, no-good-bum is still asleep on a gorgeous morning like this! We have things to do, missions to accomplish, seas to sail. Well, at least the seas to sail part."

I looked at him and laughed. "Mark, how many cups of coffee have you already had this morning? What seas are needing sailing?"

He eyeballed me with an overly dramatic, shocked look on his face. "Well, the Atlantic Sea. Actually, the Atlantic Ocean, silly girl, but you aren't going to be able to go sailing in that get-up."

I could do nothing but stand there, at a loss for words, while trying to make some sense of the discussion flow. Thankfully, I didn't have to wait long because Nick walked through the doorway.

"Lacey, didn't we talk the other day about strange people lurking the streets of Charleston? And here you go, letting one of them into the house?"

Nick had changed into khaki shorts and a blue t-shirt. Looking downward, I was relieved to see that the weathercock had disappeared. He noticed my glance and winked.

Mark took a bite of his cinnamon roll, looking at Nick, and then over at me. "You two need to get some bathing suits on because we're going for a boat ride."

Nick took a bite of his roll and looked at me, shrugging his shoulders, as if to say he had no idea what Mark was speaking about during the coffee-induced speech.

"Tom and Kitty Anderson, good friends of the Morgans, came into the restaurant yesterday. Kitty talked to Katt, who informed Kitty that the "soon to be world-renowned" photographer, Nick Atwood, and his lovely lady were in town. She suggested we all share a little boat ride before they meet us for dinner."

Mark took a breath before continuing. He needed it!

"I guess Katt and her husband were expecting to be in earlier today. The *original* plan was for all of us to go on the boat. Turns out they won't be in until later this afternoon. So, here I am, and you two need to go run and get your bathing suits on so we can get over to the dock in forty-five minutes."

Mark took another breath *and* another big bite of his cinnamon roll, then looked at Nick and me. "Well?"

CHAPTER 4

Thirty-five minutes later, the three of us walked down a dock toward the end of a pier, where I saw a charming couple moving around the deck of a boat; no, a yacht. Now, I don't know a lot about boats, and I'm not sure what makes one a boat and one a yacht, but I know a kick-ass, huge, floating vessel when I see one, and this was one of those. Reaching the floating vessel, Mark took care of the introductions.

"Nick Atwood and Lacey Coleman, this is Tom and Kitty Anderson."

Judging by the slightly graying hair and sun-toughened skin, the Andersons appeared to be in their early seventies. "Welcome, welcome, come on board."

We stepped onto a deck that spread out like a backyard patio. Double-wide padded bench-seating lined the boat deck's outer frame, and a round table sat under the overhang surrounded by six padded chairs and two more chaise lounges. The deck's teak flooring contrasted with the bright white of the furniture adding to the elegant yet welcoming feel.

The men immediately began talking about horsepower ratings, speed, and a bunch of boating jargon that slid right past my ears like a child on a wet slip-and-slide. Kitty walked over to me and presented one of those warm, genuine, southern smiles I adored.

"Come on, Lacey, let's get away from all this "man talk," and let me give you the tour."

Walking beneath the overhang, past the table and chairs, we stepped down into what was, in my opinion, one of the most incredible living rooms I have seen, on land or at sea. On a slightly elevated platform, six padded chairs surrounded a large oval wooden table. Cushioned couches and overstuffed chairs completed the cozy seating arrangement around the room's outer edges, and toward the back, three steps led right back up to the deck, whereas two more steps led down to another level. There were three bedrooms on the lower level, each larger than mine back in Cleveland. Windows were everywhere, uniting the comfort of home with the beauty of the ocean. To say I was astounded would be a colossal understatement, and that was *before* Kitty led me back outside to the front of the yacht.

More padded seating allowed for relaxed sunbathing, and shaded seating was available under one of the overhanging umbrellas. What caught me by surprise, though, was the hot tub, which seemed strange on the deck of a huge boat sitting on the Atlantic Ocean. Kitty immediately noticed my puzzled look as, of course, my inability to maintain a poker face once again failed me.

"I know. Many years ago, I thought the same thing when Tom and I first talked about getting a yacht. He had a mental image of what he wanted the yacht to look like." Kitty chuckled and shook her head. "And he got the yacht he wanted, right down to the hot tub he described thirty-years ago." Again, she chuckled. "You wouldn't think you would use a hot tub on a yacht, but trust me, dear, there are many cool nights out here, and that hot tub sure feels good!"

I smiled back at Kitty. "Well, putting it that way, I guess it does make sense."

"Uh-oh, guys, they're talking about things that make sense." Tom Anderson came up behind Kitty and wrapped his arms around her waist, winking at me.

Mark and Nick followed Tom and now joined us on the front deck.

Kitty laughed and winked my way. "That's right, talking sense and guys, well they just mix like oil and water ...," she continued looking back over her shoulder at her husband, "... and speaking of water, are we about ready to get this thing moving?"

Tom laughed and motioned for Nick and Mark to follow him. "You heard the boss, men. Let's get this thing out onto the water."

Nick leaned over to give me a quick kiss. He nudged his mouth close to my ear in a low whisper. "You better make sure I'm around you when you show off that bikini-body around these two guys. I'd hate to have to throw anyone overboard."

I giggled and shook my head while rolling my eyes back in mock exasperation.

By eleven, we were amid the vastness of the Atlantic Ocean, skimming over the glistening surface of the blue water toward a spot "farther out" where we could turn off the engines and float for a while. Mark and Nick seemed to have proclaimed themselves, first and second mate and they hadn't left Tom's side since pulling away from the dock. Kitty and I made ourselves comfortable on the cushioned seating at the back of the boat, watching the wake frothing up behind the boat. It was difficult to distinguish where the blue of the ocean met the blue of the sky, and the sun sent down warm rays of brilliant sunshine that had all of us reaching for our sunglasses.

Finally, Kitty stood, waving me to follow her back down into the belly of the yacht. I hadn't realized how warm it had become under the sun, and it took me a minute to adjust to the shaded coolness once we walked down the steps into the lower level.

Once down into the galley, Kitty motioned to the portable wine cooler, where I saw eight bottles of wine laying on top of concaved wire racks. "I'm going to get into my bathing suit. You go ahead and pick out something that looks good."

She turned and walked toward the back bedroom, as I pretended I was some sort of wine connoisseur, skilled enough to pick out something I *hoped* I would like. I saw my reflection in the wine cooler's small glass door as I read the wine labels through the glass. A momentary wave of apprehension arose from nowhere.

Wait a minute. The Andersons seem like a sweet "normal" couple in their seventies, but these were friends of the Morgans. What if they have intentions for us other than just taking us out on a boat ride? What if Mark is in on this? Heck, maybe Nick is in on this. Perhaps this is all a plan for some wild, crazy orgy or something.

I gave myself a proverbial smack upside the head. *Lacey Coleman, you need to rein in this shit.*

Arms snuck around my waist, and I jumped at the same time my mouth opened to say something that, I am sure, wouldn't have been very ladylike as my fingers closed into a fist.

"Woahhh!" Nick's surprised face reflected in the wine cooler's glass door at the same time I heard his exclamation of surprise.

I started laughing when I turned to see him standing in some kind of "karate on-guard" stance, hands up in karate-chop position.

"I will take you down, woman!"

Kitty's laughter joined with mine as she walked back into the galley from the hallway. "What in the world is going on out here?"

Nick wrapped his arms around my waist and pulled me back against him. "Not sure, Kitty, but I think Lacey was ready to show off some Kung Fu karate moves on me."

I shot a backward glance to silence him, but thankfully, Kitty's attention was focused on procuring some wine glasses as she spoke. "So, which wine is it going to be, Lacey?"

With Kitty's attention still turned toward the cabinets, I shot a "you choose" look to Nick, who thankfully caught it and reached around to open the cooler door, pulling out a bottle of wine, Iced Fantasy. While turning the screw into the cork, he looked over at me.

"You going to change, babe?"

I opened my mouth to reply. I had to take off just my shorts and top because I wore my suit underneath, but before I could speak, the boat stopped moving. I guessed this meant Tom had found the perfect resting spot, and verification arrived ten seconds later when both Tom and Mark joined us in the galley. Tom passed by Kitty, pausing to give her a quick kiss, and then opened a cabinet door above the sink. He pulled out a bottle as he smiled and winked at Kitty.

"Wine for the ladies, bourbon for the guys." Tom handed over the bottle to Mark. "Mark, I'm leaving you in charge of pouring while I go in and hit the head. Meet you all top deck."

Kitty turned to look at me and then looked at both Nick and Mark.

"Lacey and I are going to get the chairs and lounge seats situated upfront. You boys, I trust, can handle bringing the drinks up top."

With "yes ma'ams" from the guys echoing behind us, I turned to follow Kitty up the steps, back outside into the brilliant sunshine. We shuffled some of the chairs for the guys and moved two of the lounge chairs closer together to provide some shade while we engaged in some "girl talk."

I stepped out of my shorts and pulled the shirt over my head when I heard a whistle that, thankfully, I immediately identified as Nick's. *Whew!* My cheeks felt a little warm, but I was confident it wasn't noticeable because of the heat and the sun bearing down. I went bikini shopping before the trip, and Nick hadn't seen the bikini I bought until this exact moment. Obviously, the black, white-trimmed suit with the side ties on the bottom met his approval. I pulled off my shirt and was, once again, slightly embarrassed when I noticed it wasn't just Nick looking at me. Standing somewhat behind Nick, Mark was pretending to adjust an umbrella, and Tom, walking up the steps, averted his face when I looked at him.

Luckily, Kitty was already situated in her lounge chair and was busy rubbing lotion on her legs. Nick walked over and set our wine glasses on the little glass-top table between, and after taking an additional two steps toward me, he leaned over, whispering in my ear, "You look fantastic, and you're in so much trouble tonight, Ms. Coleman."

Well, I welcome *that* kind of trouble!

Music filled the air as Tom turned up the speakers to a mix of music ranging from today's popular songs, over to some Jazz and Blues stuff, some Billy Vera and The Beaters, and even some Massive Attack Radio tunes. The heat from the sun felt good on my skin, and I reached down to rub the lotion over my faded summer tan, which I was bound and determined to replace with a beautiful "last of the summer" glow.

Small talk flowed between us all, and like the music, it roamed all over the place, ranging from work, favorite restaurants, business talk, and then finally to the elephant in the room, the Morgans, and the Fantasy Play Hotel™. I felt Nick's gaze focused on me behind his shades as soon as the subject headed in that direction. I sent him a smile, letting him know it was all right.

Surprisingly, the heart's usual belly flutter and racing failed to appear at the hotel's mention. Actually, I found myself "thirsty" for some inside information about the infamous Katt Morgan and her husband. I wanted any information I could obtain from these good friends of theirs, and I wasn't disappointed.

Both couples had coincidentally been on their honeymoon cruises together, twenty-five years ago, traveling through the Caribbean. They had
quickly developed an immediate friendship, the twenty-five-year age gap between the couples, not a factor at all. Tom Anderson and Joe Morgan were
each just beginning to turn the lucrative corner in their respective business
ventures. At the same time, Katt had dreams of becoming a famous author,
and Kitty was developing her jewelry line. Driven for success — and both
couples having the financial means to back up their goals — the couples
continued their friendship throughout the years, celebrating the other's ac-
complishments as they arrived.

Tom began talking about some of the business ventures that he and Joe
shared. Kitty and I tuned out when it turned to dollars and deals, and we
continued with our "girl-talk." She sat up and reached behind her, grabbing
the bottle of wine, and refilled both glasses before she continued talking.
Kitty told me about Katt's decision to focus on her love for writing, specifically the books about sex and fantasies. Kitty said that Katt was determined
to break down the stigma surrounding the subject matter and added that at
no time had she ever doubted Katt Morgan's ability to attain literary success.
Her first book proved Kitty right, and *Fantasy Play 101* was sure to follow
the same path!

Kitty chuckled when she talked about a phone call she received from
Katt during the first book's writing. Katt had been excitedly talking a mile a
minute, and Kitty had to tell her to slow down. Katt had just developed the
concept of a fantasy hotel, and she wanted to take some of the ideas from the
books she was writing and bring them to life in the various hotel rooms, and
at that moment, The Fantasy Play Hotel™ was born!

Kitty took another sip of wine and smiled at me. "The rest is history.
That girl has created an empire, and she is not stopping."

I had many questions, and Kitty patiently answered each one without
making me feel as if I was being nosy or prying. The wine assisted in the
loosening of the tongues for both of us. I asked Kitty if the Morgans were
as sexually adventurous as her books. She paused for a moment and then
looked over her sunglasses at me, smiling.

"Absolutely, my dear. And this new hotel is taking Katt to the level she's
been wanting to reach all along."

I pushed my sunglasses up on my head and took another sip of wine. "And that level is?"

Kitty chuckled again, taking another sip of wine from her glass, scooting herself into more of a sitting position, and turned to face me. According to Kitty, Katt and her husband had always been very involved in the Dominant/submissive scene. They wanted to make sure this newest hotel would meet the growing desire among those wishing to have some opportunities to live out or "try-out" that same lifestyle. Apparently, the Morgans had accomplished precisely that. Not only did the hotel have one entire floor of rooms catering to this interest, but the Morgans also designed a penthouse intended solely for high-end events and parties where such couples could gather.

For the first time since the conversation began, I didn't know how to respond. I replied with the only input I could conceive at that moment. "Wow, that's interesting." *Always such a conversationalist, Lacey. Sheesh.*

My thoughts wandered. I was undoubtedly curious, and my interest piqued. While reading *Fantasy Play 101*, I often found myself stopping and letting my mind drift over some of the ideas in the last section, and Nick and I had ventured into some of the ideas *with* alterations. There were several times I willingly played submissive to Nick's more dominant "orders" for what he wanted me to do sexually. We flipped that several times as well, with me being the "more dominant" and Nick being the "more submissive," always agreeing, however, that it was all just "play" time, and we were just dipping playful toes into that lifestyle.

I wasn't sure I could ever allow myself, emotionally or physically, to be controlled by another. Then again, I had liberated myself sexually with Nick in ways I never imagined. The truth of the matter is, I didn't know enough about that whole lifestyle, and Nick hadn't hinted at wanting to delve any deeper, so it wasn't in my everyday thoughts — or hadn't been — until this conversation.

Has he been thinking about more fully acting upon it?

Kitty rose from her chair, and the movement halted my thoughts. A good thing, as I'm sure the mind-flow would have become an engineer-less, runaway train in my mind.

To each their own, Lacey. Let it go.

The next few hours flew by full of fun and silliness. We decided to cool off by jumping off the yacht's stern and followed that by showing off our dance moves, some of us better than others. The sun shining, the music playing, and the alcohol working its magic combined for a fantastic time on the water. I wasn't paying attention to time and would have stayed on the yacht for the rest of the day if able; alas, there *were* other scheduled events to attend. Good things always coming to an end; we soon realized we needed to head back.

Nick joined me on the back deck during the ride home. To be more precise, we sprawled over the padded seats looking out over the churning water behind us, his arms wrapped around me as I leaned back against him. The wine and the sun had warmed me inside and out. As a bonus, my skin was perfectly sun-touched. I dozed off for about ten minutes and woke up to Tom shouting at the occupants on a passing boat. We soon pulled back into the dock and, once secured, stood up and stretched our legs.

Nick, Mark, and I disembarked the yacht and transformed our sea legs back to "land legs" as we stood on the wooden dock. Tom Anderson extended Nick and Mark an invitation to go out fishing before we headed back to Ohio, and Kitty and I decided we would do some shopping while the men went fishing. The Andersons would be at the hotel's grand opening, so we said our "goodbyes" and "see you tomorrows." Mark walked to his car and said he would see us later at the restaurant, while Nick and I headed back to Rainbow Row to shower, change, and prepare for our dinner with the infamous Katt and Joe Morgan. Finally!

CHAPTER 5

Buster happily greeted us at the door with his enormous tongue threatening to drown us in slobber and his massive, droopy eyes looking at us accusingly for having left him alone. When Nick reached for the leash hanging from the metal iron hook by the door, Buster could barely rein in his excitement.

"All right, come on, Buster, let's go for a walk."

Nick leaned forward to kiss me while his sneaky hand wandered to my backside and squeezed my cheek. "You get the shower first, but I'm going to be back in a few, so save me some hot water, Missy."

The front door closed behind the two adorable males, and I turned to head toward the staircase; however, the sunroom, and beyond its doors, the patio, beckoned. I returned the mermaid's knowing smile.

Oh boy, do I have some stuff to tell you later.

I had no doubt the mermaid held many coveted stories deep within her shiny bronzed body — a wealth of hidden secrets and scandalous news about some of Charleston's elite.

She probably knows way more about the Morgans than you do, Lacey.

I closed the double doors with a "we will talk later" smile sent in her direction and made my way up the staircase to the bedroom. I could see Nick from the balcony windows, walking Buster at the end of the street. More accurately, Buster was walking Nick. By the smile on Nick's face, I could also see that he enjoyed every minute of it.

Standing in front of the full-length closet mirror, I took off my shorts and shirt and stepped out of my bikini. The sun had gloriously kissed my body, and the bikini-covered white skin contrasted nicely with the caramel-bronze. The outfit I chose for tonight's dinner would show off the tan perfectly, and I walked over to the closet to remove the coral-hued, light-cotton, loose-sleeved dress. The dress was short *and* low enough in all the right places, just enough to keep Nick's attention on me, exactly where I wanted it.

Glancing out the window again, I saw Nick and Buster beginning the trek back to the house, so I quickly headed to the bathroom to jump in the shower before they returned. Not that I held any hidden desire to still be in the shower when Nick made his way up those stairs. *No*, not me.

A light coating of salt from the ocean water covered my body, and as I lathered the soap over my body, it felt like an entire layer of skin was removed. I sensed, and then saw, Nick's outline through the fogged-up shower door, and with a smile sneaking onto my face, I feigned surprised innocence when I felt the crisp, fresh air accompany his warm body as he wrapped around me. The wine's effect still danced through my blood, and feeling Nick hard against me, caused me to push back against him in an invitation to play. He reached his arms around me and took the soap from my hands, rubbing it between his own. I covered his sudsy hands with mine as we shared a joy ride over every inch of my slick body.

Reaching between my legs, Nick slipped his hands out from under mine and gently guided my hand even further back between my legs, gently encouraging me to have some fun on my own. Nick's hands moved back up over my belly and cupped my breasts, grazing my nipples, at the same time, pulling me back even closer to him. Leaning forward, he pulled my ear lobe between his teeth, simultaneously pinching my nipples between his fingers. A moan slid through my lips.

Removing his hands from my breasts, Nick reached down for my hands and placed them on the shower wall. Jets of warm water streamed down my back as his hands found my waist and pulled me back. One hand disappeared and traveled to where my hands had just left, and a finger entered deep inside. I pushed back against it, wanting more of him and *not* just his finger. Nick's other hand left my waist, and I felt a hardness move down deeper between my legs, where he began to lead me closer to the edge quicker than I expected.

I was more than ready, and a replacement for Nick's finger was eager to take its place, completely and fully. His hands found a home back on my waist again and pulled me back up against him as he began to move, slowly and deeply, creating a rhythm I soon found myself matching. I wanted more. I wanted deeper. I wanted faster, but as much as I attempted to quicken the tempo, Nick steadfastly kept the pace slower. With each new thrust, he pushed further, intent on allowing me the pleasure of feeling every inch.

Nick reached around to grab the soap from its shelf, and his sudsy hands soon began a journey over my slippery butt cheeks. I felt him harden inside of me, and the tempo quickened. A soapy finger traced my back seam, beginning at the very top, closer to where his abdomen was joined against me, and then back down the entire length. He moved slowly, making sure to hit every nerve possible, then paused by his desired target, pressing against it gently. I pushed back, and a moan sounded from behind me as I felt him expand deep inside. As the continued steady rhythm teased me toward orgasm, I pressed back up against Nick again, this time with a little more urgency. The sudsy finger entered the previously-forbidden territory, and the next moan from Nick was joined by one of my own.

I quickly realized that all my grand plans were about to be messed up once again. I knew in a single moment that right here, in this shower, I was going to allow Nick to have complete access into the previously sacred spot. Whether it was the wine, the boat ride, or the excited nervousness over meeting the Morgans and going to the Fantasy Play Hotel™, I hadn't a clue. Whatever it was, I just knew I wanted to feel Nick inside of me, and I wasn't going to wait until some spinner on a game gave the green light. As if reading my thoughts, Nick paused and pulled out from deep inside of me, gently rubbing the throbbing thickness over where his thumb had just departed.

I pushed back gently, just enough to let Nick know it was okay, that the green light was on, that he was getting the "go ahead," and the soap returned, once again transforming my butt into a slippery sudsy landscape. He pressed against me, but before I allowed access, I needed to make sure he knew to go slow and easy; no speeding train through a tunnel for this ride, *and* I wanted him to use lots of lube.

I turned my head back toward him. "Nick."

He leaned forward to hear me over the blasting water and already knew what words were about to be spoken. Brushing wet hair from my face, he pressed his lips against my ear.

"Baby, I promise, slow and gentle."

I looked back at him. "And lots of lube, mister."

Although I risked losing the spontaneity of the moment, I wanted to enjoy the act as much as Nick did, and no complaints were forthcoming. His lips brushed against my ears again as his hand guided my hand down between my legs. "Baby, I'll be right back."

Nick returned in record time, and thirty seconds later, lube in hand, we were quickly back in the throes of passion and intent desire. Slick lube quickly replaced the soap, and my backside was soon sleek and ready; so was Nick. He gently pressed up against me. "I want in, Lacey."

I felt myself begin to relax, allowing the requested entry, and the satisfying moan drifted to my ear. Each time Nick pressed against me, I felt myself open up, allowing him to fill me slowly. The initial discomfort and newness of sensation dissipated, and a feeling that was both exciting and sensual took its place. Nick's hand reached around, and upon locating my sweet spot, two fingers began circling. As I became accustomed to the pace of feeling him slide in and out of my ass, I began to push back a little quicker. Nick's fingers glided over my clit like a skilled dancer having memorized the way to the climactic final scene. His moans let me know that the final scene would play out within the next couple of moments, and as soon as I felt the added warmth within me, his fingers became covered in the wetness of my own. So much for the best-laid plans of mice and men and *Fantasy Play 101*.

Fifteen minutes later, showered and wrapped in fuzzy towels, we fell back on the plush bed, and Nick placed his arm around me as I curled up next to him, head on his chest. His fingers ran through my wet hair.

"So, babe, what made you decide today was the day?"

I rearranged myself into a sitting position, turning to face him with a smile. "Quite honestly, I have no better answer for that than you do, mister."

I held up my "wait a minute" finger, scooted off the bed, and walked toward the closet, continuing to talk. "As a matter of fact, I had it planned out so differently."

Reaching in, I pulled out the familiar Twister box, which was quickly becoming a bit worn around the edges. Nick turned on his side, propping his head with a bent arm. "Wow, anal sex *and* more fantasy play?"

I shook my head and laughed. "No, silly, I want to show you something."

Sitting back on the bed, crossing my legs underneath me and facing Nick, I pulled off the game lid and removed the spinner, all triangles now replaced with only one category: Anal Play. I turned it so he could read the triangles.

"*This* is how I was going to let you know I was ready for anal sex, Mr. Atwood, and I hadn't been planning on it until a few days from now!"

Nick moved closer and reached over, taking the spinner from my hands. He placed it on the bed next to himself and looked up at me.

"Hmm, we could always go for round two, you know?"

There was no way I was going to agree to anal sex, round two. I would be talking with Nick a little later about anal sex *not* being a frequent addition. It wasn't like his penis was the smallest thing, and even though it was an enjoyable experience, there were many things I enjoyed more; a *lot* of things I enjoyed more. I pushed Nick back gently and scooted over to sit on top of him. Looking down into his brownish-green eyes, I removed my towel.

"I'm all for round two, but that round is going to be my way! *This* time you need to finish where you originally started thirty minutes ago."

Very quickly, we were on a mission to finish off round two.

I glanced at the clock as the alarm signaled our little afternoon nap of forty-five minutes was over. We needed to get ready to meet the Morgans. A few hours of sun and saltwater, some wine, two rounds of fantastic sex, and two showers had knocked both of us on our asses.

I sat up and bent over, kissing Nick. "Come on, handsome guy, we have to get ready."

Nick stretched and smiled. "I love you, beautiful."

Once again, my heart turned all warm and melty. I bent over for a second kiss. "I love you, too."

Rising off the bed, I walked toward the closet, taking the coral dress and its hanger off the rack. Nick watched through each motion, his head resting against the crossed arms behind his head. I walked over to the mirror and pulled the dress over my head.

"Oh, man, Nick. I forgot to fill you in on what Kitty told me about the Morgans." Popping my head out the top of the dress, I looked over at him. "Well, unless you know more about them than you've told me already?"

I silently hoped Nick didn't already know everything Kitty told me on the boat. My heart momentarily paused its beating until he replied. "Lacey, I've told you everything I know about the Morgans. I promise." Nick sat up on the bed with his back against the headboard. "So, spill it, woman. What juicy secrets do you know that I don't?"

I chuckled and threw the towel at him. "Spill it, woman?"

He grinned. "Okay, okay ... please, oh beautiful, sexy, fantastic woman of mine ... dare tell me what secrets you hold within."

I walked toward the vanity table and sat down on the padded seat, flipping on the lamp to apply my makeup. I directed my gaze to the reflected Nick as I spoke. "That's better, but you need to get your butt up and start getting ready."

Nick arose from the bed and began to put on his clothes, occasionally glancing at the "reflected me" as I began to tell him all about the Dominant/submissive lifestyle the Morgans lived. I added that I had been unsure how to respond when Kitty first told me. Nick replied with timely smiles and "no shits." I was curious about his thoughts, and after makeup was on and hair brushed, I turned around on the padded stool, watching Nick put on his shoes.

"So, Mr. Atwood, what do you think about all of that?"

Nick looked up at me and smiled. "Hmm, let's see if I can read the great Lacey mind that's behind this question."

He knows me, oh so well.

Nick stood up and walked over to me, reaching down to take my hands, pulling me up to him. "First, there is no way I could even imagine wanting to be involved in that lifestyle with anyone but your sexy, beautiful self. Second, I wouldn't ever want either of us doing anything we didn't want to do under some sense of obligation."

He pulled me closer, capturing my soul with his eyes. "Now, that said, the thought of having my way with you, in all kinds of ways, using all kinds of toys and devices...," Nick traced my lips with his finger, keeping his eyes locked on mine. He stopped at the rise of my upper lip and then moved down, placing his finger just inside my mouth, against my teeth "... now that's an entirely different story."

I gently bit down against his finger as I looked into his eyes, a warmth coursing through my entire network of veins. I grinned around his finger. "Hmm ... that may be a fascinating story, Mr. Atwood."

Nick lifted my chin with his forefinger and thumb, intense liquid heat seeming to transfer directly from his eyes into mine. "Fascinating indeed, Ms. Coleman. To be continued, as it is time for us to leave. We need to go."

CHAPTER 6

Santauris was hopping; it was 7 p.m., and the patio tables appeared near capacity. Laughter mixed with conversation and drifted through the air as we walked toward the front door. Nick looked at me and winked before pulling the wooden door open. "You ready for this, beautiful?"

I returned a smile that was full of confidence, although it steadily wavered with each step. "As ready as I'm going to be, I suppose."

Nick leaned over and kissed me. "Lacey, I love you. You'll be fine."

We stepped inside the bustling coziness that is Santauris on a Friday evening.

I breathed in deeply. *This is it, Lacey. The long-awaited meeting with the notorious Katt Morgan.*

The same smiling hostess, Marci, was situated behind the reception stand. "Hello again, you two. Reservations?"

Nick started to reply. "I believe Mark has a table rese ...," but before he could finish, Mark came walking around the corner.

"I thought that was you two walking in." Mark welcomed us with hugs and then turned back to me. "But, then again, it's impossible not to recognize a beautiful face."

Nick shot a side glance, complete with squinting eyes and raised eyebrows. A grin followed two seconds later. "You flirting with my woman again, dude?"

Mark returned the grin and, with a mock look of surprise on his face, pointed to his chest. "Who me?" A wink in my direction chased after the question.

I smiled and shook my head. Boys in men's costumes!

Mark turned to Marci as he spoke. "I'll take them back to their table."

Marci reached down to grab two menus, but Mark shook his head. "No need for those, but the Morgans are due soon, so when they arrive, can you please walk them back to join us, Marci?"

Mark gifted the overly, smitten hostess another smile, and I almost heard Cupid's wings fluttering from within her eager body. Ahh, the rush of infatuation and imagined true love. I had met many "Marks," all charming and handsome but "oh so dangerous" for fragile hearts.

From the earlier view of the patio, I had assumed full occupancy. I was delightfully mistaken. Snaking our way around the tables, Mark stopped several times, greeting familiar faces, shaking hands, kissing cheeks. He led us back past the stone fireplace to a secluded spot, unseen from the restaurant's entranceway, a perfect hidden oasis.

A cobblestone wall surrounded a hidden patio. One round, wooden-topped, cast iron-legged table awaited us, large enough to seat eight to ten patrons. Today, the table held six place settings. A wrought iron tree branch sat in the center of the table with candles strategically placed atop the metal leaves. Six padded wooden chairs surrounded the table, intended to comfort the diners as they filled their bellies with food.

Across from the secluded spot's hidden entrance, flames danced within a crafted stone fireplace, and behind that, a towering tree stood full of twinkling white lights that adorned the willowy branches. I looked to my right, my ears hearing the gentle sound of splashing water. There, a "mini-me" version of *my* mermaid smiled back at me, water cascading over her outstretched hands. To my delight, upon *these* cupped, copper hands, a little bronze bird perched. The water cascaded down to the stone-surrounded small pool where fish swam under the tiki torches' reflected light standing guard around the fountain. I ventured this little mermaid had her tales to tell as well.

The soft jazz sound drifted from speakers hidden within the stone walls, effectively muting the patio crowd's conversations and noise. It was almost magical, and I found myself so enchanted by the beauty that I nearly jumped when I heard Nick's voice beside me. His hand pressed against my lower back.

"I'm pretty impressed. How about you?"

I looked from the mini-me mermaid toward Nick while nodding my head. "This is beautiful, and do you know what it reminds me of, but on a smaller scale?"

Nick chuckled, nodding his head. "Nicholas Ventricci's patio where I proposed?"

Memories of that night flashed through my mind. I turned to face Nick, placing a hand on each side of his handsome face. "Exactly! The best day of my life so far, Mr. Atwood."

Mark appeared next to us, chuckling, shaking his head. "Okay, you two, enough of this envy-provoking love you have going on. I have a couple bottles of wine heading back to us. Katt just texted. They're running fifteen minutes late."

I took a deep breath. *Relax, Lacey.*

The waiter returned with the wine. We spent the next fifteen minutes talking about tomorrow's grand opening, the planned haunted tour, and Nick's new upcoming Charleston photo project before Nick suddenly looked at me, then at Mark. "And there's still the surprise she knows nothing about yet."

I looked, first at Nick, invisible question marks appearing all over my face, and then over at Mark, who returned my questioning expression with a suspicious grin. "Sorry, sworn to secrecy, Ma'am."

I returned my look to Nick. "What do you mean, you have a surprise for me?"

He replied with a smile and wink. "It wouldn't be much a surprise if I told you, would it?"

I narrowed my eyes at him, attempting a look of seriousness. "I have ways of making you talk, you know."

Nick started to reply, his mouth shaping into a mischievous grin. Suddenly, a woman's voice, slightly tinged with a southern drawl, filled the air.

"I am so sorry we are late."

I turned my head, and there she was, the incomparable — the one and only — Mrs. Kattrina Morgan. Walking next to her was her husband, Joe, and following them was the ever-smiling hostess, Marci. Katt was beautiful, yet not in an "over-the-top" way. She projected a self-assured and self-confident beauty, but it arrived wrapped in the same warmth to which I had grown accustomed in Charleston. She reminded me of Kitty Anderson, only twenty years younger.

Tall and on the slender side, Katt Morgan emitted an aura of casual southern class. Her auburn hair fell way below her shoulders and cascaded in that perfectly messy, just rolled off the beach, wavy style. She wore a loose, maxi-length, white dress with billowy sleeves. I had seen her photo from the book cover and had googled her image several times. It was different seeing her standing in front of me, and I felt nowhere near the sense of intimidation I had anticipated. She was beautiful in a big sister or a "girl next door" kind of way. Joe Morgan and Nick would get along great if their personalities matched their taste in clothes. Joe wore jeans and an off-white, button-down shirt, which appeared as if handpicked by his very own designer, which it probably was!

Mark walked the few feet over to greet the Morgans as they made their way to the table, while Nick reached for my hand and gently pulled me toward the group. Katt looked past Mark and took the few steps over to us, arms outstretched.

"Nick! It is so great to see you again!"

Nick reciprocated the hug and then stepped back to introduce me, although he didn't need to. Katt smiled at me with unmistakable genuineness.

"Lacey Coleman! You, my dear, are refreshingly stunning, and I feel like I already know you!" Katt wrapped her arms around me and then stepped back, looking up at her husband. "Lacey, this is my husband, Joe. Joe, Lacey."

Joe wrapped me up in his big arms and gave me a hug mirroring Katt's but squishing me just a bit more. He was a big guy!

We spent the next couple of minutes determining the seating arrangement. Nick and I sat across from the Morgans. At the same time, Mark settled into the chair nearest the patio's entranceway, anticipating a summoning before long. The waiter arrived to pour the wine, and I was surprised to see it was Nathaniel, the waiter from our first visit; Nathaniel, with an endearing crush on me. Nick looked at me and winked before returning his attention.

"Nathaniel! This is cool! Two for two, having you as our waiter."

He looked at Nick and nodded. "Yes, sir. As always, my pleasure."

Walking around the table, Nathaniel filled each glass with wine, and when he arrived at my setting, he smiled, his face becoming flushed. He was so sweet, and his innocent infatuation was endearing.

"It's nice to see you again, Nathaniel." I thought he would drop the glass.

Nathaniel asked if there was anything else he could get for us before turning to look at Mark. Chef Mason wanted to know when he should begin the meal process.

Mark stood and smiled, lifting his glass. "A toast before I head up front." We all raised our glasses. "To old friends and new friends. To new adventures and the insatiable curiosity to always explore the unexplored. Cheers!" Turning to walk away, Mark looked back over his shoulder. "Appetizers will be out momentarily. New menu for you guys tonight, so enjoy!"

Katt reached across the table and placed her hand over mine. "So, I hear this is your virgin trip to South Carolina, Lacey. Tell me, what do you think?"

I looked across the table into her cheerful, smiling face and returned the smile. "I have unequivocally fallen in love with Charleston, and quite honestly, the thought of having to leave here next week already makes my heart hurt."

Katt nodded her head and looked over at Joe. "That's exactly the way we felt when we first set foot in Charleston and the main reason we decided to build the hotel here. What better way to spark the curiosity and excitement of fantasy play than with sun, sand, history, and old-fashioned southern hospitality!"

Katt took another sip of wine and winked at me.

What was THAT for? Luckily, Nathaniel's return with steaming bowls of lobster bisque and baskets of buttery biscuits interrupted the runaway-thought train.

It was a good thing I had chosen a loose-fitting dress to wear! The wine and food continued to flow over the next two hours, with blackened catfish, garlic potatoes, a fresh vegetable mix following the bisque, and Crème Brulé to delightfully complete the dining experience. The shared conversation flowed as effortlessly as the wine, and the establishment of friendship developed with an ease I had never experienced. Joe's wicked sense of humor had us laughing just as much as we talked. However, I was no fool, and the elephant in the room would soon demand its presence be known; of this, I had no doubt.

And it did. The conversation eventually turned back to the Fantasy Play Hotel™ and the grand opening. Katt Morgan teased us with some of the affirmative RSVPs while I made sure to keep my lower jaw from dropping. I had past superstar crushes on some of the invited people. These were the same people who would soon be setting eyes on bright, shining images of me, Lacey Coleman, in all sorts of provocative poses and outfits — just one more reason I was thankful for obscuring my face in the photos. Under the table, I pinched my forearm to remind myself that, yes, this was really happening and, no, this wasn't just a dream.

Katt hadn't stopped talking, and I began to catch up to her words again. "Just so you know, if you ever decide you've had enough of northeast Ohio, you two can move on down here. We would have so much fun!"

Nick and I looked at each other and chuckled, shaking our heads. He snuck a hand under the table. Reaching and finding my leg, he began rubbing his thumb slowly along my inner thigh as he turned with a smile toward Katt. "Don't go putting any ideas in Lacey's head. I think I'm already going to have a tough time convincing her to go home in a few days. That said, I think we both would love to relocate down here eventually."

Katt looked at both of us and raised her wine glass. "A toast then! For future possibilities and opportunities ahead!"

Mark rejoined us, and the men continued the discussion on tomorrow's party while Katt and I picked up our wine glasses and walked over by the fireplace. Gentle wisps of cooling night air balanced the warmth of the fire.

"So, Lacey, are you excited to see your image decorating the walls of the Fantasy Play Hotel™?"

I shook my head and looked at her. "You know, Katt, if someone told me one year ago that I would be engaged to Nick Atwood, that I would be sitting here talking to the one-and-only Katt Morgan, and that hundreds of people would soon see LED images of me in little, frilly outfits, I would have deemed them crazy!" I took another sip of wine. "But now it just seems almost pre-destined. I'm truly excited for tomorrow to arrive!"

Katt reached over and put her hand on top of mine. "I want you to know, as added appreciation, you and that handsome guy of yours have your choice of a fantasy room for a night this weekend, on the house."

I almost choked on the sip of wine I was swallowing. "Get out! Are you serious?"

She laughed and winked at me. "As long as it's not one of the same rooms that Joe and I will be using."

I shook my head and laughed. "Okay, that's a deal."

Katt added one more titillating item, leaving me unsure how to respond. "Also, Lacey, you and Nick should think about attending one of our special 'invitation-only' events we have planned over the next couple of months."

I looked at her with a questioning expression, prodding her to explain more.

"You know, one of our Dominant/submissive events … just to check it out. No pressure." Her hand returned on top of mine, and she leaned over closer to me. "You may really enjoy it, Lacey. You just never know."

AWKWARD!!!

Thankfully, Nick sensed that same awkward thought as I was thinking it. I was never so relieved to hear his voice next to me, sparing me the need to respond to Katt's statement. "Well, my dear, are you about ready to head out?"

I looked up at my rescuer with thankfulness. "Yep. I'm ready if you are."

We parted ways with Mark and the Morgans, thanking them for dinner and passing around hugs. The evening had most definitely been an interesting one. Nick and I decided to stroll through the streets, recapping the evening before returning home. I told him about the offer for the comped hotel room, and he stopped walking and turned me to face him. Wrapping his arms around my waist, Nick pulled me close, and I saw a darkening of his eyes.

"Hmm, you up for that?"

I let my hand drift down to Nick's butt, where I gave it a couple of pats. "I'm up for it if you are, Mister."

Nick leaned in to kiss me. "Okay, so here's the deal then. After we get the tour of the place, I'm going to let you choose the room. Agreed?"

Hmm. Interesting tactic. "You sure you want me to choose, Nick?"

He leaned back in, but instead of giving me another kiss, he found his way to my ear. "I am sure, but right now, beautiful lady, I need to take you home because I feel an increase in appetite, and this time, it is *not* for food."

I looked up at Nick and smiled. "I guess you'll just have to catch me first!"

Turning, I began to run back toward the car, not getting too far before I was swooped up, like Tarzan's Jane, and thrown over his shoulder. I laughed all the way back to the car.

Arriving back at the house, Nick left to take Buster for a short walk. Somewhere along the line, this dog-walking chore had become Nick's without any discussion, and that was perfectly okay with me. I loved giving Buster lots of hugs and kisses, but I was less than enthusiastic about the thought of being dragged halfway down the street by a massive bundle of fur. I would stick with sharing my early morning coffee time in the outside garden with him, his big body lying by my feet while I silently conversed with my bronzed friend.

I stopped by the patio before heading upstairs. My mermaid was there, still splashing in the water with the patio lights reflecting off her bronze skin.

Ohh, I have some juicy things to tell you. I'll meet you for coffee in the morning.

I swear she smiled and nodded her head. I fully realized the two glasses of wine might have led to the propensity for hallucinations like that. I giggled, closed the doors, and as I headed up the staircase, my mind wandered to the delectable things about to happen over the next hour. It was going to be a good night.

CHAPTER 7

Nick was still sound asleep. I heard the steady, low snoring above my head, which was resting on his chest. Last night had been more than fantastic. The wild fantasy I created in my head while Nick walked Buster had been met *and* satisfied. I scooted from under his arms, being careful not to wake him, and grabbed the satin robe hanging on the door hook, wrapping it around me.

Stepping into the hallway, I quietly closed the door and descended the steps toward the kitchen; I needed some coffee to shake the remnants of slumber. Buster strolled into the kitchen, where he promptly plopped down on the floor on a spot where the sun's rays beamed through the window. I bent down to pet him, and he responded with a heavy sigh. His droopy eyelids closed; Buster was ready to return to his interrupted sleep.

Coffee in hand, I walked toward the garden door, eagerly anticipating the silent conversation ahead. The beep from the phone seemed to echo in the silence, and I jumped at the sound. I must have woken Nick, and this was probably a plea to return to bed. I looked down at my phone, a grin beginning to appear on my face. I was already turning to rush back up the stairs, eager to jump back in bed with Nick for some extra cuddling. I pressed the little blue envelope icon. It wasn't Nick. **Good morning beautiful. Where have you been? I've missed seeing you. I found what you left for me**.

WTF? Not Here!! It was happening again, and I stood, hand on the railing, slowing my breathing. *I thought this was over.* Jack Turner must still be up to his tricks, somehow, some way. There was no way I was going to allow anything to hamper this vacation.

I then remembered my promise to Nick to inform him if I ever received any additional and unwanted messages. It had been an easy promise to make at the time as I thought this was behind us, and I also knew a disclosure would destroy the day. So, I decided to take matters into my own hands and quickly typed a message back. **I am reporting this to the police, and you WILL be caught. You better leave me alone.** I pressed the send button. Another blue icon immediately greeted me. **Unable to send message. Message sending failed.** *Damn it!* I made a mental promise to talk to Lt. Bob Chandler when I returned to Cleveland. Obviously, the creep was still lurking somewhere. I had no enemies. The only radar-blip of a jerk with a self-imagined conviction to harass me was the asshole himself, Jack Turner.

Deal with it later, Lacey. You're safe here. Deciding to heed my inner voice's sage wisdom, I shoved all thoughts of the matter into a "save for later" box. For now, I had some juicy info for the bronze mermaid, *and* there was also a big event for which I needed to prepare mentally.

I walked into the patio garden into brilliant sunshine, already warming up the day, and stretched out on the chaise, laying my head back on the pillow. I looked at the mermaid. *How many stories had she silently listened to? How many hopes, dreams, and wishes had others shared with her? How much sadness, how many tears had she borne witness? How many joys and smiles had reflected off the splashing water under her scaled tail? Would this evening's affair produce additional shared secrets?*

I closed my eyes and mentally rewound the tapes from the previous night. I had finally met the one and only, Kattrina Morgan; THE Katt Morgan!! Where fear and apprehension once ran rampant, nervous excitement and curiosity had taken over. I was also excited about Katt's offer of a free hotel room, and I was bound and determined to select one that would provide a memory of a lifetime.

I took a sip of coffee and looked at the mermaid. "What do you think about that?"

If it is possible to jump straight up from a chair, I think I achieved exactly that. When I posed the question to the mermaid, I had not expected an answer, specifically, a response in a male's voice. "What does who think of what?"

Thank goodness for decent health. If not, a heart attack may have been immediately forthcoming.

I jumped from my chair and looked at Nick, standing in the doorway, wearing an expression of humored confusion. I breathed in deep to slow the speedy heartbeat locomotive.

Nick laughed. "Who in the world are you talking to, Lacey?"

I shook my head. "You scared the crap out of me, Nick!" I continued to talk as I walked over to him. "Who do you think I was talking to?"

I pointed at the mermaid and imagined a smirk on her face. She was no help to me in this situation. Reaching Nick, I snuck my arms around his waist and looked up into his intoxicating hazel eyes and sleep-ruffled hair.

"You know, Nick Atwood, sometimes a girl just needs to have some girl talk, and since there is presently a lack of female companionship, my friendly mermaid offered her ears." I kissed Nick briefly on the lips and smiled. "So, in the words of another handsome Nicholas, we know, 'Nonna youse bizness!'"

He reached down and scooped me up, pretending he was going to throw me headfirst into the fountain. Instead, he carried me back toward the chaise and set me down before pulling over one of the other chairs and placing it across from me. Nick reached over and held both my hands within his hands, leaning forward until our faces were a mere few inches apart. His eyes captured my gaze and locked in on it, and I sensed something was on his mind. I immediately feared he somehow knew about the morning's random text.

I opened my mouth to ask what was wrong, but Nick put his finger against my lips to silence any words, shaking his head slightly. "Lacey, I want to talk to you about something we've been joking about, but now I need you to take me seriously."

Ugh! What was this? I hate the feeling of not knowing what's coming?

Nick took a deep breath before continuing to speak. "When I proposed to you, I knew I wanted to spend the rest of my life with you. I know your feelings about us merely living together as well as your fears that we'll become comfortable in 'living together' mode. I don't want to wait to be married, Lacey. I want to be your husband, and I want to look at you and see my *wife*."

He paused.

I took that opportunity to speak. "I feel the same, Nick, so what are you are getting at."

Nick squeezed my hands, and an endearing, childlike grin erupted on his face. "What I'm saying, Lacey, is that I want us to be married before we go back to Cleveland. I've made some calls, and if you're on board with this, I have a plan."

I wasn't sure what to say or how to respond as there was actually nothing standing in the way of this happening. Nick looked at me with an expression of mixed apprehension and uncertainty.

I paused before nodding my head slowly up and down, a smile beaming on my face.

"Nick Atwood, I would love for Charleston to be where we start our married life together. Let's do this."

He breathed in deeply and then exhaled as a smile spread over his face. "You sure?"

I nodded again. Nick stood and grabbed my hand, pulling me up, so we were face-to-face. He reached up with his finger and traced my lips. "So, now the question is, do you want to know the details, or do you prefer it to all be a surprise?"

Well, that was an interesting question, and I again had to pause before responding. Not only was I lost in my thoughts, but I was also somewhat lost in the feeling that Nick's finger, still tracing the outline of my lips, was creating. Little invisible sparks traveled throughout my body. This year, so far, had been one of challenges, shared vulnerability, several unexpected surprises, and adventurous exploration. No reason to stop that runaway train now!

I looked at Nick. "It's all in your hands, Mr. Atwood, but I do have one condition." He waited. "I don't want to be married at the hotel. Please, just promise me that isn't part of the plan."

Nick laughed and pulled me close to him. "I promise it isn't part of the plan. Actually, it will be closer to the day we leave, and that's all I'm saying about it. Now come on, get your sexy ass moving. Let's go enjoy some of this sun before we have to get ready for tonight."

Arriving back at the house three hours later with sun-kissed sandy bodies, Nick embarked on his dog-walking duty while I jumped into the shower. Exiting ten minutes later, I laid down on the bed. The sheet was refreshingly crisp under my warmed, tanned skin, and with the deck doors open, the ceiling fan helped send gentle waves of cool air over me. I fell asleep and didn't even hear Nick come in the room, jump in the shower, or sneak under the sheet next to me. He must have fallen asleep as quickly as I had, and we both woke to his phone alarm. Thankfully he set it, or I think we would have, quite possibly, slept for several hours more, and *that* wouldn't have been good. We had a grand opening to attend! Not that I was one 100 percent ready for it, but as the saying goes, ready or not, here I come!

CHAPTER 8

The thirty-minute drive to the hotel seemed to pass at an excruciatingly slow speed, and any prior thought or belief that my nerves were back under control was obviously untrue. Thirty minutes earlier, I had walked from the bedroom in a form-fitting black dress, matching high-heels, with my hair cascading over my shoulders in beachy waves. Nick's mouth-gaping expression affirmed the success in pulling off the look I attempted, which was one of cool, calm, and full of self-confidence. Outward appearances can be *so* deceiving; my nerves were a mess, and I was a jittery wreck. I reminded myself, repeatedly, to stay in the here-and-now with no expectations. My goal was to fully enjoy the experience or at least smile like I was.

Old Charleston is a continually morphing city, and The Fantasy Play Hotel™ is situated about fifteen miles from the hub of its laid-back charm. I first glimpsed the hotel as we rounded the corner onto the street; elegant and welcoming, the hotel's design intended to project an atmosphere both trendy and classic. The cream-colored hotel rose five stories high, and individual room balconies, bordered with a wrought iron railing, jutted from the building at each of the upper four levels. I was eager to see what awaited behind each of the tall multi-paned doors beckoning the room's occupants to re-enter for endless adventure.

I looked upward through the windshield toward the upper levels as Nick drove past the hotel to turn around for valet parking. Colored strobe lighting streamed from the open windows. *That must be the "event" level.*

Above the ever-changing strobe lighting was the rooftop, bordered by tall shrubbery, peppered with little white lights. A deep blue glow filled the night-time sky, oozing of suggested sexuality. *And that must be the famed rooftop lounge and pool.*

Nick turned the car around and placed the gear in park. I knew Katt Morgan would ensure that the hotel theme, maintained continuity through-out every detail, and the valets standing along the curb were no exception. Quite possibly, Katt had hand-selected these fine specimens of the male gen-der directly from a *GQ* lineup. The uniform of made-to-fit-oh-so-perfectly jeans and colored t-shirt; each valet sporting a different color was delightful. Most of the men sported tattoos somewhere on their visible skin, and all hair, including facial, was deliberately styled to project a vibe of "bad guy/ good guy" sensuality.

A valet reached in for my hand to help me from the car. "Let me help you, beautiful."

Nick walked around the car and smiled at the valet. "She's quite stun-ning, wouldn't you say?"

The valet replied with a smile. "Yes, sir, that she is!"

He motioned with his hand, directing us toward the entrance where a steady stream of party-goers made their way inside. Nick grabbed my hand and smiled as we strolled over the brick walkway toward the large wooden doors. "You ready for this, Lacey?"

Managing to reach down and pull one of my confident "no sweat" smiles from my cache of inner goodies, I replied with a nod and a "Yep, let's do this!"

A couple more steps forward, and we were inside the surreal lobby of the hotel. It was at that moment, although not consciously realized for many more months, my life switched tracks. It was a subtle shift. On a subcon-scious level, I recognized, registered, and accepted this awareness shift as something for my future self to process more fully. It was something Nick and I would have many discussions about over the years. I'm somewhat sure that Nick experienced a shifting of the train tracks in those initial few mo-ments as well. For now, all we knew was that we had just entered a very awe-inspiring atmosphere.

The lobby was grand and bridged old-style structures with modern-day technology. As evidenced by the food-covered tables taking over half of the space, Mark was here somewhere, and the mouth-watering aroma drifted past my eager nostrils. As found in most upscale hotels, a gift shop was open for business to my immediate left. The sign above the door proclaimed it as the Fantasy Play Toy Store, and from what I could see, it offered everything a curious or adventurous individual could desire during their stay. Katt had mentioned that safety and health guidelines deemed it necessary to have guests bring most of their "more intimate" toys; however, she assured us there was plenty of fun stuff and apparel waiting beyond the store entrance.

The aroma from the food tables continued to tease while music, now emanating from somewhere past the lobby desk, began to stream through the speaker system. Both the aroma and the sound kidnapped my senses; however, it was neither of those that caused me to stop dead in my tracks and render me motionless. I breathed deep a few inhalations as I drew to a standstill. There, in front of me, shining in huge full-size LED on the wall behind the front desk, were a couple of images of me. ME!!

Hanging to the front desk's left was a shining, displayed image of me sitting in a chair, clad only in knee-high socks and pearls with hair covering the turned face. On the wall to the front desk's right, my shining image hung, this time adorned in garters, teddy, and stockings with a hat angled down on my head to shield my identity. The brilliance of the LED made it challenging to wrap my brain around what I was seeing.

Nick hadn't moved yet, either. I looked at him with my mouth still slightly agape. Returning my look of amazement, he smiled, shaking his head. "Those turned out pretty damn awesome, babe. That's YOU!!!"

Lowering my voice, I placed my mouth next to Nick's ear. "Nick, people are actually standing here looking at the images. This feels so unreal."

He wrapped his arm around my waist. "Nope, it's all very real, my dear. I'm standing here with my arm around *that* woman everybody is standing here looking at, and she happens to be *my* fiancé."

Intending to respond, I was distracted by movement near the far side of the lobby desk. There stood a giant LED Fantasy Play wheel that I hadn't noticed previously. I had been too focused on the illuminated displays. A small gathering of brave-hearts began cheering as a woman stepped up and gave the large spinner a turn. This wheel undoubtedly put my little Twister invention to shame, and *this* wheel held numerous mini photos, each symbolizing a suggestion for adult fun from *Fantasy Play 101*. Laughter erupted from the group as the wheel stopped on a picture of a woman bent over a man's lap, his hand holding a paddle. The woman burst into laughter and turned. It was Kitty Anderson from yesterday's yacht excursion, although I hadn't recognized her with her hair up and makeup on her face.

Kitty noticed Nick and me standing there watching and nudged her husband, nodding in our direction. After urging one of the other women in the group to give the wheel a spin, the Andersons headed over to where we stood. Kitty wore a fairly sheer, flowing caftan, and the thinness of the fabric allowed a glimpse of the alert and lifted, "enhanced" seventy-year-old breasts. She hugged me and then stood back a step.

"Absolutely gorgeous, my dear!" She then leaned closer to me and whispered in my ear. "You know, Lacey, after seeing you on the boat yesterday, I do see a remarkable resemblance to these beautiful pictures throughout the hotel." My stomach turned, and I felt a warmth on my cheeks. Kitty let out a short laugh. "Don't you worry. Your secret is safe with me."

I turned and smiled at her, ready to reply, but stopped, deciding instead to play it cool for the time being. Better not to affirm her intelligent and on-target observation. Besides, Kitty was already smiling and waving to someone from behind Nick and me.

I heard Katt's voice moments before I felt her hand land gently upon my back from behind. "There you two are!!"

Nick and I turned to see Katt Morgan wearing a white jumpsuit that was cut low enough in the front that bending over would present a challenge in keeping the "girls" corralled. Looking quite *GQ* himself, Joe Morgan stood at her side dressed in suit pants and a button-down white shirt, no tie. He didn't need one. There are certain costly clothing brands that one can wear without any extra accessories, and from the looks of the hotel, money was *not* an issue for the Morgans.

Following shared hugs, Katt immediately began talking a mile a minute.

"You two ready for the tour?" Neither one of us had a chance to answer before she continued talking.

"What am I thinking? First, let's get you two some drinks!"

"Getting us something to drink" took almost as long as the car ride to the hotel. Being stopped every few paces to exchange hugs and swapped kisses, introductions, and small talk, we would then set off *again* toward the nightclub down the hall. To say that it took a concentrated effort to maintain an aura of nonchalance in the presence of individuals to whom I never dreamt I would be face to face and shaking hands with would be an understatement. An overwhelming sense of surrealness hung in the surrounding air, leaving me slightly discombobulated, and I had to remind myself to remain "in the moment" several times. However, the "to be reviewed later" box, somewhere in the back of my brain, was quickly nearing capacity.

We *did* eventually make it down the hall and through the nightclub doors into a throbbing atmosphere of sensuality, sexuality, fun, and excitement, where colored strobe lights projected over the dance floor, currently brimming with movement. A beat-pumping, air-fisting DJ, seamlessly blended musical magic from an elevated circular platform in the center of the room, as five additional raised platforms offered the opportunity for those seeking extra attention. Dance cages sat atop two of those five, both occupied, with a mini-skirted woman in one and a shirtless jean-clad man in the other. Neither lacked dancing skills, and both caused heads to turn upward in their direction, including mine. That is until a now-familiar brilliance caught my eye.

LEDs beamed from the surrounding walls, and after pausing midbreath in anxious anticipation of what would momentarily fill my vision, I sighed in relief upon seeing that, instead of reflecting my image, these displays were ever-changing to showcase the dancers.

Joe immediately took over as bartender once we finally made our way over, and within minutes, six curvy, sexy-looking, long-stemmed glasses appeared before us. Sexy glasses for the Fantasy Play Hotel™, no surprise there! Joe picked up his glass and raised it in the air.

"I give you the S&M — guaranteed to capture your attention — sometimes sooner, sometimes later, but always successfully." We all lifted our glasses for the toast, and Joe continued. "To friends, new adventures, and who knows what the hell else. Bottoms up!"

The drink was tasty, a mixture of scotch whiskey, melon, lime, pineapple, and cherry liqueur. Joe was right; it was an unusual taste uniquely designed to awaken several senses. The change in beats filling the air awakened one of the other senses, and after Joe joined us on the other side of the bar, we all turned to watch the dancing crowd as we, too-quickly, finished the first round of drinks. It was impossible not to soak in the dancers' intoxicating movements, and I informed Nick that I would be dragging him out on the dance floor before the evening's end. We connected in the bedroom, and that same natural rhythm followed us onto a dance floor whenever presented with the opportunity.

But first things first, we had a tour to take. The first drink went down *way* too easy and succeeded with allowing a nice little buzz. Joe — not having to be asked twice — refilled our glasses and then rejoined us to begin the hotel's formal tour.

Arriving back at the lobby, we found ourselves stopped in front of another LED. This one showcased a diagrammed listing of the hotel's layout and a short, detailed sentence or two that explained the theme corresponding to each hotel floor. The different floor levels matched the different categorized sections of *Fantasy Play 101*, so I was surprised to see three additional rooms in the hotel's basement. According to the display's description, the hotel's underground level offered three fully-equipped sexual dungeon playrooms, each available in one- to three-night packages. *Hmm, very interesting!*

The main floor, which we were currently on, was home to the lobby, bar, nightclub, gift shop, and restaurant. A clerk at the front desk greeted guests with a more detailed listing of the rooms, the hotel's rules and regulations, the zero-tolerance policy designed to ensure all visitors had a safe and enjoyable stay, and a listing of the package deals available for more extended stays.

Katt presented both Nick and me with a brochure describing the theme of each floor and every room. I briefly skimmed over the vast variety of offered themes ranging from bath and sensory play on the first floor, movie-making on the second floor, and over to intimate erotic massage rooms, nipple play, and restraint use on the third floor. There was so much more, but my mind wasn't allowing me to process it all at once as I became a bit "heated" just looking over all the provocative descriptions. Nick squeezed my waist, and I looked over at his smiling face.

Hmmm. What thoughts are traveling through that handsome head of his?

The fourth floor encompassed the last and most openly adventurous category; On Fire! I could only imagine what went on in the rooms beyond those doors! Bondage, physical discipline, Dominant/submission, sadism and masochism; all areas that waited for exploration by the bolder couples. An added directive next to the fourth-floor description advised visitors to check in with the front desk for additional rules, safety guidelines, and consensual agreement signing before room use.

The fifth floor was devoted to rental space and special events, and I already knew from yesterday's conversation with Katt, the Dominant/submissive parties. Katt added this floor would be the location of numerous workshops and instructional classes they had scheduled for the next six months, and my curiosity and interest piqued upon hearing the titles of some of these. The first workshop, the Art of Shibari Weekend, was already filled and had a waiting list. From what I remembered, Shibari has something to do with erotic rope tying and the now- formulating image of being tied up by Nick, well … luckily, Katt interrupted my thought.

Turning to Nick and me, a mischievous smile slowly appeared on Katt's face. "You know, you two are more than welcome to sign yourselves up for the Dominant/submissive 101 classes beginning in early spring."

I opened my mouth to reply, but Joe came to the rescue. Placing his arm around Katt's waist, he squeezed as he spoke. "Sweetheart, they may need to work their way up to that; don't want to scare them away just yet." *Thank you, Joe.*

The uncomfortable moment passed, and we all shared a laugh. However, I was now more than ready to begin the rest of the tour as I usually found comfort in movement amidst uncomfortableness, and besides, I was eager to check out the rooftop bar and pool. Grabbing a set of keys behind the desk, Katt looked at me and winked.

"Some rooms, not *everyone* is allowed to see."

My curiosity piqued once again, and I grabbed Nick's hand as we began to trail behind Katt's beckoning wave. We passed Mark Santauri, hovering over food-laden tables, on the way toward the elevators and stopped for some hugs before beginning the fun part of the tour.

"Lacey, you look beautiful as always, and Nick, you always clean up well, buddy."

Hearing his name called by one of the catering staff, Mark chuckled and shook his head. "Always something, I swear. You guys come grab some food after you get back from the tour." Turning to walk toward the beckoning staff member, Mark stopped and wheeled back to look at us. "Enjoy, you two."

We turned and resumed following Katt down the hallway, where I immediately found myself face-to-face with "Lacey in Lights." While it still boggled the mind to connect those breathtaking images to the person looking up at them, I was finally able to view them in a more detached way, and I was humble enough to admit that Nick's skill behind the camera deserved most of the credit.

Halfway down the hallway, we stopped in front of the elevator and waited for the door to open. When it did, a visual delight beckoned me to step deeper inside toward the far wall. One of the hotel staff members called out to Katt the moment she stepped into the elevator. While she spoke with the staff member, Joe stood with his hand against the elevator door, keeping it open for her. This short delay in our journey was insignificant to me as I attempted to absorb the sight before me.

The elevator's back wall was created entirely of glass, allowing a clear view of the central courtyard. A giant palm tree fountain, its height level with the fourth-floor balconies, sprayed water from the top, the water then pouring down over large leaves on its way to the stone basin below where changing colors danced beneath.

Scattered around the fountain, chairs — each glowing with a different color — awaited hotel guests. I noticed another glass-sided elevator in motion directly across the courtyard. Looking around the perimeter, I saw three others on the move, each in the process of transporting guests who were also enjoying the tour of this incomparable hotel.

Nick joined me. "Damn!"

I responded, looking up at him with a smile. "Um, yep, a little stunning, I would say."

Katt's voice interrupted our focused stupor. "So sorry about that, guys, comes with the territory!"

Katt turned to us and smiled as she pressed the #1 button.

"We need to go up before we go down ...," and Katt being Katt, added, not surprisingly, "...pun most definitely intended, my dears."

What am I in for?

CHAPTER 9

The elevator door opened onto the first floor, where I came face-to-face with a shiny image of myself dressed in the nurse's outfit, complete with white stockings, garters, and a stethoscope hanging between my breasts. Walking through the opened elevator door, I looked down the hallway in both directions, seeing several more LEDs adorning the walls. Nick grabbed my hand to slow me down while allowing the others to walk a few paces ahead.

"You doing okay, Lacey?"

I looked over at Nick and smiled. "I'm perfect, Nick. Just focused on determining which room we're going to test out tomorrow night."

He leaned closer, his mouth grazing my ear. "Maybe we should try several."

I was just about to respond when we realized the group had abruptly stopped. One more step, and it would have been a human pile-up. Katt explained the hotel floor plans; each floor consisted of sixteen rooms, four rooms per each of the four sides of the hotel's square shape. Two of the sixteen were designated honeymoon or bridal suites, complete with a hot tub and a massage table.

The rooms' spacing ensured the complete privacy and seclusion of the hotel's visitors, which was a good thing, as I'm sure that plenty of noise occurred behind the doors!! In each room, as I was about to discover soon, a standing Fantasy Wheel awaited use. Opened doors beckoned in each direction, unlocked, and opened for tonight's grand opening, and I saw curiosity-seekers entering and departing rooms — not surprisingly, with smiles on their faces.

The first several rooms we entered pertained to the role-playing suggestions found in the Mild Sizzle section of *Fantasy Play 101*. The attention to detail was astounding, and it provided added testament to Joe and Katt Morgan's desire to please their clientele. There were doctor offices with examination tables, Tarzan and Jane jungle rooms, and the law-enforcement themed rooms even come equipped with flashing lights and a variety of handcuffs hanging from the walls. Guests can also preorder costumes or props from the hotel's gift store and have their purchases ready and waiting in their room upon their arrival.

I held back a giggle as I recalled the first visit to Nick's loft and our Tarzan and Jane conversation. *Maybe I should revisit that whole scenario.*

The next set of rooms we walked through catered to the artistic suggestions in *Fantasy Play 101*, with several of them painted in UV colors and lit solely by black lights. The LED hanging from the wall near these rooms was one of my very favorites, and my mind traveled back in memory. Nick and I had finished covering each other from head-to-toe with our Day-Glo artistry, and we stood in front of the full-length mirror. Nick stood behind me as we reveled in the visual glowing reflection, his face obscured behind mine. If not for the darkened room and the paint on my face, there was no way this image would have passed my approval. It was the only picture that could be identifiable to someone who knew me well.

The last of the first-floor rooms were rather basic compared to all the other rooms but far from boring; each came equipped with an elevated dance platform complete with a stripper pole. A leather oversized chair was placed at the edge of the round platform, allowing a very up-close-and-personal view.

We exited the room, and having toured the first floor's full circle, found ourselves back in front of the elevator. My mind felt a bit overloaded. I loved the journey Nick and I were on toward discovering new and exciting sexual adventures, but I found so much full-on "sex focus" at one time, a bit overwhelming. I was aware of the thoughts flitting through *my* brain during the tour, but I had no idea what Nick was thinking. Was he, like I was, picturing us "playing" in each room we walked through? I noticed him glancing over at me several times with a questioning look, a "what do you think of this?" look, and I had little doubt that this evening's conversation would be an interesting one!

The brilliant image of my butt-naked self, bent over Nick's naked lap, his hand poised to strike again as my flushed ass cheeks awaited another sting, greeted us as the elevator door opened onto the second floor. I sensed Nick standing close behind me as the elevator doors closed. His hand traveled down my back, and his thumb began to gently rub the top of my fabric-covered ass. A smile and a wink met my face as I turned to look at him, and I reached down, grabbed his hand from behind me, winked back, and tugged him toward the rest of the group.

The rooms on the second-floor split into three sections: spanking options, movie watching and making, and the introduction of some of the more adventurous sex toys. The beds in the erotic spanking rooms were all four-posted and massive, perfect for the adventurous couple! My eyes drifted over to the heavy, dark wooden chairs, wooden benches, and padded kneeling posts strategically placed in the corners next to mirrors.

One of the rooms contained a three-holed, wooden yoke and reminded me of the many excursions made to Fall festivals and the token photos taken with my head and arms dangling through the openings. This yoke was quite different, with a padded kneeling bench waiting nearby, ready for use. A variety of leather belts, wooden paddles, and some whips hung from wall hooks, while an assortment of ties, handcuffs, and blindfolds lay on the wall shelves. These rooms also provided a sex swing that hung securely from a rafter, and additional ropes "for play" hung nearby from ceiling hooks, which I assumed were for Shibari play.

Nick looked at me and smiled before exiting the room with the yoke. "Hmm, this room may be an interesting choice, yes?"

I grinned back, not saying a word. I would provide no clues to the forthcoming room selection!

The second-floor tour completed, we once again headed back to the elevator. There hadn't been much conversation until now, with Katt Morgan doing most of the talking. However, it appeared she was now eager for some feedback, and before pushing the elevator button to head up to the third floor, Katt turned to face Nick and me.

"So, what do you two think so far?"

Nick and I exchanged glances, and then we both looked at Katt. I wasn't sure how to respond, and he wasn't opening his mouth to "magically" save the day, so I replied with the most honest statement I could make.

"I'm at a loss for words, Katt. I think I'm slightly stunned."

A little bit too late for my liking, Nick finally rediscovered his voice and looked first at Katt, then at Joe. "Well! Without question, managing hotels is your calling, and the attention to detail is just staggering!" He shook his head. "I wish I had even half of the ability to execute something like this. Whatever you guys are doing, you're doing it successfully."

Joe nodded his head while releasing a chuckle. "It's not easy, that's for sure. But, hey, remember, we can always find a dual-management position for you two if you wanted to give it a try."

Thankfully, the elevator door opened, and we piled inside. The others began discussing various business details while Nick and I quietly laughed at the absurdity of even wanting to venture into the hotel business. Visiting hotels was one thing; managing one was something else!

Seconds later, the elevator opened unto the third floor; this one devoted to the "Aflame" section of *Fantasy Play 101*; this one greeting us with a blindfolded Lacey on the bed, limbs spread wide, and tied to Nick's bedposts.

Nick leaned in from behind me with a voice low and husky. "Do you remember, Lacey?"

I turned and smiled back before following Katt toward the first door. "As if I possibly could forget something like that."

The rooms on the third floor offered a greater variety of restraint options for the entire body, including nipple clamps, body chains, and wrist-to-ankle restraints. The four-poster beds came with wrist and ankle cuffs already attached, and the heavy chairs offered the same. Interestingly, a headrest topped off one of the chairs, complete with a strap designed to keep one's head immobile. *I'm not so sure about that thing.* LEDs hung on the walls and displayed numerous suggestions and ideas for the usage of "toys."

On the third floor, I fell in love with the three "special" rooms; these three being slightly more expensive and available only to those who possessed the Gold Fantasy Card. The Pink Room, wholly decorated in shades of pink, was a true princess's dream! A pink frilly robe hung in the closet. Pink curtains, pink sheets, pink phone, pink *everything*, in every shade of pink possible. I had always been more of a deeper color kind of girl; that is until I walked through that pink door. There was something so surreal and different about it. I don't know why, and I had no logical explanation, but I immediately became enamored with that room, a pink cotton candy orgy for the eyes!

The second secret room was the Mirrored Room. Everywhere I looked, my reflection stared back, and intriguing thoughts of Nick and me enjoying each other in a multitude of reflected ways flashed through my mind. *Maybe this would be my room of choice.* Coincidentally, it seemed Nick's thoughts mirrored mine. He moved to stand next to me and caught my reflected eyes. His wink told all; yes, he was sharing the mental visions playing in my mind.

Arabian Nights of Romance aptly described the third "special" room, which invoked an aura of mysterious sensuality through the chosen deep colors of crimson red and rich, brilliant gold. Heavy drapes of gold and that same crimson red surrounded a massive bed, elevated to a height necessitating the three steps located at the foot of the bed; it was that high off the floor! Another delightful perk of this room was the personalized one-hour belly-dancing lesson given to all overnight guests. If that wasn't enough of a hook, each female guest received a complimentary beaded and coined hip scarf to jumpstart their belly-dancing career!

Our small group exited the Arabian-night-themed room into the hallway. Expecting to head down the hall immediately, I was somewhat perplexed when both the Morgans and the Andersons stopped and turned to look at Nick and me, amusement lacing their smiles. Nick and I exchanged a glance, puzzled by this sudden stoppage.

Katt Morgan smiled at us and chuckled. "It's always so fun to see the reaction of couples getting the tour for the first time." She walked over and placed an arm around our shoulders, pulling us in for a makeshift huddle. "Watching the two of you and trying to guess your thoughts; that's what makes this whole Fantasy Hotel concept so exciting for Joe and me." Katt kissed both of us on the cheek. "You guys haven't seen anything yet!"

Boarding the elevator once again, I walked to the back and looked down into the central courtyard. All the chairs held occupants, and at least fifty more people milled around, with some of them waving from below. The elevator began its ascent and then stopped parallel to the top of the spraying palm tree fountain. From this fourth-floor view, I watched as the jets of water shot from the top, reminding me of a particular part of the male anatomy. It hit me like a brick in the head; that was Katt's intention!

The elevator doors opened once again. We had arrived at the floor dedicated to the final category of *Fantasy Play 101*; the one focused on Dominant/submissive play. Each room on this floor offered spanking benches, four-poster beds equipped with cuffs, ties, attached ropes, and hanging racks holding various restraints and sexual tools of pleasure to those couples eager to have a "home away from home." A menu of additional accessories shone from the LED above the bed, and with a quick phone call to the lobby store, any purchase would arrive in minutes. According to the Morgans, these rooms would be in high demand once the Dom/sub events kicked off next week, and five were already under lease for one year.

Each room on this floor was identical to the next, so we toured only two of them; one was fully equipped, and the other awaited the master's desire for decoration. It was apparent Katt and Joe aimed to please, with the full intention of procuring a full roster of repeat customers.

It was at the fifth-floor level that we found ourselves slightly above the top of the courtyard fountain. The elevator doors opened, not into a hallway, but into a grand event room that spanned the hotel's length. Massive in size, the room was capable of being sectioned off into three smaller-sized rooms. Double doors interrupted wall-to-wall windows in several locations, and a balcony wrapped around the outside perimeter, providing a perfect view of the courtyard from any spot.

Joe Morgan happily showed off the inner workings behind the room's darkening windows, *much* needed in a hotel where full windows abounded, and "special" events routinely occurred. During the conversation with Kitty on their yacht, I was told the fee for access to one of the selective private events, and with a price that steep, ensuring the secure privacy of all VIPs was a must! Three bars were set up in the room, stocked, and ready for use when needed. Speaking of bars, we had one last stop to make, and I was now more than ready for a reprieve! Rooftop, here we come!

The elevator doors opened to fresh air and a party atmosphere. Little twilight-white lights encircled the tall shrubbery lining the rooftop edge, and identical to the seating found in the courtyard below, glowing chaises, couches, tables, and chairs were scattered around the roof, creating a kaleido-scope of color. The glowing-blue pool, complete with a swim-up bar, already held several dozen people, and the occasional sprinkling of water touched upon my warm skin as we walked around the roof. Making our way around the perimeter toward the far end, I was thrilled to have a bird's-eye view of Old Charleston, visible on the horizon, connecting the hotel with the city it called home.

A "tiki-themed" bar beckoned from a bit further, and it was there we decided to take a break before heading down to the basement. Once again, Joe slid behind the bar to mix up six fresh glasses of the S&M drink, of which I already was quite fond. The delightful concoction, already successful in creating a full-blown buzz in my overloaded head.

That full-blown buzz in my head may have been the reason it took me several seconds before I registered the pungent smell. Somebody nearby was smoking weed, and I inhaled again as I turned to my left, where I discovered the inviting aroma's source, Katt Morgan. I experienced a momentary lapse of mental capacity to form a thought while attempting to figure out if it was real or if the S&M drinks were working better than I thought. Nope, it was undoubtedly real.

Katt put her lips to the end of the pipe, inhaled, and passed it to Kitty, who then passed it down the line to Joe, who took a hit and then handed it to me. I tried to play it off as casually as possible and tried not to emit any expression other than a "hey, it's cool" look.

I shook my head and smiled. "Sorry, not for me, I get drug tested."

The pipe headed over to Nick, and I breathed a sigh of relief when I saw him shaking his head no. "No, but thanks for the offer. I haven't touched that since my high school days. The older I get, the more I have to stay on top of my game, you know?"

Joe shrugged his shoulders, grinned, and took another hit, after which he passed it back to Tom.

Tom smiled, and his voice danced with amusement when he spoke. "Well, I guess we won't get to share any good stuff later, then. Will we?"

It was times like these when I questioned my ability to read people as well as I thought I could. Of course, I knew the Morgans and the Andersons enjoyed alcohol, and the smoking of weed wasn't much of a shock, either. I know of only a few who *don't* treat themselves occasionally, but what was meant by Tom's last statement about the "not having to share the good stuff?"

What is that supposed to mean?

Sharing what?

Sex? Drugs?

This was the Fantasy Play Hotel™ after all!

Nick looked over at me, and in his infinite wisdom, immediately deciphered the invisible thought-bubble hovering over my head. He stood up and reached for my hand.

"Come on, let's take another walk around the roof before we head back in."

Turning to the others, Nick announced we would return in a few minutes, and with raised glasses, the group smiled and went back to passing the peace pipe.

Silently, we walked hand-in-hand toward the opposite end of the roof. The sun was setting, and I could see the city of Charleston in the distance. We stopped to look at the beautiful view for a few seconds before Nick finally turned to face me and began chuckling.

"I figured I needed to get you away before those thoughts started transforming into words spoken from that gorgeous mouth of yours."

My eyes widened, and I opened my mouth to speak, but nothing came out. I just shook my head, a smile spreading over my face as Nick wrapped his arm around me.

"Nick, I don't think I want to know what Tom meant by the 'good stuff' comment. Was he talking about sex or drugs?"

Nick laughed again. "You dirty-minded woman you! I didn't even think about him insinuating anything sexual. I assumed it was about drugs of some kind because Mark told me that both couples dabble in coke and acid. Anyway, let's get back to the thoughts flitting around in that curious mind of yours, Lacey Coleman."

I smiled before leaning my head closer to Nick's face. "What do you think about everything here? The hotel? The rooms? The Morgans? The Andersons?"

Nick lifted his hand, and with his thumb and forefinger, turned my face toward his.

"Lacey, I could care less about any of this. I could be standing with you on that beach right now and be just as happy." He leaned forward and kissed my forehead before continuing to speak. "This is all pretty impressive, but if a couple doesn't have what we have, none of this means anything." Nick paused, and a smirk slowly appeared. "Well, wait a minute. I need to take some of that back." I looked up at him questionably. "There *are* a couple of rooms I probably would enjoy a whole lot better than standing at the beach right now!"

I could only laugh as I fake-punched him in the belly. "Ohhh, who has the dirty mind now, Mr. Atwood?"

We were interrupted by approaching voices I recognized as those of our hosts for the evening. "There you two are! Ready for the rest of the tour?"

Nick and I followed the slightly intoxicated and buzzed couples off the rooftop and back onto the elevator. This time, instead of going up, the elevator didn't stop until it reached the basement level. No courtyard view to see here. Instead of the expected hallway leading to rooms, the space we stepped into was a vast round lobby with three wooden doors, each secured with brass hinges. A large key, identical to the one imagined in Katt's book, was centered on each.

A fourth door stood left of the elevator, barren except for the brass knob. There was, however, a digital keypad mounted beside the door.

Wonder what that's all about?

Katt walked toward the center door, and slipping the key into the lock, she turned it and pulled it open. *Medieval Chamber* came to mind immediately; the main space — the one we stood in — was something beyond my imagination. At least seven feet in height, a large metal cage hung from the ceiling and rested lightly on a raised platform to which several wooden steps led. I looked up and noticed a pulley system used for the lowering and raising of the cage. A table, comparable to a wooden medieval massage table, waited to the right of where we stood. At the opposite end of the room, a large bondage cross invited the bold.

Nick waved me to follow, and we walked into a bedroom. Another large bed stood ready with its four massive posts, each equipped with leather straps. Mirrors lined the walls and the ceiling, from which heavy chains hung down around the bed. To the left of the bed, a familiar raised-platform, stripper-pole set-up, complete with ringside seating.

The others joined us in the bedroom, and as they did, Nick turned to face the four of them. I could tell that he was a bit dumbfounded by all he was seeing. He released a half-laugh, slowly shaking his head a couple of times.

"This is fucking crazy! Where in the world did you find all of this stuff?"

That was a question they were more than willing to answer. Conversation over the next fifteen minutes focused on the rapidly growing interest held by so many in the world of sex dungeons, S&M, and the Dominant/submissive culture. The demand for products and furniture to sustain such a lifestyle was growing and expanding in response. Katt informed us of the worldwide trade shows and underground markets geared toward the exact items we were all ogling.

We made our way back out to the basement lobby, and after Katt unlocked the door to the next room, we all obediently followed her inside. The room we walked into was more of what I envisioned a Dominant/submissive playroom to look like and was similar to the one on the fourth floor, yet on a much grander scale. The same bed, the kneeling benches, the bondage cross on the wall, and the usual chains, were all strategically placed for easy access;

however, the adjoining bathroom and shower, accessible through a door at the far end, made this room something "extra-special."

Spanning the entire length of the wall, the shower, which contained a long bench with straps attached to it, caused my jaw to drop. A variety of shiny, polished, hand-held shower sprayers hung from the walls above, leaving little doubt about the sprayer's purpose. Thoughts drifted back to shower-play with Nick and his magical hand-held shower wand. *Oh, the fun we could have in THIS shower!*

Closing the second door behind us, the group made its way toward, and through, the third locked door. I struggled with putting my finger on the room's purpose; it was part medieval, part rodeo, part doctor's office, and part mechanical shop class. There were various machines scattered around, and I allowed my imagination to decide each machine's intent. However, the elongated dildo on the end of one of the devices allowed for ease in defining its purpose. A mechanical bull was front and center with fluffy, padded mats surrounding. Shelves around the room offered "available for purchase" sex toys duplicated in the hotel's shop and hanging above the headboard of the bed; a LED illuminated possible uses for each one.

I was a bit confused by this room, and a glance at Nick confirmed he was also trying to make sense of this hodge-podge of a sexual playground. It seemed to be just a little bit of everything.

Katt noticed my perplexed look and smiled, nodding her head. "Yes, my dear, I know what you're thinking, and it's exactly why this room is called 'Little Bit of Everything,' and actually, it is one of our most requested rooms."

Nothing, absolutely nothing, about the Fantasy Play Hotel™ could surprise me anymore!

Exiting the third room, Katt led the way back over to the elevator. "So, there you have it, the grand tour. What do you think?" I opened my mouth to ask about the final door, but Katt continued talking as the elevator door opened. "And remember you two, you get your choice of any room, so good luck choosing! Just let me know before you leave tonight, and I will put a hold on it."

I was still curious about what lay behind that final mysterious door, but my attention quickly turned to the elevator's rising back to the main floor.

Nick and I had an exhilarating evening ahead of us, and I was more than ready for it to continue.

The party was in full swing by the time we walked back into the main entrance. No less than two-hundred revelers milled in and around the lobby and store.

Mark Santauri waved us over. "You guys better get over here and grab some of this food before it's all gone!"

Food sounded heavenly at this time, and I welcomed something substantial in my stomach. Before the night was over, I knew more S&M's would make their way down my throat, and I needed to provide some sort of absorbent cushioning! Katt and Joe excused themselves to crowd-mingle, and at the same time, some friends waved Kitty and Tom over. It was nice to be just "Nick and me" again, and we grabbed some plates, filled them with more food than I thought I could eat, and made our way out past the lobby to the center courtyard where, luckily, we found a secluded table.

We "people-watched" in silence, quickly devouring the food from our plates. Nick spoke first. "So, are we ready to leave social work and professional photography behind so we can build a Fantasy Play Hotel™?"

I almost spit out my food with laughter at the insanity of the question. "I don't know which would be more far-fetched; my clients or this hotel."

Nick nodded. "I have to agree with you on that one." He took another bite of food. "So, speaking of fantasy play and hotels, which room are you picking for tomorrow. Did you decide yet?"

I nodded and then shrugged my shoulders once, narrowing my eyes as I looked across the table. "Well, yes and no. It's a tie between two rooms."

Nick reached under the table and placed his hand on my leg, immediately moving it up toward the hem of my dress. He leaned closer across the table and accosted my eyes with his stare. "Well, I'm just going to say that the Mirror Room looked pretty sweet!"

That caught me off guard. I was so sure Nick would have chosen either the spanking or the restraint room. He had stopped talking as he focused on sliding his hand under my dress, and I soon felt his finger sneak under the trim of my panties. I looked over at his face. His eyes were closed as his finger slid over the silkiness and then continued to move between my legs while my internal alert system triggered a familiar throb. Nick opened his eyes to see me smiling at him.

"Well, that suggestion is a shocker, Nick; not what I had figured you would have chosen."

Nick pulled his finger from under my panties and traced it down my inner thigh. "Seeing you from every angle while I have my way, in *every* way possible? It's a 'no-brainer.' Nick picked up a grape from his plate and placed it in my mouth, running his finger over my lips on the retreat. "So, come on, Lacey, time for a decision. Which room are you choosing?"

I narrowed my eyes. "You sure I can pick any room I want? No complaints?"

A look of immediate acknowledgment fell over his face. He knew what I was about to say. "Lacey Coleman, please don't tell me you're picking the Pink Room."

I threw my arms in the air. "Jackpot, babe; you got it!"

Now, mind you, I know Nick enough to recognize his "poker face," and he was wearing it. He sure wasn't "chomping at the bit" at the thought of heavenly pink delight surrounding him for an entire evening. No worries, though, I would make sure he would enjoy every second of it and already planned an early morning visit to the mall to purchase some fun pink "frillies." I was *also* planning on allowing Nick *full* access to *every* nook and cranny. He would be delighted when he exited the Pink Room, and I wouldn't be surprised if the color pink was thought of differently after our visit.

Nick shook his head slowly back and forth. "Pink? You?"

I laughed and nodded. "I promise it'll be okay, babe. I promise."

Nick stood up and leaned over the table to kiss me. "I'm going to hold you to that promise, or I may have to reserve the spanking room for a follow-up visit."

Bellies, now full of food and still slightly fuzzy from the alcohol, we decided to check out the lounge. I wanted to pull Nick out on the dance floor for some sharing of body space! Walking into the lobby, we found the Andersons engaged in conversation with a famous "reality" star and her current "boy-toy." Ironically, the week before we left for Charleston, the same reality show had been playing on my client's television when I went to visit. Kitty Anderson waved us over.

Introducing us as two of her closest friends, I tried my best to stay calm and collected, which was the exact *opposite* of what I felt behind the smooth exterior. The woman, proclaiming herself as a fan of Nick's work, inquired about purchasing one of his photographs. I couldn't believe I was standing with my fiancé and talking to a multi-millionaire reality star about buying one of his prints, our lives taking a one-hundred eighty-degree spin over the last few months!

Finished with the business talk, we resumed making our way toward the lounge with the Andersons now joining us. At the same time, Mark rounded the corner, his voice traveling across the room. "Hey, Nick, ready to do some partying, buddy?"

Nick waved him to follow. "Yep, you got it! Time for some fun!"

The next two hours encapsulated a brief period of my life that I would *never* forget. Giddy and relaxed with alcohol, we headed to the dance floor to bump-and-grind with the "rich and famous." Knowing the coworkers back home would question the legitimacy of my brief claim to fame, I was sure to corral some of the same "rich and famous" for a few selfies as I needed some proof this night was a reality. Nick and I were like two giddy, awestruck kids at an amusement park, albeit an adult one.

At one point during the evening, Nick dared me to climb the steps up to the dance cage. The alcohol increasing my boldness, I happily took the dare, but only *after* he bribed me with a sexy wink and a juicy kiss. After a few minutes, he joined me in the cage, our images beaming in LED from the walls, once again, providing validity to the "skill on a dance floor being a measure of skill between the sheets" old wives tale. Judging by the encouragement from the crowd dancing around us, we received enough affirmation verifying our ability to "hold our own" on the dance floor.

It was nearly 2 a.m. when Nick and I finally walked out of the lounge and back toward the lobby. The Morgans arranged for an Uber to take us back to our vacation home and assured us that our car would be safely transported there before morning. Katt reminded us to stop at the front desk on our way out to let the clerk know which room we wanted for the next night, and after securing the Pink Room, Nick and I walked outside into the warm night air toward the waiting Uber. As the car drove away from the hotel, neither one of us spoke, both of us processing the last few hours.

The experience overload and the late hour sent me off to slumberland before we arrived home, but I remember Nick wrapping me up in his strong arms, holding me close as he climbed the stairs. I vaguely remember him undressing me and tucking me under the sheet, then, with a gentle kiss, whispered that he was going to take Buster for a quick walk. That was it. I was out, and *that* was a relief because I was going to need as much sleep as possible before returning to the hotel in less than twenty-four hours!

CHAPTER 10

Thank goodness for Buster's fluffy big ol' head and wet nose waking me. I would indeed have slept in for several more hours, and thanks to that cuddly canine, I had time to run to the mall. I left behind a short note, explaining only that I would be back shortly, and arrived back as Nick was pouring his first cup of coffee. I hid the pink packages behind my back as he turned to greet my entrance. The evening's goal was "Pink Power," and I didn't want him to espy any of the new pink frilly items contained within the bags.

Nick looked at me and smiled. "I was wondering where you had gone. What's that behind your back, mysterious woman?"

I grinned over the counter. "Oh, you'll find out soon enough. I promise!"

That said, I backward stepped out of the kitchen, turned, and sprinted up the stairs to add my new frilly items to my overnight bag. I couldn't wait to see Nick's reaction later, and I was more than ready for the evening to arrive, an evening we would not soon forget!

Nick and I walked back through the front hotel doors at the scheduled check-in time of 5 p.m., this time with two overnight bags in tow. It was a completely different atmosphere today; no music streamed from the night-club down the hall, no food-covered tables filled the lobby, and instead of hundreds of people milling around, perhaps only twenty to thirty people strolled about. The nightclub doors opened at 7 p.m., so I was sure this was just the calm before the storm that would, once again, descend upon the hotel.

We checked in at the front desk, picked up our key card, and took the elevator to the third floor. Opening the door into our pink paradise of a room, the boldness and brightness of everything pink smacked me in the face. It was as if I had just walked into a sweet pink cotton-candy factory on steroids. I could see into the bedroom where the three pre-ordered packages lay on the bed. Nick noticed them and tried to outrun me, but I arrived at the bed first as he was too busy laughing while trying to run.

"I still can't believe I'm going to be spending the next twenty-four hours surrounded by pinkness!"

I stood in feigned indignation and waggled my finger at him. "No complaints, remember?"

Nick plopped himself down onto the oversized, leather, pink-lips sofa and leaned back with his hands laced behind his head. I watched his eyes dart around the room until they stopped, and I followed the direction of his halted gaze. *When did that magically appear?* I hadn't noticed it during the tour the previous evening; maybe the alcohol had dulled my senses, perhaps I had been blinded by all the pinkness, or quite possibly, one of our tour guides had unintentionally obscured it.

Nick nodded his head over in the chair's direction. "Now, I'm not exactly sure what that is, but I *do* think I'm going to have some fun figuring it out with you, Lacey."

I walked over to the chair, which despite its bright pink coating, resembled a doctor's examining table complete with some sort of reclining chair contraption. A round foot, or knee, padded circle hung below the front of the chair, and two hand grips jutted up from near the chair's bottom edge. Two levers, one on the back of the chair and one closer to the front, adjusted the chair's slant and height. *Well, this could prove to be exciting!*

I looked back at Nick. He was no longer sitting on the pink lips couch and now walked over to where I stood. Coming up behind me, he reached around and pulled me back against his body. His face nuzzled through my hair and found my ear, and whispered words of seduction crept near, traveling down through my body.

"I think I changed my mind about this pink room idea of yours."

Nick's right hand reached up under my shirt and snuck under my bra. His finger rubbed across a nipple, suddenly erect and rigid, eliciting a moan as I envisioned myself on this chair with Nick in front of me, doing all those things he does best.

Focus, Lacey!

I wriggled out of his embrace, something I very much hated to do at that moment, but I was determined to succeed in my plan. Returning to the bedroom, I grabbed the suitcase off the bed and turned back around to look at Nick, still standing by the chair.

"I need to go change before we head down to the bar. Be right back, sexy guy!"

Walking into the bathroom, I closed the door behind me and placed the pink bags on the floor. I pulled out the dress I bought to wear for the evening from the larger bag, a sexy pink, loose-draping V-neck. I had fallen in love with the sleeveless, hollowed-out, crisscross design, and it hung at "perfect" length, just skimming my upper thigh. The dress's color provided a beautiful contrast to my sun-kissed skin, and as I stood back from the mirror, the reflected, smiling woman sent a silent affirmation. *Lacey Coleman, you are looking pretty damn sexy tonight!*

Exiting the bathroom, I found Nick lying on the giant, pink-framed, pink-covered, pink-frilled bed. For someone who protested having to spend the evening in a hot pink room, Nick is probably the only man who could make a hot pink bed look even hotter. I crossed the room and stood; Nick following me with his stare as I made my way over. I twirled around, waiting for a response that quickly arrived in the form of a massive, beaming smile.

"Ms. Coleman, I wholeheartedly approve. You, my dear, are stunning."

I walked over to him and reached down for his hand, motioning him to stand up. "Well, for your information Mr. Atwood, I know I'm stunning. I also know you better be ready for an adventurous evening. So, get up and get moving!" I didn't need to say it twice.

By the time we made it back downstairs to the lobby, the atmosphere had started to liven. A few couples stood at the front desk, waiting for room check-in, and I noticed the store looked rather busy with curious customers. Many individuals headed down the hallway toward the elevators, while others headed in the other direction toward the nightclub. I looked past the front desk out to the center courtyard, where the phallic-shaped palm tree sprayed water over the tall leaves, and although I did want to take a closer look, the music started to filter down the hallway. The fountain would have to wait, and I grabbed Nick's hand, tugging him toward the beats.

Entering the nightclub, we headed straight over to the bar. Last night, the S&M drinks went down quite smoothly, but Nick and I wanted to try something new, and after considering, The Teaser, Twisted and Tied, Spank Me, and many more, I settled on the Teaser, while Nick opted for the Twisted and Tied; both sweeter vodka drinks. Garrett, the bartender, asked if we had attended the grand opening the previous evening. We informed him that we had left at the "early" hour of 2 a.m., and to our amusement, he was quick to offer condolences. According to Garrett, a famous musician had arrived around 2:30 a.m. and took turns cranking music with the DJ, the resulting party not settling down until the sun's glow began to fill the morning sky. By that time, I had been dancing with Mr. Sandman for quite some time. Two women moseyed up to the bar, diverting Garrett's attention, providing us the perfect opportunity to make our exit toward the elevators with drinks in hand.

Arriving at the rooftop, we heard the music and laughter before the elevator doors opened. All the bar stools were full, as was the pool, where an impromptu game of water volleyball was in motion. We located a double lounge chair and settled in to watch the competition while planning out the last four days before heading back to Ohio. Even *saying* the name triggered a slight rise in anxiety. I didn't want to leave the perfect little world we had created in Charleston, and the *only* thing making the return to Cleveland bearable, was returning to Cleveland as Mrs. Nick Atwood. I allowed the thought to permeate my brain and concluded that it didn't matter to what city I returned; Nick was "home" to me.

The fun laughter from the wild volleyball game eventually grew too loud for continued conversation, so Nick and I returned to the nightclub where we engaged in some teasing, "feel-my-body-move-this-close-to-yours" dancing. It didn't take long before we made a unanimous decision to return to the room; we wanted to be awake and alert enough to enjoy the Pink Room, and we had no time to waste!

Card swiped, Nick held open the door, allowing me leading entrance, and as the door closed, I turned to face him. "Now, Mr. Atwood, you need to take a seat on that lovely-looking, kissy couch while I go get some things ready in the bedroom."

I started walking toward the bedroom and stopped midway, turning to see if Nick was following my orders. He hadn't moved, so I pointed to the couch. *"Ahem."*

A smile and a salute preceded his walk toward the couch.

Before entry into the bedroom, I noticed the main room's double wall-switch and flipped up both; the first turned on some music, and the second, to my amusement, switched on the pink ceiling fan. Nick looked up and shook his head.

Giggling, I looked back over my shoulder before closing the bedroom door behind me. "NO PEEKING, EITHER!"

I pulled the bags from the closet and began removing the previously purchased items: pink handcuffs, pink scarf, pink leather cuff-restraints, a pink vibrator, a pink butt-plug, pink anal beads, a tube of lube, and for the pièce de résistance, a small, pink-tasseled whip. Nick's money was paying for this vacation, so the two-hundred dollars I spent on the toys and the outfit for the evening's fun seemed perfectly justifiable, and as the evening unfolded, I was confident that Nick would think it justifiable as well.

Hmm. What to put on first?

I stepped into the pink panties, my first ever crotch-less pair, and then slid on the pink lacy garter. Next came the pink stockings, unrolled carefully up one leg at a time, and then hooked the tops to the garter clips; the bright-pink, silky, back-laced corset followed. I had left it, for the most part, loosely laced and tied, for without the salesgirl's help, I knew I would waste two hours trying to figure it out on my own, and I had no plans on wasting any time!

I stepped back from the mirror and spun around, checking all angles. The cinched-in waist provided the impression of a plumper bootylicious bottom, and the underwire pushup-bra created the same mirage at the other end. Thank goodness for the magic of illusion!

The brush slid through my hair one more time, my mouth received a renewed minty rinse, and a fresh coat of bright pink lipstick slid over my lips for a refresher. Let the Pink Adventure begin! I walked out past the bed where the fun toys awaited and proceeded to the main room. Nick stood at the balcony window, looking out over the courtyard, and *now* I fully understood the importance of the darkening windows! Anyone looking into this room would receive an eyeful of Nick, and the only one I wanted to get an eyeful of Mr. Nick Atwood, was *me*.

His glance reflected off the glass as the sharp intake of breath traveled to meet me. I also witnessed the change of expression as it occurred, the predator first seeing its intended prey. I was familiar with that look, and immediately, nervous goosebumps sprouted over my arms.

Nick's a man of a thousand different expressions, from the playful, mischievous one, the "sometimes I'm a jerk" one, the "I'm in love with you, Lacey" one, the "business and all-work-focused" one, and the one he currently wore. My composure melted like a bowl of warm jello. He knew the exact effect he was causing, and I immediately felt a vulnerability that, one second earlier, had not been present. No matter how much I thought I was in control of the evening, I was fooling myself. I just didn't want him to be aware of that!

Nick grinned. "Yes, I am *definitely* changing my mind about the color pink."

I slowly spun around, providing him the full view. Nick took the few steps over to me and ran his hands over the silkiness of the corset, slowly following the curves of my body. When his hands reached the bottom of the corset, they traveled around to my ass, where they lingered for a few seconds. His warm breath glided down my neck, and a soft, rolling current of erotic electric-like sparks coursed from head to toes.

Kneeling in front of me, hands still firm on my cheeks, Nick's tongue found its intended target, and a startled gasp floated past my lips as the teasing flicking began. I knew I would reach the brink soon if he didn't stop, and while that sounded pretty damn good at the moment, I still wanted to prolong the evening a bit more. I took a step back and looked down at his now-upturned face.

"Nope, not yet."

He stood with an exaggerated sigh of protest and a pointing finger directed toward the "special" pink chair in the corner.

"Now, Lacey, you need to get yourself settled in over there while I un-change into something more comfortable." He turned me around and pressed up against me, his mouth close to my ear. "I hope you're ready because I'm going to have a lot of fun exploring you *and* this room tonight."

I headed over to take a closer look at "the chair" while Nick headed into the bedroom, and from behind the door, his voice floated over to me, "No way! Someone has done a little planning." A loud laugh followed. "Woman, you have no idea what you're asking for. Do you?"

Oh, how wrong you are, Nick. I know exactly what I'm asking for.

By the time Nick walked into the main room in all his glorious nakedness, I was lying back on the slightly reclined chair. Nick carried some of the items from the bedroom, well, actually, *all* the items — minus the restraints and handcuffs. While devouring my body with his eyes, he placed everything on the pink table and then walked toward the chair's bottom. Bending down, he moved the pink kneeling pad to the side, allowing him to stand directly against the reclining chair's edge. Neither of us said a word as Nick lifted my right leg, bending it gently over the leg-rest, and then did the same with the left one. I could do nothing but wait for his next move, and I was excited to see what it was. Thankfully, I didn't have to wait long.

Nick picked up the pink vibrator and pressed the button, turning it into a powerful tool of delight. He gently touched it against my already over-sensitive sweet spot, and in less than one minute, I had my first orgasm of the evening. No worries, however, there would be many more to follow! Reaching over, Nick pulled me closer to the end of the chair, and with one more little step forward, he was inside me, moving with urgency and rhythm no longer under control. As fast as I reached my orgasm, Nick was on his way to having the same, or so I thought. Unexpectedly he stopped and stepped back, pulling out of me. I was confused. Reaching out for my hand, Nick pulled me up, guided me off the chair, and then held up his finger in a "wait-a-minute" gesture before proceeding to readjust the kneeling pad to the front position.

Oh, I know what he's up to now!

Nick gently turned me around, then urged me to kneel over the edge. I quickly realized the purpose of the handles on each side, and after I wrapped a hand around each one, my backside presented for Nick's pleasure.

I felt the shifting body movement and turned to see Nick reaching over to the side table, returning to his previous position with lube in hand. A cold splash of the gel dripped down my butt crack trailed by his finger one second later. Another squirt of lotion welcomed his finger's arrival around the entrance, and I immediately tensed. Reminding myself to relax and trust my tush to Nick's loving care, the buzzing of the vibrator reassured me that my comfort was his priority. As the vibrator rested against my clit, Nick's finger entered the coveted territory.

I relaxed into the finger's slow, in and out motion and had just started to enjoy the feeling when he unexpectedly removed it. Another squirt of wetness hit my warm skin, followed by another shift in body movement, and I turned my head in time to see the anal beads lifted from the table.

"Relax, baby."

Nick gently guided in one bead at a time until I was pretty sure the whole strand was deep inside. The buzzing started again, and the vibrator was repositioned against my clitoris, this time with a little more pressure. With each quickening spasm, Nick slowly pulled out the strand of anal beads, and with each little bead's passing, my orgasm neared. I fought to keep from exploding as he tugged out the final bead; I now wanted something *else* deep inside my ass.

Nick was quick to oblige, and with a bit of lube and a gentle slowness, he slid inside me, immediately able to reset my momentum. Meeting the urgency from my end, Nick picked up the pace as he moved deep inside, sending us both jumping over the orgasmic cliff at the same time, our bodies shaking and our hearts beating a rapid congo beat.

I needed a break!

Afterwards, Nick stood up, helped me do the same, and then turned me around to face him. "Have I told you I am one hell of a lucky man?"

I returned his offered kiss. "Yep, that's right, Mister Atwood, and you had better remember that the next time you complain about the color pink."

Nick and I jumped in the pink shower. We lathered each other up with the pink sudsy soap, dried ourselves off with the fluffy pink towels, and then laid down on the pink-sheeted and pink-blanketed bed. The night was far from over, but we both needed to re-energize, and I was also suddenly famished. Proclaiming the dire emergency of pending starvation, we grabbed the room-service menu from the bedside table and fell back on the bed. Not surprisingly at all, the Pink Room offered a unique selection of menu items.

Consistent with the "all things pink" theme, the food choices were a humorous read: pink shrimp cocktail, pink "bunned" beef sliders, pink pasta-salad cups, pink ham and salami roll-ups, pink pancakes, pink cookies, pink cupcakes, pink grapefruit salad, pink ice cream and even, believe it or not, pink watermelon-flavored, penis-shaped popsicles. Indeed, we could always stay on the safe side and order from the *"yawn"* "boring "un-pink" menu, but Nick and I agreed the color pink was working in our favor, and it wasn't the time for any jinxing.

While Nick opted for the shrimp cocktail and the sliders, I desired sweets and selected a sweet, pink-surprise cupcake accompanied by a bowl of pink cherry ice cream with pink sprinkles and pink whipped cream on top. One call on the hot-pink room phone down to the kitchen, and we were a scant thirty minutes from satisfying our hunger.

Nick and I laid back on the bed, his arm nestled under my neck, and both of us looking up at the pink ceiling fan. Passing the time until the food arrived and trying to stay awake, we took a walk down memory lane through the last week and a half. It seemed forever ago that we had walked into our Rainbow Row vacation house and first met Buster. We reminisced about our first visit to Mark's restaurant and the "private party for two" in the secluded little dining room.

We reminisced about the fascinating trip to Magnolia Plantation, the unhurried stroll through the street market, and the fun boat ride with the Andersons; all the reminiscing, successfully compiling into a lengthening list of justifiable reasons to remain in Charleston — forever. There was still much to do, so much to see, and not enough time to do it, and I will admit, I was also feeling somewhat spoiled, having so much one-on-one time with Nick. The thought of returning to reality and the time-compromising demands filled me with dread.

A knock at the door announced the arrival of our food, and after wheeling in the pink cart, we wasted no time. We had worked up a serious appetite and made quick time devouring all our pink food, so quickly, in fact, that within minutes, we were lying back down, bellies satisfied and full of food.

The plan was to re-energize with nourishment; however, Nick was sound asleep within five minutes, and I soon followed. That's why backup plans are essential!

I awoke to the sound of a soft knock at the door. The powers "that be" must have been looking out for us as I'm a pretty sound sleeper. I looked over at Nick as I rose from the bed. He remained sound asleep, which meant I could still move forward with my plan. Slipping into the fluffy pink robe, I made my way to the pink door and opened it; nobody stood there. I was perplexed for a couple of seconds until I noticed a pink bottle sitting in a pink ice bucket at my feet. I bent down and picked it up, closing the door quietly behind me. Setting the bucket on the pink table, I noticed a pink card attached to the bottle's neck.

> *Hope you two are having lots of fun in the pink room ...*
> *Here's some pink champagne on the house ...*
> *Love Katt.*
> *P.S. If you two need anything at all, don't hesitate to call.*

My first thought was, "oh, that's so nice." My second thought was, "oh, that's kind of intrusive," but before I even allowed my mind to start dissecting the motives and meanings behind the gesture, which I honestly believed was one of thoughtfulness, I refocused on the task at hand. I had a man to take captive and seduce, and besides, the champagne would taste great in a couple of hours after I had my way with Nick.

Treading as quietly as I possibly could without fully tiptoeing over the pink shag carpet, I returned to the bedroom door and gently pushed it open, silently praying Mr. Sandman still held Nick captive. Okay, not really. The only person I wanted holding Nick captive was myself, and thankfully, he remained asleep, mouth slightly open, allowing just the smallest bit of a snore to escape. It may seem peculiar, but I loved watching him sleep, as, without exception, the bed pillow would find a home halfway over his face, covering his eyes. I once asked him about this unusual but endearing sleeping habit, and he shared the fears of a young boy, petrified of the dark. The pillow became the shield to thwart all approaching monsters from entering his room. Old habits die hard, and as I stood there in the doorway, watching Nick sleep, my heart swelled when I saw the pillow covering half his face.

Only good things are cumming in this room tonight, Nick.

Continuing my silent approach into the bedroom, I walked over to where I initially set the purchased items; there was not much left! Nick had made fair use of most of the purchases, but the ones I needed remained untouched. Glancing again at Nick, I picked up the four, leather ankle/wrist restraints and walked back toward the bed. I was afraid he would wake up as soon as I touched his arms and legs, so I wanted to have my goodies as prepared as possible.

Hmm, which first, Lacey?

I decided to start with the leg and arm closest to the bedposts on Nick's side of the bed. Luckily, he was sleeping in a stretched-out position, and his right leg was close to the edge of the bed, his right ankle almost touching the corner bedpost. I was thrilled to see there were restraint cuffs and clips around each of the four posts, making the task so much easier! Laying the four leather cuffs on the empty side of the bed, I stepped back to the dresser and grabbed the pink silk scarf I was going to use as Nick's blindfold once he awoke.

The first cuff slid effortlessly through the space between Nick's ankle and the mattress, and I avoided touching his ankle any more than necessary. I guided the strap through the metal buckle and, "oh so slowly," tightened it enough to where he couldn't slide out, but not enough, that he would awaken. I didn't want to hook it to the post yet. I looked back up toward the head of the bed. Nick hadn't moved, and the soft snoring continued. Walking over to the other side of the bed, I picked up another restraint and followed the same plan with his other ankle. Two down, two to go, and there was no way I could proceed with the last two restraints without Nick's partial cooperation.

My original plan was to have all the restraints on Nick and be ready for action before he awoke, and I realized the improbability of that occurring. It was time for Phase 3; I would quietly hook the wrist restraints to the bedposts last. Walking back over to the first cuffed ankle, the one closest to the post, I very carefully pulled the metal clasp from the bed restraint and clicked it onto the leather cuff wrapped around Nick's ankle. Restraint number one now fully secured.

Grabbing the two wrist restraints, as well as the pink scarf, I silently padded over the pink carpet to the top of the bed by Nick's head. Setting the items on the floor by my feet, I bent over and kissed his forehead and then his lips. His eyes opened slightly, and he grinned.

"Hey, beautiful."

I returned his grin. "Hey, handsome."

Nick tried to scoot up in the bed, which, of course, was now impossible. He looked down at the end of the bed. "What in the wo ...?"

I didn't allow him to finish the sentence. I bent down and kissed him once more, stopping to look in his eyes after the kiss. "You, Mr. Atwood, get to play by *my* rules this time."

Picking up the pink scarf, I held it up in front of his face. "And just to keep you guessing, it's blindfold time."

Nick looked at the scarf and then back at me. "Hmm, pretty sneaky, Lacey. You better hope those restraints are pretty strong, though, because if I get out of them, somebody's going to get her pretty little self, restrained, belly-down, so her pretty little behind can get a spanking."

I grinned, shook my head, and sighed. "I guess I'm going to have to get the Man-Muzzle as well, huh?"

The grin never left his face. "Well, unless you want to hear everything I'm going to do for payback, you just may have to go get the muzzle."

Nick was undoubtedly enjoying this turn of power. I glanced downward to witness Frankie rising under the blanket, just another confirmation of that enjoyment. Directing my eyes back upward, I saw Nick's eyes beginning to darken, and I felt a familiar ache start between my legs; the intensity of animalistic passion within those dark eyes was dangerously intoxicating. While I most certainly had no complaints about being Nick's "prey," this time, Nick was *my* prey, and I needed to get back to business.

"Man Muzzle, it is. But first things first, Mr. Atwood!"

I tied the scarf around Nick's eyes and then stood up, reaching down for the two remaining restraints on the bed. It just made more sense to simultaneously have access to both top bedposts, and straddling Nick would be the perfect way to accomplish that. Lowering myself down on his naked torso, I reached over and pulled his right hand in front of me, laying it on top of my left thigh, when a finger reached out, moving slowly across my skin, sending waves of heat down deep. I wrapped the leather restraint around Nick's wrist and lifted his arm back over his head toward the bedpost, hooking the clasps together. Halfway there!

I had to shimmy up a little to reach over to the right bedpost, pulling the strap over to me as far as it would go, then reached over to grab Nick's other hand, pulling it over to my other thigh.

His voice broke the silence. "Seems like someone's a little excited, huh?"

He could feel the dampness from between my thighs against his warm skin. I was more than a little excited, but Nick didn't need any further verification of that.

"Keep it up, Mister, I'll find that muzzle. I swear!"

I wrapped the leather wrist restraint around his left wrist, and with two clicks, the third restraint was in place with one more to go. Before dismounting Nick, I bent down over him, my breasts within millimeters from his face. Reaching back and placing my right hand behind his head, I lifted it gently, allowing his mouth to graze my hardened nipple.

"I believe you know what to do with this, Nick."

His mouth opened and engulfed my nipple in warm wetness as his tongue sucked, licked, and flitted over the hardened nub. As good as it felt, I reminded myself that I still had a job to finish, so I lowered my hand, easing his head back down on the pillow. Un-straddling myself, I climbed off the bed and walked over to the last post and the final restraint, and with two clicks, my handsome fiancé laid, spread-eagled, and thoroughly restrained.

I stood at the foot of the bed and conjured up the most serious and sternest voice possible. "Okay, so here's the deal, Nick. I don't want to cover up that mouth of yours because I plan on putting it to work, *but* I will not tolerate any, and I mean any, talking back or directives from you. Am I making myself clear?"

Nick smiled. "Ms. Coleman, I would never, ever think of doing anything like that, but just in case I slip, what exactly do you plan on doing about it?"

I walked over to the dresser and picked up the pink-tasseled little flogger. "I had a feeling you were going to be a little nosy about it."

Walking around to the side of the bed, I stood near Nick's right thigh. I sent the tassels whipping with a flick of my wrist, not too hard, over his right leg, causing him to jump slightly.

In a voice serious enough but still laced with just a hint of sarcastic humor, Nick spoke, "Ahhh, okay. You mean business, woman! I'll try my best, Mistress Coleman, to obey your wishes, but I can't promise I won't need some reminding again."

Of course, I was fully aware that Nick would enjoy this exchange of erotic power, and I thoroughly planned on creating a memory for him, not quickly forgotten.

"I'll be back."

I walked out into the other room, closing the door behind me, and headed over to the little pink table. Picking up the plastic pink remote, I pressed the musical note button, and music instantly streamed throughout the entire suite. The ice bucket was the next targeted destination, and after uncorking the gifted pink bubbly, I poured myself a glass and plopped myself down on the cushiony pink lip chair.

Taking a sip of champagne, I began to mentally plot all the deliciously devious deeds awaiting my sexy and willing captive lying in the next room. I wanted to tease Nick until he begged for mercy while I exhausted every ounce of his energy in the most exciting and satisfying ways imaginable. Draining the rest of the champagne from the glass, I refilled it and then carried the glass, as well as the bottle, back into the bedroom while shutting the door behind me. Time for some fun!

Nick remained as I had left him; actually, he really had no other chance to do anything else. My only fear was that he had possibly fallen back asleep in the five minutes that I was gone; however, I was reasonably confident the curiosity toward upcoming events had rendered that an impossibility. I gathered the remaining tools of pleasure from the dresser and returned to my willing victim.

Bending over, I brushed my lips against Nick's ear. "You still comfortable, babe? You're okay with all this, right?"

Nick turned his head toward me and gave me a "Nick" grin. "Oh, yeah. I definitely am okay with all of this."

I leaned forward again right next to his ear and whispered, "Good, just checking," before taking his ear lobe between my teeth and biting it lightly, at the same time, reaching for one of the nipple clamps. I released Nick's ear lobe and moved over to his mouth, where I proceeded to run my tongue over his lips, and while keeping his mouth occupied, I brought the clamp up to his right nipple. As the cold metal surrounded the erect nipple, enclosing it with a painful-pleasurable squeeze, I pushed my tongue into his mouth, feeling the moan as much as hearing it. Our tongues continued to dance as I brought up the second nipple clasp and placed it around Nick's left nipple, again eliciting a moan from deep within him.

Climbing on the bed, being careful to keep my body far enough away so Nick couldn't feel it, I removed the sheet, moved my hand down, avoiding the one bit of anatomy craving the most attention, and gently grazed "the boys." Another moan escaped, and Nick pulled against the restraints. My right hand drifted down his inner thighs, while my left hand returned to the nipple clamps, ever-so-gently, flicking, first the left one, and then the right one. The sounds coming from Nick alternated between moans, small gasps, undecipherable words, and the more decipherable words of "babe," "yes," and "FUCK!!"

Reaching over to the glass of champagne, I stuck my finger in and brought the wet champagne-covered finger over to Nick's mouth. Like Picasso painting his favorite scene, I brushed my fingertip slowly over his lips, parting them gently along the way before inserting it further. Nick's tongue eagerly removed any leftover traces of champagne, and I repeated the same action several times.

Each time I leaned over, I gently brushed against the nipple clamps, sending another jolt through his body. Feeling entirely in control at that moment, I decided to test how far I could go with Nick or, to be more accurate, how far Nick *wanted* me to go with him.

I bent over one more time, placing my mouth gently against his ear. "I think we should test out these nipple clamps in some other places. What do you think?"

Nick shook his head slowly back and forth, a grin across his face. "Not so sure that sounds like a good plan."

I looked down at his blindfolded face. "Hmmm, sounds like someone is refusing something I want to do." Rising from the bed, I walked to where the little pink-tasseled flogger lay on the dresser, all the while continuing to address my captive. "We both know what happens when you refuse. Right, babe?"

Nick chuckled. "Technically, I didn't refuse yet."

I slowly dragged the tassels down past Nick's clamped nipples, over his belly, and continued down, ending with his inner thighs, and paused.

"I don't know about that, Nick. It sure sounded like you were questioning my suggestion, and *that* deserves some sort of punishment."

I lifted the flogger, and with a light snap, sent the tassels across Nick's left inner thigh, resulting in a tug on the restraints again and a "DAMN" from Nick's mouth. I looked down at his face; he was still grinning.

"You better make sure you hide that little whip of yours later. I can already visualize how red your ass cheeks are going to look when I have my turn, Lacey."

I sent the tassels over Nick's other thigh, causing another tug on the restraints and another "DAMN!"

"Nick, Nick, Nick. Must I remind you who's in control at this moment?"

His face turned toward my voice and answered back with a "no ma'am."

Scooting over on the bed, I straddled him and bent down to peek under his blindfold. "Still okay?"

Nick laughed. "Lacey, I can handle whatever you can dish out. Game on."

I replaced the blindfold over his eyes. "I should've known better."

Reaching down, I undid the nipple clamps and shimmied my body down, hovering briefly, just barely allowing Nick to feel me above him, before moving between his legs. With the knowledge that extreme gentleness was in order, I ever-so-lightly clamped some of the skin beneath. Nick gasped and tightened against the restraints as Frankie reappeared and rose in height, as well as widening in girth, reassuring me of the clamp's effectiveness.

Fantastic partner that I am, I decided to *allow* Nick the opportunity to release some of that pent-up excitement. I bent down between his legs, one hand gripping him firmly and the other just millimeters from the clamps. I had a feeling it wasn't going to take long at all, and I was right. Engulfing the rigid thickness with my mouth, I reached down and jiggled the clamps, and within seconds, a familiar taste filled my mouth as he pulled against the restraints with each spasm, inaudible sounds coming from his mouth with each tug.

After removing the clasps as gently as possible, I inched back up Nick's body, straddling his belly. Leaning forward, I untied the pink make-do blindfold and was met with narrowed eyes and a grin as he laid his head back on the pillow. His eyes closed again, but the grin remained.

"You, Lacey Coleman, definitely have some tricks up your sleeve."

I returned the smile and nodded my head. "That I do, Mr. Coleman. That I do!"

Reaching to grab the champagne bottle and glass, I continued to sit on Nick's belly while pouring some more champagne into the glass. "You want some?"

Nick nodded and lifted his head off the pillow. I placed the glass against his lips and tipped it, allowing the red sweetness to pass through his lips. I looked at the clock; 2 a.m.

Nick opened his eyes again. "That was incredible, Lacey."

I pulled my leg back over his belly so that I could lie next to him, my head resting in the crook of his outstretched underarm and looked up at his peaceful face. "You need to take a short nap because *that,* my love, was only round one."

That statement was for me, just as much as it was for Nick. Within five minutes, we were again both asleep. I learned my lesson last time, and before I dozed off, I reached over and set the alarm for one hour. I didn't trust myself to awaken on my own, and I needed a refill of energy!

The phone's vibration seemed surreal, as I swore only five minutes had passed; however, a glance at the time verified it was, indeed, one full hour. Nick was still asleep, so I quietly rose from the bed and walked to the bathroom, smiling at the reflected image; I had "after-sex" hair, but no sex yet, but that would change shortly!

I quietly walked toward the dresser back in the bedroom and picked up the vibrator before returning to the bed. "Wake up, sleepy-head, time for some more fun."

Nick's eyes opened as I reached over to place the extra pillow under his head. I smiled down at him. "Someone still a little sleepy?"

He nodded. "Just a little bit."

I reached over and placed my hand in the ice bucket, pulling out two ice cubes, one disappearing inside my mouth, the other remaining hidden in my hand. Bending down, I placed my mouth over Nick's right nipple, allowing the ice cube to rest against it, then repeated the same with his left one. As each of Nick's nipples entered deep-freeze level, I left a trail of icy wetness past his bellybutton and continuing down to his inner thighs. Nick was now fully awake! Like a sped-up, time-lapsed series of pictures capturing a flower sprouting from a seed beneath the dirt, Frankie grew to full height within moments.

I climbed back on top of the bed with lube and vibrator in hand, straddling Nick, and looked down into his face. "Blindfold on or off?"

Nick smiled up at me. "If you're going to do what I think you're going to do, I want to see the whole thing."

I let out a tiny breath of air, just loud enough for Nick to hear. "That's what I thought you would say, but on second thought, I've changed my mind. I really don't think you deserve the final say on *anything* this morning, so ...," I reached up, pulling the blindfold back down over his eyes, continuing, "... time to rely on your other senses!"

Nick looked up at me in feigned astonishment. "Oh, I think I underestimated your wicked side, Lacey."

I pressed the button on the vibrator and leaned back, still straddling Nick's belly, simultaneously placing my left hand on the top of the bed frame for support. Already at heightened sensitivity, it took only moments after the vibrator nestled against me to reach the orgasmic edge and plummet overboard. I wasn't waving any white flag yet.

I picked up the tube of cherry lube, unscrewed the cap, and squeezed some of the gel on Nick's belly. Sticking a couple of fingers into the lube, I placed them between my legs and coated myself with cherry goodness while thoughtfully providing Nick with a detailed account of every move. By this time, Frankie could have doubled as a sissy bar against my butt and lower back. Feeling him so close to my ass made my fingers speed up, and Nick happily assisted by urging me on. His words, the feel of the hardness against me, the body-generated heat; all had me crossing over the brink of ecstasy one more time. I bent forward, laying my chest on top of Nick's chest, and looked up at his face with a satisfied smile.

Nick's head turned downward. "Someone getting a little tired?"

I moved up until we were face to face and placed my mouth near his ear. "No, but you soon will be."

Moment of reprieve at an end, I returned to my quest for complete satisfaction and sat back up, looking down at Nick. Reaching over and picking up the tube of lube from the bedside table, I squeezed a little bit on my finger and slowly, teasingly, traced it over Nick's lips. "You like the taste of that?"

Nick nodded. "That, my dear, is better than any champagne or pink food they can send up here."

"Exactly what I wanted to hear, and *just* because I'm such a sweet person, I'm going to let you have use of your hands back." In all reality, I was craving the feeling of his hands on my skin. "Can I trust you to behave?"

Nick replied with only a smile, not saying anything for a few seconds. "Do you really want me to?"

I reached over, and after releasing his arms, Nick stretched them in the air before leaning forward and running his hands over my thighs. I had no intention of remaining on his belly; I wanted to feel his tongue on me *and* inside me.

"How much did you say you liked the taste, Nick?"

Nick's hands moved up to my waist. I didn't need to hear an answer, as strong hands helped me scoot up past his chest until I hovered just mere inches overhead. I reached forward, grabbing the pink headboard, and lowered myself down until I was only millimeters from Nick's face below me. His hands returned to my waist, and he swiftly pulled me down to his face, where his tongue spent the next few minutes, exploring every nook and cranny. The grip stayed firm, ensuring no possibility of escape, and before long, that magical tongue of his had me reaching a third *and* fourth orgasm.

My needs now completely satisfied; it was time to return the favor. After all, Nick had been a very cooperative captive, and he deserved a special reward!

Lifting myself off Nick's face, I moved down over his chest, past his belly, and hovered over the *very* patient, *very* hard, and *very* erect Frankie. I rubbed myself back and forth, just barely brushing against the thick head, and to Nick's credit, he maintained great restraint and resisted pulling me down on top of him. Instead of lowering myself on him, I moved one leg back over Nick and turned around; it was time for some Reverse Cowboy, which provided an additional tease for Nick, leaving him solely with his imagination.

I squeezed some lube into my hand before rubbing it over Nick. His hands moved down to my ass, kneading each cheek, before returning to my waist, where his grip tightened. As I lowered myself more, a sound escaped from Nick — half groan, half exasperation. I smiled over my shoulder as I dropped down, even more, feeling him fill me up an inch at a time. Nick's patience was finally waning, and with his hands gripping my waist tightly, he pulled me down on top of him, completely stuffing me and leaving me gasping in pleasure. I was surprised he had maintained control for as long as he did, but everyone has their limits, and Nick had reached his. He knew what he wanted, and he wasn't going to waste any more time getting it!

The strength of Nick's hands provided extra force as I moved on top of him, and as my pace began to match his, his hands moved from my waist down to my ass. Maintaining pace, Nick reached over for the lube. The thought of what was to come resulted in my quickened tempo. Nick's hands returned to my waist, slowing me down.

His voice was husky with exerted desire. "Baby, wait. Not yet."

I slowed my pace just a little as I felt Nick's lubed fingers move closer to my "back seam." Another squirt of lube met his finger as it arrived at its target, sliding through the lube, and entering, where it began to keep pace with the hard thickness already deep inside me. Nick removed his finger, and I felt another squirt of lube.

He halted my movement on top of him. "Lacey?"

I knew what he wanted, and without a spoken word, I lifted myself off him, scooted forward an inch, and hovered over him. Anal sex, from a sitting-up position, was new to me; it would have to go slow. Nick picked up the lube again and squeezed some onto himself. There was now enough lube on our bodies to slick a raceway.

Nick gently pulled me down, so my ass was just touching the tip, and I continued to lower slowly without his assistance. Nick and I moaned in unison as I allowed him entry, gradually, inch-by-inch, until he was deep inside, after which I paused for a couple of seconds, allowing myself to relax before I started to move again. I felt Nick grow within, and his hands on my waist tightened as our pace picked up speed once more. It didn't take long; we reached the summit and leapt in unison.

Every ounce of energy now depleted it took every bit of strength to pull myself off Nick. I desperately needed a shower; enough lube covered me that I could have slid through a Fantasy Play Hotel™ keyhole. Standing next to the bed, I reached down and removed the pink scarf from around Nick's head.

His eyes were closed, but he was grinning. "I believe I just died and went to heaven … don't move me."

After unclasping the ankle restraints, I headed toward the bathroom for a shower. Nick was *not* budging one little bit.

"You, Mr. Atwood, need to join me in the shower. We are both a mess, so get your sexy ass off the bed and meet me in there."

Nick opened his eyes and peered over at me. "I don't have the restraints on now. You better watch it."

I turned to look back over my shoulder, laughing. "You, Nick Atwood, don't scare me."

Nick jumped out of bed and chased me to the bathroom, where he joined me under the warm water as we washed away three hours of glorious and taboo sex.

CHAPTER 11

We crashed, and we crashed *hard* after we changed the sheets and climbed back into bed following that last round of sex. Therefore, it came as no surprise that we slept until noon. I laughed when Nick said his body felt run over by a Mack truck — until I arose from the bed. That Mack truck had made a double hit.

We planned to head up to the rooftop, snatch something to eat, and then spend a few hours swimming in the pool before heading back to the condo. There was no need to rush; we had the room for the day, and Mark was dog-sitting Buster while we were gone.

I changed into the bikini I wore on the Anderson's yacht. Nick wore white club swim-shorts and a tight blue t-shirt, and if my muscles had not been screaming, I might have pulled him back into bed with me. No chance! I threw on a button-down, white, linen beach shirt over my bathing suit, and after grabbing the sunscreen on our way out the door, we were ready for food, sun, and some relaxation.

The lobby was busy, but then again, it was the second half of the weekend. After stopping at the desk to ask that our room not be disturbed, we continued to the elevator, where the glass interior view showed several people mingling around the impressive phallic palm tree in the courtyard.

The elevator doors opened onto a rooftop of laid-back revelers who were already in party mode. The DJ was already at work, and a small group of five females in skimpy bathing suits provided entertainment for the group of guys sitting at the bar. A water-volleyball game was in process at the far end of the pool, and a decent number of hotel guests were either lying on recliners, sitting at the small tables, or spectating the game.

We headed over to the bar to get some coffee and order some sandwiches. Nick gave no more than a cursory glance at the skimpily clad, young ladies, encircling my waist with his arm and pulling me close, always the consummate gentleman! We bypassed any alcohol and opted for shots of espresso and iced coffee instead. After the previous two evenings, a detox was in order, and although coffee isn't exactly detox stuff, it would help wake us up, and so would some food!

Everything on the menu looked good, although any option pink-colored was now an agreed-upon veto! We decided on the sampler with offered bruschetta, grilled shrimp and pineapple on skewers, mini-sliders, and fresh-baked pretzel squares with a variety of melted cheeses *and* a large grilled chicken salad we could split. I had no fear of any leftover food; we were both *that* hungry! Any excessive calorie intake I amassed over the past ten days had been entirely offset over the previous twelve hours. No need for me to worry about vacation weight gain with Nick around.

Finding two chaise loungers in the shade, we threw our towels over the backs and sat silently for a few minutes, drinking our coffee, and watching the volleyball game. The water looked refreshingly inviting, and after a few more sips of coffee, Nick and I walked to the pool's edge and slid into the refreshing blue water. I sank underneath the water before popping back up and running my hands back through my hair. Nick did the same and then smiled while pulling me close to him, his back up against the side wall.

"Lacey, I want to tell you something. I've *never* been as satisfied and content as I am right now, and *no,* I don't just mean sexually satisfied ..." Nick's hands gently squeezed my waist as he continued, "... but, make no mistake, I am sexually satisfied, too."

I looked at Nick's tanned, handsome face and his newly sun-kissed hair. *This guy is really mine. All mine!*

"Well, you handsome guy of mine, just to let you know, I feel the same. This vacation has been perfect, and I can't believe in four days we'll be back in Cleveland, back to reality."

Nick put his hand under my chin, lifted it slightly, and looked into my eyes. "I know, I know, *but* no time to think of Cleveland just yet. You have some shopping to do in the morning, woman, and I have to talk with Jim at the gallery. I'll drop you off in Charleston and then head over to the gallery, and after that, we can grab an early lunch. Sound good?"

I had almost forgotten. How could I have almost forgotten? I would return to Cleveland as Mrs. Atwood. Lacey Atwood. Mr. and Mrs. Atwood. I did a little happy dance in the water and threw my arms around Nick's shoulders, giving him a big chlorine-tinged kiss.

"I am *so* excited to be your wife, Nick!"

His response? Nick picked me up and tossed me back into the water, from which I emerged, laughing and splashing.

The food arrived, the aroma teasing us out of the pool, and after pulling the shirt back over my head, we began to devour everything on our plates until I heard a familiar voice. A few more familiar voices followed that initial one; The Andersons and Morgans were heading our way. *Oh, joy.* Luckily, there were only two chairs at the table.

Kitty spoke first. "Soo, how did you like your stay last night?"

Nick and I looked at each other. I took a bite of a slider, rendering me, purposefully, unable to answer. He squinted his eyes at me before smiling up at Kitty. "It was quite an experience. Wouldn't you agree, Lacey?" I smiled, nodded, and continued to chew my food.

Kitty nudged Katt. "Aren't they just the most adorable couple?"

Katt nodded and smiled back at us. "Are you sure we can't convince you to stay another night?"

I looked at Nick, who was stuffing a slider into his mouth. He smiled and winked across the table; apparently, it was my turn to reply. "Aw, thank you, Katt. We really wish we could, *but* we have only three nights left, and there's stuff we still want to do. We do, however, truly appreciate your generosity."

Kitty spoke again, smiling at both of us. "You two should reconsider and join us for this evening's penthouse party." She followed her statement with a wink. *Geez.*

Katt had noticed my expression and chuckled. "Okay, come on, you guys, let's let these two lovebirds enjoy their food before it gets cold!"

I smiled at her, and she winked in return as if to say she had our backs, and putting her hands on Kitty's shoulders, she turned her around. Walking away, Katt looked back over her shoulders. "Tell the front desk to page us before you leave."

We assured her we would.

Nick and I spent the next four glorious hours swimming in the pool, drinking another cup of iced coffee, and talking about the remaining vacation days. The return flight left Charleston on Friday at 1 p.m., which left us four more nights. I had already accepted there would be no visit to Cypress Gardens this trip, so the only thing we hadn't crossed off our to-do list was the Charleston Haunted Ghost Tour. We decided to do the tour on Wednesday evening and a final get-together with Mark late Thursday afternoon. That left the evening ahead and tomorrow. One more day and I would be marrying the man of my dreams!

Sun-kissed skin and bellies, now full and satisfied, we made our way back down to the room to jump in the shower, and after rinsing suntan lotion and chlorine from our golden skin, we changed into our clothes. I did the final room-check to ensure we had left nothing behind and made our way to the door with suitcases and bags of purchased "accessories" in tow. Pausing at the door, I looked around one more time, saying a silent goodbye to the pink "chair," the pink-lip couch, the pink ceiling fan, and all the other items of "pink."

Nick looked at me and shook his head. "There's *no* way anyone could have convinced me that I would like the color pink so damn much."

"I told you, Mr. Nick Atwood. Never doubt my intuition!"

With the door's close, the Pink Room became one more memory to add to our mental scrapbook of adventure. It had been a "once-in-a-lifetime experience!" Katt had assured us that we had an open invitation to return whenever we wanted, and there *were* many more rooms to sample.

We walked down the hallway toward the elevator, and it dawned on me that I had developed somewhat of an immunity to seeing myself in LED. I stopped in front of the last one before the elevator door and stepped forward. *That's YOU, Lacey Coleman!* My life had changed so much over the previous several months that it still felt unreal at times, but looking at myself, handcuffed to the bed, in bright LED brilliance as the elevator door opened, I smiled. *Oh, this is real, Lacey. This is very real.*

I silently said farewell to the courtyard and the squirting palm tree as we descended to the main floor. Upon arrival, the elevator doors opened to the main lobby and an increasing number of people, through which we made our way to the front desk. Nick informed the clerk of Katt's request for paging before our departure, and while we waited, we joined the crowd cheering on a couple as they spun the giant fantasy play wheel, the woman giggling nervously.

We had to wait only a few minutes before the Morgans walked into the lobby. Katt had changed into a beautiful coral jumpsuit, and her hair dangled from a chic ponytail; Joe wore his usual shorts and polo, and after walking over to us, they showered us with cheek kisses and hugs.

Katt turned to me, grabbing my right hand with both of hers, and held it as she spoke. "It was such an absolute pleasure to meet you, Lacey. I am *so* honored you agreed to grace our walls. We couldn't have asked for a better model to assist in promoting our hotel."

I felt myself blushing. More accurately, I felt a little choked-up. My initial hesitation and worry, long forgotten and replaced with the recognition that the Morgans are just genuinely caring and generous people, and I would miss Kattrina, or Katt, Morgan.

I swallowed before speaking. "I want to thank both of you for giving me the opportunity you did. I will admit, it pushed my comfort zone, but it challenged me, and we all know that challenges provide growth opportunities. I did some growing. That's for sure!"

Katt smiled and hugged me again.

Joe looked at Nick with raised eyebrows. "Remember, you two can always come aboard to help us out down here. This place can be a madhouse!"

Nick briefly laughed and shook Joe's hand. "I have full confidence you and Katt have this under control."

The Morgans walked us outside, where the valet waited with our car doors open and ready. Nick popped the trunk, and the valet loaded the suitcases and packages inside. One more round of hugs followed, and Nick and I promised to call when we traveled back to Charleston. With a wave, we pulled away from the hotel and headed back to Rainbow Row, to Buster, and to my mermaid, who would be getting an earful of titillating information over coffee in the morning.

Chapter 12

True to my word, I met my mermaid friend for coffee early the next morning before Nick awoke. He was still lightly snoring when I closed the door to the bedroom and headed down to make some coffee. The clock above the stove read 6:05 a.m., which in vacation time meant, "what the hell are you doing up this early?" I knew I would regret not sleeping in on the vacation mornings when I had the chance. Once I returned to work, it would be tough to get up and leave my bed on those early mornings; however, sometimes, a girl needs some girl talk, and I surely did!

I took one of the coffee cups from the drying rack, filled it with dark coffee, added the creamer, and made my way toward the garden patio. There she stood, my permanently silent friend, with water flowing over her bronzed body, her arms reaching out, and a knowing smile on her face. I was perplexed by the connection I felt with the mermaid; it was as if she was a kindred spirit of sorts. Perhaps she represented serenity to me. Maybe it was because she was a keeper of *so* many of my secrets. Possibly, it was due to her being around Charleston for so long, a witness to hundreds of years of history. Whatever the reason, I would miss my bronze friend. I would miss her more than Katt, Joe, the Andersons, or even Mark.

Over the next hour, except for one brief coffee refill, the mermaid remained a captive listener. She intently listened to the mental replay of the last forty-eight hours, my thoughts of returning to Cleveland, and the big event that would happen *sometime, somewhere*, over the next twenty-four hours. I took another sip of coffee and sat silently, watching the water flow over the glistening body and splash into the water below, where her tail remained half-submerged. I laid my head back and looked up at her serene, smiling face. I spoke softly, lest some neighbor walking nearby hear me talking to myself.

"So, what do you think of all that? Pretty exciting, don't you think?"

She remained silent. After all the time spent together, she could have warned me, at least!

"Think of all what? And what is pretty exciting?"

Nick's voice joined with his laughter as he walked up behind me, practically giving me a heart attack, again! I looked up at the mermaid and mentally laughed. *Some friend you are!*

Nick bent over and kissed my head. "I hate to tell you, Lacey. She can't talk."

I reached back with my hand, hitting him lightly in the stomach, as he turned to head back toward the kitchen. "Smartass."

"I'm just saying, Lacey."

Prying myself from the chaise, I shook my head slowly at the mermaid as if to say, "*Unbelievable! After sharing all those juicy details with you!*" I'm not crazy; I *knew* she couldn't talk, but oh boy, could she keep a secret!

Joining Nick in the kitchen, we split a bagel with cream cheese while searching his phone for the weather forecast.

"Perfect! High seventies with zero chance of rain!" He looked over at me and reached out with one hand, brushing a piece of hair that had fallen in front of my eyes. "You ready for today, Lacey?"

The expression on his face caused a lump to form in my throat. Nick looked at me with so much love in his eyes. I know how rare it is in today's world to find someone who loves as Nick loves me, and when it's mutual, with the same intensity and depth of passion, at the shared moment in time, it's like "finding a needle in a haystack." If there is such a thing as a soulmate, Nick was mine.

"Yes, Nick. I am one-hundred percent ready for today."

Walking around the counter, he stopped in front of me and pulled me up off the stool. "Well, in that case, young lady, you need to move your pretty little behind into the shower and get ready to go wedding dress hunting."

Nick bent over to kiss me and placed his hands on my shoulders, turning me around toward the hallway. He lightly slapped my behind. "Get moving, beautiful, and while you're getting ready, I think I'll have a little talk of my own with the mermaid to find out *everything* you've been telling her."

I had just placed my foot on the first step leading to the second floor. I turned around and looked at Nick, standing in the kitchen, shit-eating grin on his face. I returned his sly smile.

"You know what they say about mermaids and men, Nick. I would be careful!"

Forty-five minutes later, I retraced my steps to the kitchen, but now, I wore a pair of white Capri pants and a coral-colored, sleeveless blouse that had little sailboats on it. Nick and Buster were nowhere in sight, so I figured Nick had taken him for a walk before heading out. I poured myself another cup of coffee, sat on one of the island stools, and proceeded to engage in one of my over-thinking silent conversations.

You're going to be married today.
What are you thinking?!
But it's Nick. So, it's okay.
You haven't known him for even a year!
BUT IT IS NICK! I do know him! Now, be quiet and be happy!!

The door closed, and Buster came strolling into the kitchen, wagging his enormous tail. Nick followed, wagging his sweet "tail," as well. The mental door to my indecision slammed shut.

"Looking gorgeous as always, I see. You ready?"

I nodded. Nick stood on the other side of the island and leaned over. "So, here's the deal, Lacey. After you get your dress, we're going to grab some brunch, probably around eleven-thirty or so. Then you have two appointments; one's for your hair, done up in whatever way you want for your special day, and the second appointment is for a manicure and pedicure. After that, bear with me now, and you need to trust me on this one; at around 3:30, Mark will be picking you up and driving you to meet me someplace special. Okay?"

I hesitated before speaking. Nick had put some thought into creating a memorable day, and the reality of what was happening hit hard. My eyes quickly filled with tears that I was not expecting, and Nick's expression changed to one of concern. He walked around the island, and upon reaching me, placed his hands on my cheeks, lifting my face.

"Lacey, do you not want to do this?" He wrapped his arms around me, and his voice became muffled within my hair. "Babe, why are you crying?"

I began giggling (talk about emotional!). Nick looked at me, a puzzled expression on his face. Poor guy! I shook my head and smiled up at him through my tears.

"Yes, I want to do this, and I'm crying because you are just so damn sweet, and you thought of impromptu ways to make this day so special for me, and I love you, and I can't wait to be Mrs. Nick Coleman!"

I took a breath.

Nick stepped back and put his hand over his heart. "You were about to give me a heart attack. Don't scare the shit out of me like that again."

He kissed me and then kissed me again before picking up the keys from the counter. We ordered Buster to "hold down the fort," and we were on our way.

Nick dropped me off at one of the clothing boutiques where I had *"oohed"* and *"aahed"* over beautiful summer dresses earlier in the week. The chimes above the door clinked together as the rush of air from the opened door hit them. A friendly "Hi, welcome to Cassandra's" came from somewhere between the dress racks. I returned the greeting and headed toward the summer dress section.

I had an image of what I was looking for, a simple maxi dress in any color *but* white. When I questioned him about his dress preference, Nick told me that any dress I picked out would be perfect. I needed to find some matching sandals as well.

Cassandra, well, I assume it was Cassandra, walked toward me as I arrived at the maxi dress rack. She was beautiful. Her long red hair flowed past her shoulders, just touching the top of the green pantsuit's scooped neckline, and she was eager to be of help.

"So, what are you looking for, and what's the occasion?"

I told Cassandra a little bit about Nick and me and what was planned at some point today. She clasped her hands in front of her chest, and I was surprised to see her eyes glistening.

"Ah, I am so excited for you!! How beautiful!"

Romance will do it every time!

Cassandra and I started sifting through the dresses, dress after dress *not* meeting my approval. And then, there it was!

Cassandra looked at the dress upon which my hand rested and smiled. "Yep, you're right. This *is* the one!"

The dress was soft beneath my fingers and a light peach shade, precisely what I had envisioned. Anxiety crept in as I flipped over the tag to check the size and cost; it was a medium which was perfect, and the price was under one-hundred dollars. I was ecstatic!

Cassandra steered me over to the far wall shelved with sandals of every color, and it took no time at all to locate the perfect pair to complement the dress. However, the real test awaited, and I headed toward the dressing room, eager to try it on. Closing the dressing room door behind me, I reached up and hung the dress on the wall hook for a better look. The light polyester fabric was perfect for Charleston weather, and there were a few layers of chiffon hanging from the fitted waist down the length of the dress. The spaghetti straps supported the lacy halter bodice and crisscrossed in the back. It was stunning! I stepped out of my Capris and shirt and slipped the dress over my head, silently praying the size would fit perfectly. Walking up to the mirror, I was happy to see it did precisely that, and without a doubt, I knew this dress had been waiting all this time, just for me. I slipped on the sandals and turned, facing the mirror again as a knock sounded on the dressing room door, followed by Cassandra's voice. "Need any help, sweetheart?"

I lifted the latch and became even more excited when Cassandra jumped, clapping her hands excitedly. "It's perfect!!"

Turning around, I asked her if she could zip up the dress, and as the zipper traveled over the tracks, the fabric began to melt over my curves like a well-fitted glove. Stepping back into the dressing room, I spun around for the full view, catching the reflection of Cassandra in the mirror, still standing there with a smile on her face.

"I'm saying YES to the dress, Cassandra!"

Fifteen minutes later, the door to Cassandra's Boutique closed behind me, once again sending the little chimes tinkling in the breeze. Walking down the two steps toward the stone entry, two bags in tow, a black, wrought iron bench a few feet from the store, came into view, so that's where I headed. After placing the bags next to me, I pulled the phone from my purse; I still had a twenty-minute wait until Nick would pick me up. I didn't mind at all, as it allowed me the opportunity to absorb the sights and sounds of Historic-Old Charleston. For a weekday in October, quite a few people were out and about. School had started again. The sounds, sights, and smells of autumn filled the air, and speaking of smells, a delicious aroma drifted over from the little restaurant across the cobblestone street, resulting in a familiar internal rumble. Maybe, I *would* need to hit the gym when I arrived back in Cleveland after all!

Our rental car turned the corner and pulled up in front of me. "Hey, pretty lady. Need a ride somewhere?"

I shook my head. "No, I'm sorry. I don't think my fiancé would approve."

Nick sighed out loud. "Can I bribe you with brunch at an incredible little restaurant? I've heard it's the go-to place if you want the best lobster, shrimp, and corn-on-the-cob in all of South Carolina."

I tilted my head as if pondering the offer, then smiled as I rose from the bench. "You got it. I'm sure he wouldn't mind!"

Closing the car door, I looked over at Nick, sitting with eyebrows raised and eyes squinted. "Oh, yes, he would mind!" He leaned over and kissed me. "Find everything you needed?"

"I most certainly did, soon-to-be-husband of mine."

Whoever told Nick that Henner's Family Restaurant had the best grilled shrimp and corn-on-the-cob in all of South Carolina had not lied. The food was delicious and eating it all kept my nerves at bay and my thoughts focused. Nick kept glancing at the time, and I could almost see the mental clock ticking in his brain, but we were having a tough time waving the white flag of fulfilled appetite. One or two, or maybe it was five bites later, we set our napkins on top of our plates. Enough was enough! It was time to head back to the house to prepare for the rest of the momentous day.

Walking back into the house, thirty minutes later, I asked Nick if I needed anything other than the dress and sandals. He assured me he had it all taken care of, but there would be no more hints. He did tell me we wouldn't be gone all night and would be returning to the house at the end of the evening. I was pleased to hear that. I loved sleeping in our "home away from home," and we didn't have too many nights left there. Nick headed upstairs to gather what he needed, so I decided to take Buster out for a quick walk, returning ten minutes later to Nick walking down the steps, ready to go.

Back in the car, Nick reached over for my hand and asked if I was still okay with Mark picking me up, which I assured him I was. He didn't have to know about the hundreds of unleashed butterflies fluttering against internal walls or the silent deep breaths assisting in remaining calm and centered. The trip to the salon took ten minutes, ten *quick* minutes. Nick pulled alongside the curb and stepped from the car, reaching back to grab my packages from the back seat. He walked around, opened my car door, and we walked up the three steps to the salon entrance, the tinkling chimes announcing our arrival.

Nick stepped from behind me and addressed the girl at the counter. "I called yesterday about the appointment for "the works.""

The girl nodded her head and smiled as she extended her hands to take my packages. "Let me take these to the back room. We'll be ready for you in about ten minutes."

I nodded and told her I was going to walk Nick to the car. I was simultaneously nervous, sad, and excited, and although I knew I would be seeing him again in a few hours, the next time would be to take our vows. The thought sent my emotions immediately on an internal roller-coaster ride, and I attempted to blink back the tears because I didn't want Nick to think I was having second thoughts. He turned to me before opening the car door, and wouldn't you know; *he* was the one with teary eyes. I reached up and wiped the drop beginning to fall from his eye.

"Hey, you better stop that, or I'm not responsible for the weeping mess I may become, Mister!"

Nick chuckled and pulled me close to him, looking eye-to-eye. "This will be the last time you hear me say this; I love you, Lacey Coleman." He gave me a quick kiss on the lips and hugged me again before jumping into the car. "See you in a little bit."

I leaned down and stole another kiss. "Bye, babe."

Driving off, Nick waved, and I turned to head back into the salon for "the works."

The salon girls must have known the reason behind the "special" appointment because all eyes and a bunch of smiling faces turned to me when I returned.

One of the stylists stepped forward and extended her hand. "Hi, I'm Tonya. I'm going to be doing your hair today, and ...," pointing over to one of the other girls who waved, continued, "... that's Kara, and she'll be doing your nails."

I waved over to Kara. "Sounds good to me."

Tonya and I looked through some hairstyle books. I didn't want anything real fancy, so I combined a few ideas from two different books and finally decided on a bunch of loose curls, half up, half down, and pulled from the back, around to one side. I also wanted a few small white flowers and baby's breath tucked within the curls. Tonya had her work cut out for her; my job was to chill and be pampered. Nick had covered all bases, and after leading me to my chair, she walked away, returning seconds later with a bottle of wine in her hand. I recognized it immediately as one from Ventricci's, our favorite. Tonya uncorked the bottle and filled the glass while I unfolded the note she had handed me as well.

From Nicholas Ventricci ... he insisted on sending out a bottle when I called to tell him what I had planned ... I love you; have a glass for me!
Love, (Your) Nick

A smile appeared on my face as I thought of our "adopted" Italian father and not wanting to disappoint anyone, and since he *did* insist, I lifted the glass to my lips and sat back so the magic could begin.

One hour later, I sat in front of the mirror, staring at the incredible magic Tonya had performed with my hair. It hung over my shoulder in long beachy twirls, and the flowers added the pops of color I wanted. She turned my chair around and handed me a hand-held mirror so that I could see the back. It was a masterpiece of beauty! I wasn't going to take my hair down for weeks. Okay, many hours, at least!

Tonya walked me over to the other side of the salon for the manicure and pedicure, and, thirty minutes later, nice and relaxed from the glass of wine, I slid my fingers from under the setting-lamp and removed the toe-spacers from between my toes. I glanced over at the wall clock. It was already 3 p.m.; I had only thirty more minutes to go!

Tonya appeared in front of me. "Mr. Atwood requested you get dressed here before his friend picks you up."

Hmm. I was somewhat surprised. I had assumed Mark would be taking me to where I would change outfits, but knowing Nick had everything figured out, I trusted the plan and followed Tonya toward the back of the salon. I was pleasantly surprised to see a quaint, little sitting-room adorned with vintage-framed photos of brides dating from the early 1900s to the present day. A vintage-looking, patterned chair sat next to a small table, positioned near the quaint little powder room. Fresh flowers filled the vase atop the table, and a tall wooden-framed, full-length mirror stood in a corner.

Tonya walked over to the powder room, hung my dress from the door hook, and placed the shoebox on one of the chairs. "Take your time, and if you need anything, just holler."

Smiling, I hugged her, thanking her for everything. As the door closed behind her, I closed my eyes and took a deep breath; thank goodness for the glass of wine.

I walked around the little room, looking at the photos hanging from the walls. Every framed photo had been taken in the same room in which I stood, and it was fascinating to see the different styles of wedding dresses adorning the beautiful brides throughout the years. They were so fascinating that I lost sense of time, and as I returned to the table where the little clock sat, panic quickly hit! I needed to get my butt moving; Mark would be arriving in twenty minutes.

It took me only ten minutes to pull the dress over my head and buckle the sandals on my feet. I needed the other ten minutes to conceptualize the fact that it was me reflected in the mirror. Spinning around, I looked back over my shoulder and was pleased to see the back of the dress looked just as great. I was so excited to see Nick's initial reaction when he first laid eyes on me.

Lost in the moment of processing the image in the mirror, it took a moment for my brain to become conscious of the soft knocking at the door.

Tonya's voice followed the knock. "Lacey, someone named Mark is here. Are you dressed? Can I let him in?"

I turned to face the door and told her to let him in, and as the door opened, both sets of eyes widened as Mark and Tonya stood frozen in place. I hoped it was a good sign.

Tonya smiled. "Beautiful!" Telling me to "take your time," she turned and walked away.

Mark still hadn't moved, nor had he taken his eyes off me.

Before it became awkward, I broke the silence. "Well, what do you think? Will it pass Nick's approval?"

I spun around so he could get the full view, and as I returned to face him, I could tell Mark had returned to the living.

He smiled and nodded, still standing in the doorway. "Sorry about that. I didn't mean to stare. You look beautiful and, yes, Nick will approve. I'm still trying to figure out how Nick ended up getting so lucky." He released a sigh. "But then again, if that boy can wind up with someone like you, I guess I still have hope for myself, right?"

I walked over to Mark and gave him a quick hug. "Mark, thank you for the compliment, and don't you worry, I'm sure you're going to find someone special. The girls are already falling at your feet wherever you go."

Mark nodded his head. "True; however, falling at my feet is *not* the same as standing by my side."

I was at a loss of how to respond to that one, knowing full well Mark enjoyed the attention from those "falling at his feet young women." He didn't give me a chance to reply as he glanced at the clock.

"Come on. Not to rush you, but we need to get moving! No way am I going to have you show up late. Nick would kill me."

I walked around *the* room, picking up my belongings. Mark took everything from my hands, except for my purse, and stood back from the door, allowing me to walk through. As I walked back into the salon, heads turned in my direction. The smiles on the stylists' faces and a few *"Awws"* and *"Wows"* triggered a blush to warm my face.

I reached the front desk, and Tonya walked over to hug me. "You do look absolutely beautiful, Lacey. Enjoy your moment!"

I thanked her again and headed for the door, and after closing the door behind him, Mark followed me down the steps. I was two steps away from the car door when Mark stopped me.

"Wait a minute, Lacey."

He walked around to the driver's side of the car, and after placing all my things in the back seat, stepped back with something in hand; it was a scarf. I looked at the scarf and then at his face.

Mark laughed and raised both hands in front of him. "No, it's nothing freaky or anything like that. Nick warned me you would give me exactly the look like you're giving me right now, and he also told me when you did, I was supposed to remind you to trust him."

I looked at Mark skeptically. "Well, I guess it all depends on what you plan on doing with that scarf."

Mark chuckled and shook his head a few times. "Lacey, I promise, nothing bad is going to happen. Nick just wants the destination to be a total surprise. I promise that's all it is."

I inhaled a breath of air and released it with emphasis. Nick owed me for this one, big time!

"Okay, I guess. But you must talk during the ride, or it's going to be totally weird for me."

After promising me he would talk the entire way, Mark turned me around to tie the scarf around my eyes. Satisfied that I could not see anything, he opened the car door, guided me to the seat, and closed the door after I was inside.

Mark kept true to his word, and the conversation flowed. He covered everything from childhood memories of Nick and himself to the ten-year plan he had for his restaurant. It still felt rather odd to be blindfolded in the passenger seat of a car, and as hard as I attempted to figure out our direction, I still was clueless.

Mark started laughing, and I turned in his direction, with my finger pointing at him. Well, I assumed it was. "Oh, no!!! That's not cool. You aren't allowed to laugh without telling me what you're laughing at!"

He explained through his endless laughter. "Lacey, you're missing all the looks people are giving us as I pass them. A blindfolded woman in the passenger seat isn't something they see every day, I'm guessing!"

I hadn't even thought about that. Mark continued laughing, and this time I joined in.

"They're probably saying, "That damn hotel!! Look what it's doing to our city!!"

We both began laughing harder. "Lacey, I'm going to be lucky if one of them hasn't called the police already and reported my license plate!"

Luckily for us, no 911 calls were placed, and I was happy no sirens sounded behind us. We drove for nearly fifty minutes until I felt the car turn and slow down, continuing a few hundred feet more before stopping completely. The time had arrived. For the first time in my life, I felt as if I was having an out-of-body experience as I opened the car door and stepped out into the last few minutes of being Miss Lacey Coleman.

CHAPTER 13

I had no idea where I was. I heard Mark open and close his door, followed by footsteps as he walked around the car. Opening my door, Mark reached in for my hand, helping me from the car, and then proceeded to guide me even further.

"You ready for me to take the blindfold off?"

I giggled nervously. "I think I am."

Mark reached up and untied the scarf. I stood, momentarily, stuck in place and processed the sights and sounds surrounding me.

I was at the start of a walkway, and as I looked around, realization and emotions took over, my eyes welling with tears; I was getting married at Cypress Gardens. I turned to Mark, now standing to my side with a broad smile on his face, and only then did I realize a photographer standing to the side, and, no, it wasn't Nick. Mark introduced me to Sean, one of the photographers Nick would be working with on the Charleston Project. Again, I was amazed at how much thought went into making this a day I would always remember.

Mark reached up and took my arm, leading me to a bench at the edge of a walkway that disappeared into the tall trees and brilliantly colored bushes ahead.

He turned to me. "You, my dear, are good to go. I'll catch up with you two tomorrow. Dinner is on me at the restaurant. Nick already knows."

I leaned over and kissed him on the cheek as I felt a lump form in my throat. "Thank you for everything, Mark. Obviously, we couldn't be doing this without you. Nick was right, you're a fantastic guy with a great heart, and I'm so glad we have you in our lives."

Mark smiled, and I saw the beginning of brimming emotion fill his eyes; however, Mark being Mark, he quickly regained control and handed me an envelope. "Nick wants you to read this before you begin your walk to the bridge."

I took the envelope from his outstretched hand and again smiled at him. He leaned forward and again kissed my cheek before turning to head back toward the car. Halfway there, he stopped and turned. "Oh, and no crying before you get to him. You'll make your eyes look all funky and stuff."

I laughed and waved as he got in his car, pulled out, and headed back down the long driveway.

Sitting on the bench, letter in hand, I forgot that Sean was even present until I heard a couple of clicks. After about a minute, he stopped taking pictures and walked past me down the path, heading to where I assumed Nick awaited. Sliding my finger underneath the envelope flap, I lifted the triangle shape and took out the folded piece of paper.

> *My dearest Lacey,*
>
> *One year ago, if someone told me I would be standing here, waiting for a gorgeous woman, thief of my heart, to arrive so I could become her husband, I would have asked for two of whatever that person was drinking. That was a year ago, and that was before you changed my life! I have never been so sure of anything in my life. I fell in love with you, Lacey Coleman, the first time I walked into that Cleveland bar and saw you sitting there. Yes, even way back then, I knew there was no way I was ever going to let you walk out of my life. I am looking forward to the life ahead with you, the adventures, and the memories. I give you this promise, as I stand here, waiting to see you walk into my vision, moments away; I will show you, every day of my life, it is you and only you, forever, who holds my heart within your hands. I want nothing more than that smile of yours to be the first thing I see every morning and the last thing I see before I go to sleep at night. I love you, Lacey. See you in a minute ... Nick.*

Okay, I lied. I cried, but I didn't allow my eyes to get all funky. Joy, excitement, and contentment battled for acknowledgment. I stood up, filled with an urgency to be with the man I loved, and began to walk down the path, the aroma of fall flowers and brilliant colors surrounding me as I passed and with excitement growing with every nearing step.

A bridge soon spanned before me, and I noticed a few people scattered around, having stopped to see this fairy-tale romance play out in front of them, and now, I was the princess in the fairy tale.

Ahead of me, walking up the far end of the bridge, was Nick, dressed in a black suit and looking as perfect as I knew he would. I felt the lump in my throat return, threatening to trigger emotion-filled tears. I registered the click of the camera, but from that moment on, there were no other people around; Nick and I were the only ones who existed.

Nick stood in the middle of the bridge, and I continued to walk toward him, in total control, until I saw him reach up and cover his mouth with his hand. As I neared, seeing Nick overcome with emotion, all emotional power of my own vanished, and as I walked the last few steps over to him, my heart continued to swell with love as the tears cascaded over my eyelids and down my cheeks. Nick's hand remained over his mouth, and when he removed it to speak, he was momentarily unable. I smiled at him through my tears, reaching up to wipe the wetness below his eyes as he took a deep breath and reached for my hands, taking them in his.

Emotion laced his words. "Lacey, you look beautiful."

Movement caught my eye; I hadn't noticed the young man standing a few feet behind Nick until he walked toward us. I assumed this was the minister, and that was verified when he shook my hand and introduced himself as Pastor Eric. Nick seemed to have found the perfect person to marry us, as Pastor Eric seemed no older than us, and he stood, dressed in shorts and a Led Zeppelin t-shirt. He smiled at me and then looked over at Nick, who gave the "all systems go." After positioning himself, centered and facing us, he began as the photographer's camera clicked away.

Pastor Eric spent five minutes reading some Scriptures and feeding us wisdom for a successful marriage: communication, respect, and the ability to bite one's tongue if, and when, needed. The three of us shared a laugh, helping to dissipate any pre-vow jitters and lingering nervousness. There was no nervousness present, only a growing excitement as Nick and I stood, smiling, hand-in-hand, anxiously waiting for the magical words to fill the air.

When Nick suggested being married in Charleston, I had shared my concern about not having a wedding ring for him; it was something significant to me. Standing on that bridge, preparing to share our wedding vows, I remembered the conversation, and as if reading my mind, Nick looked up and me, reached into his pocket, and retrieved not only my wedding band but a simple gold wedding band for himself. I looked at him curiously. Nick just smiled and winked, placing both rings into Pastor Eric's outstretched hand. Have I mentioned Nick's attention to detail?

The vows' time arrived, and Nick and I took turns repeating Pastor Eric as he led us through the wedding promises. It felt surreal, yet authentic, simultaneously. *This is really happening!* I heard Nick say he wanted me for better or worse, in sickness and health, till death do us part. My lips moved, and the words flowed over my lips as I repeated the same vows to Nick. Pastor Eric took a step back and smiled at both of us.

"I now pronounce you, husband and wife. You may kiss your bride."

Unbeknownst to us, quite a group of people had gathered to watch the fairy-tale dream unfold, and to the eruption of applause, Nick and I shared our first kiss as husband and wife. It had happened; I was Mrs. Nick Atwood.

The next hour was pure bliss as we strolled around posing in, what seemed to be, a hundred different places. Nick's keen eye knew the photogenic spots, and it was interesting and slightly amusing as well to see Nick put through the motions on the other side of the camera. More than once, he found it impossible to remain a passive subject in front of the lens, and at those times, Nick would run over to Sean, peek at the camera angle, or suggest a different position for better lighting. Sean would laugh, look over at me, and shake his head as Nick — ever the Dominant one — ran back to stand next to me, smiling as if he hadn't moved. Luckily, Sean understood the idiosyncrasies of a passionate perfectionist, and Nick and I joined in the laughter each time it happened.

And yes, for the final set of photos, we even recreated the famous boat scent from *The Notebook*, with Nick rowing the boat through shimmering colors reflected from the surrounding trees.

As we stepped from the boat, Sean looked up at the sky and then his watch. "I think that's a wrap here, Nick. We should arrive at the beach at prime sunset time."

Nick put his arm around my waist. "Ready for our first meal as husband and wife?"

What else had Nick planned?

Walking behind Sean, we made our way back to the parking lot, where Nick helped load all the camera gear into the car trunk before reaching out to shake the outstretched hand. "See you in about fifty, buddy."

We pulled out after Sean, following him down the entry, the same one where only three hours previously, I had traveled as a single woman — an eternity, yet only moment ago.

Nick reached for my hand. "So, Mrs. Atwood, how does it feel to be my wife?"

Intertwining my fingers through Nick's, I squeezed and looked over at my dashingly handsome husband and smiled. "It feels fantastic, and *you*, Mr. Atwood, made me feel like a princess. Thank you for that."

Nick turned and smiled. "Mrs. Atwood, you *are* a princess, and the evening has just begun."

CHAPTER 14

Precisely forty-five minutes later, Nick made a final turn, and we pulled down a street that Nick traveled down a bit before pulling along the side and turning off the car. I had no clue where I was.

"Welcome to Sullivan's Island Beach, Lacey."

Sean had already parked and was walking with his camera gear toward, what I assumed, the beach ahead, and he had been correct when he stated we would arrive at prime time. The beautiful sunset had just begun to fill the sky with colors, and I wouldn't put it past Nick to have somehow ordered an extra dose of brilliance for our special day.

Nick stepped out of the car, walked around to my side, and opened my car door to help me out like the gentleman he is. Either he was a true gentleman, *or* he was hoping to get lucky later; that was something Nick didn't need to worry about at all, as I was just as eager for our first night together as husband and wife.

"Lacey, when I tell you to close your eyes, you need to trust me, ok?"

"What do you have planned now, Mr. Atwood?"

He took hold of my hand and gently began leading me forward. "You will see, Mrs. Atwood."

At the end of the road, we began down a pathway leading through a span of tall beach grass, and as soon as I spied the sand ahead, Nick gently tugged me to a stop.

"Okay, Lacey. Time to close the eyes, but first, the shoes."

Nick knelt beside me, placing my hand on his shoulder, after which he removed both my sandals, and after removing his shoes, he turned to me again. "Eyes closed."

I closed my eyes as Nick tucked my arm around his and then gently led me several more steps until I felt sand, like a warm liquid carpet under my feet. We continued walking forward for another minute or so before we stopped again.

"Okay, Lacey, you can open your eyes."

I gasped at the vision before me; pastel colors filled the sky, creating a true-to-life masterpiece, a wedding present of magnificence. I looked over the horizon, trying to burn the beauty into a lifetime memory, when my eyes fell upon a mirage. But, it wasn't really a mirage; it was just another of Nick's magical surprises. A wooden, four-post, framed cabana stood like an illusion in the vastness of the nearly empty beach. Drapes of white cloth hung taut from the top post, met at the middle, allowing access to the entrance and exit, and provided a framed view of the ocean. Sheets of flowing white hung from the sides and gently billowed with each soft breath of the ocean breeze, and in the middle of the magical oasis, a round white linen-covered table with matching white padded chairs sat facing the ocean view. A tiki torch burned at each corner, flames dancing with the gentle breeze while seemingly hundreds of white candles burned in the sand surrounding the cabana. I was speechless with awe at the heart-stopping beauty Nick had created, and when I looked over at him with tear-filled eyes, I attempted to push words past the lump in my throat.

Nick smiled. "I guess I did okay, huh?"

In some far-off "other" world, I heard the clicks of the camera; in my world, at that moment, it was only Nick and me. I reached up, placing my hands upon his tanned cheeks. "I am a lucky girl, Mr. Atwood." I continued moving my hands up to the back of his head and pulled his face close to mine. "I love you."

A throat-clearing sound came from nearby. Turning to look, I was surprised to see our very favorite waiter standing in full restaurant attire at the edge of the cabana. *No way!* I looked over at Nick and shook my head. "No fair, Mister!"

Nick and I walked over, and Nathaniel greeted the two of us with congratulations before turning to me and smiling, his face reddening slightly. After nervously clearing his throat again, he informed us that he would be at our service whenever we were ready and added that the main course would arrive in approximately one hour.

"However, while you wait." Nathaniel pointed to a side table of appetizers to which the three of us walked. A display of deliciousness tempted; crab dip waiting to accompany still-warm pita bread, fresh fruit kabobs, and bruschetta, piled high with pieces of shrimp, diced tomatoes, and salsa, silently summoned some underlying hunger pangs.

Nick looked over at Nathaniel. "This looks fantastic! Can you give us about fifteen minutes to catch some last pictures? We'll be ready after that."

Nathaniel nodded and smiled. "Yes, sir."

With the breathtaking view changing colors before our eyes, Sean went to work, the camera's clicking becoming white noise in the background. I was sure the photos would turn out just as impressive as the morphing sky, which was now turning a deep blue as it followed the sinking sun into the ocean.

"That's it, Nick. I think it's a wrap!"

Nick held up a finger. "Hold on there, Sean."

Looking over at me with mischief flitting over his face, and before I could even react, Nick swooped me up in his arms. He carried me out into the ocean, pretending he was going to throw me in but stopped at the water's edge and carefully set me down. Turning me to face him, Nick then placed his warm hands on my face, and I immediately became lost in his gaze as he pulled me near, kissing me passionately as the warm ocean lapped against the bottom of my dress. If there is anything similar to heaven on earth, I was there at that moment, and I genuinely believe that I experienced absolute serenity — a full, pure, and complete peace for the first time in my life.

Nick walked Sean back to his car while I made my way over to the appetizers. I was starving, and as I neared the table, I saw Nathaniel straighten himself, lifting his hands to his tie to ensure alignment. Reaching the table, I picked up one of the small plates and smiled in his direction. "So, how were you so lucky to be picked for beach waiter duty, Nathaniel?"

As Nathaniel returned my smile, a hint of redness appeared on his cheeks, and it wasn't from the candles *or* the tiki torches. "Well, to be honest, I volunteered for tonight. I love the beach, and this doesn't happen very often. Also, it gave me another opportunity to see you."

Did I hear him say that? I looked up to see him grinning, and I cocked my head in response. "Nathaniel, are you flirting with me?" He laughed briefly. "Yes, ma'am, I am."

Nick's voice carried over the short distance as he neared us. "I hope you aren't letting her eat all the appetizers, Nathaniel!"

Nathaniel laughed and smiled at me again before turning to face Nick. "No, Mr. Atwood. There are plenty of appetizers left."

Arriving at the cabana-enclosed table with plates full of appetizers, Nick and I settled into our chairs, watching the waves hit the beach. Nathaniel appeared a moment later to fill our wine glasses with none other than our favorite wine from our favorite Italian. As expected, with no detail forgotten, music began to stream in through two small speakers placed inside near the cabana corners, and I tried to soak in every single moment as the outside world seemed to cease existence.

A wide variety of music, jazzy, bluesy, and seductively romantic, serenaded us through our appetizers and then through the lobster, which arrived thirty minutes later. Dessert was Cherries Jubilee, set on fire by Nathaniel and served with a scoop of vanilla ice cream, and yes, I ate every single bite!

Nathaniel reappeared at our table as the last bite of decadent sweetness disappeared into my mouth, asking if we needed anything else. Nick asked him to leave the bottle of wine, still half full, to which Nathaniel replied he "would do just that," adding that there would be someone coming by to remove the cabana after we left but assured us there was no rush. After sharing congratulations with us one more time, Nathaniel walked away, leaving us to a nearly empty beach. I looked in both directions, seeing only one other person walking a dog in the distance.

That was one positive aspect of a beach in October; it's almost always empty; the downside is the possibility of an evening chill, and a chill was present in the air. Nick walked back to the car, returning with his jacket, which he wrapped around my shoulders, and a blanket, and after gently pulling me up from the chair, he led me a few feet from the cabana.

The glow of the candles and tiki torches illuminated the makeshift beach dance floor. As the music drifted over, I melted into the warmth of Nick's body as we danced for the first time as husband and wife, swaying under the glow of moonlight and candles as the sounds of the waves accompanied the musical notes drifting in the air. I couldn't have asked for a better wedding day, and quite honestly, I didn't think a better day was possible.

We danced three body-to-body dances before Nick went back to the cabana and returned with the blanket, after which we located the perfect spot, near enough to our cabana, but far enough away to not be caught up in the bright glow. After stretching out the blanket, we sat down, both of us releasing an audible sigh at the same moment; a lifetime had seemingly occurred over the last twelve hours!

We talked about the day's events and the tomorrows ahead, the conversation ebbing and flowing in rhythm with the gentle waves. Nick had us wrapped up in the blanket, and he soon pulled me on top of him, both of us obscured from the *hopefully* empty beach. Still, I looked around once more to ensure no spectators were in view. And then, we made love. We made love for the first time as Mr. and Mrs. Nick Atwood; glorious, romantic, newlywed love to the sounds of the waves hitting against the shore and Frank Sinatra crooning through the speakers. I was now a married woman, and I was married to the man who held my heart in his hands; for better, for worse, for richer, for poorer, in sickness and in health, to love and cherish until death, do we part. It was a done deal!

CHAPTER 15

Wednesday morning arrived via brilliant sunshine streaming in the windows, proclaiming it was way past time to be up and at 'em. After the romp in the sand the previous evening, Nick and I eventually made our way back to the car. I would venture to guess that even though Nick and I were discreet enough, the two men waiting to take down the cabana were fully aware of what had occurred. Well, they were either aware, or perhaps the smirks on their faces, as we passed them in the parking lot, merely meant they were enjoying the evening's ocean view. Regardless, no sooner had we walked past them, the two men headed toward the cabana for take-down.

Arriving back at our vacation home twenty minutes later, Nick had looked over at me and held up his finger. "Don't even think about it, Lacey Atwood."

I giggled as Nick exited the car, walked around to my side, held out his hand to help me out, and then literally swept me off my feet, proceeding to carry me up the few steps to the front door. A few amusing moments passed as he attempted to maintain a hold on me while fumbling with the key; however, I was soon carried over the threshold of our home away from home, where Buster greeted us with unrestrained delight and a crazily wagging tail.

Nick set me down once we made it into the kitchen and then grabbed the leash off the hook; Buster was demanding attention, and while Nick took him for a short walk, I briefly apprised my bronzed friend of the events of the last twelve hours. I must say, I think she was rather impressed, and I swear she even nodded her head slightly during the shortened re-cap of my wedding day.

Closing the patio doors fifteen minutes later, I almost bumped into Nick, back from his Buster-led walk, and together we climbed the staircase. A unanimous decision was made; we were too exhausted to do anything but remove our clothes and fall onto the bed, and we fell asleep wrapped up together like a warm twisted pretzel until the streaming sunlight saved us from sleeping away the entire day.

I turned my head and looked at Nick, who was just opening his eyes. "Good morning, Mr. Atwood."

Nick turned over on his side to face me and then planted a kiss on the center of my forehead. "Good morning, Mrs. Atwood."

I scooted closer to him, nuzzling my head against his warm chest while he wrapped his arm over me, and tilted my head up toward him with a sleepy smile. "This isn't a dream, right? I am really lying here in bed next to my husband. We are now married, right?"

Nick squeezed his arm around me and laughed. "Ironically, I had the same thought this morning, and if it's a dream, we are both in it together, so it's all good."

I laid my head back against Nick's chest. "I think we should stay in Charleston forever. I'm not looking forward to going back to Cleveland at all!"

I could tell by the change in his voice he was looking down toward me. "Well, speaking of Cleveland, the first thing I'd like to do is to figure out a different job for you, maybe. I'm not thrilled with my wife putting herself in all kinds of danger out there. Lacey, you don't have to work at all if you don't want."

I scooted up, so I could look directly at Nick. "I know I promised to look for something else, and I'm still planning on it. I feel an inner itch to discover where my true passion is, but I just don't feel comfortable not working and helping bring in some income."

Nick turned his head and looked at me. "Lacey, I think you already know we're doing great financially. You made more than your annual salary with the hotel displays, so you can take your time and figure out what you want to do. Maybe start a nonprofit of your own or something?"

I started to reply, but Nick placed his finger against my lips. "You're an awesome social worker, and you kick ass for the agency as well as all of your clients. We both know you have so much more to offer, and I just want you happy doing what you want to be doing. You know I support you in whatever decision you make, Mrs. Atwood."

Nick kissed me on the forehead and continued speaking as his arms pulled me closer, and his hands moved down my back. "Besides, I may just keep you so busy you won't have time for your job anymore."

I stretched my leg over Nick's turned body, gently pushing him over, so he was lying on his back, and then slid on top of him, my bed-hair falling into his face as I zoomed in for a kiss. "Hmm, now *that*, Mr. Atwood, is a job I think I would enjoy. But for now, we need to get out of this bed and enjoy our last two days!"

Those last two days in Charleston sped by like the second-place race car in the Indy 500 on the final lap. We met up with the Anderson's for breakfast early Wednesday morning, and after our bellies were full, Nick and Tom left to go fishing for a couple of hours while Kitty and I ventured around historic Charleston. We stopped in to say hi to Cassandra and Tonya, showing them some of the pictures already up on Sean's website. And Kitty being the perfect southern hostess, treated me to some quiche and tea at her favorite little cafe before heading back to meet Nick and Tom.

Appetite sated, we walked over toward the street to meet the guys at the Street Market. Nick was sun-kissed, and fish blissed. The guys had scooped up Mark along the way, and from the smell of fish, beer, and sunshine, they had a great time. Nick and I said our goodbyes to Kitty and Tom and thanked them again for all the kindness and generosity offered to us over the last week, and they made us promise to return soon, which was not a difficult promise to make at all!

Later that evening, Nick held to his promise of a Charleston haunted ghost tour. We remain in disagreement over what I know I captured on my phone's camera, a specter peeking out from behind a gravestone. Nick continues to be adamant that it was just some kind of weird lighting; however, I was there, and no other light shone in that graveyard!

Thursday came, and with it, a somewhat somber mood for both of us. Friday's flight home was 1 p.m., and that meant we had to be at the airport by ten-thirty or so. We also needed to have the house looking as it did the day we arrived and pack everything up by evening.

We took one last walk along the beach in the morning, shuffling our feet in the sand, splashing each other gently as we walked near the water's edge. We walked through some of the shops once more, so I could show Nick the ones we had missed, and we picked up some more souvenirs for our shared condo.

Later in the evening, we joined Mark at his restaurant, where the three of us spent a couple of hours on the patio, sharing dinner, some wine, and good conversation. Mark promised he would come to Cleveland around Christmas, which seemed to be light years away from my thoughts at that moment. I had grown closer to Mark during the past two weeks, and as I hugged him goodbye, I found myself choking up a bit, with tears threatening to appear. Nick hugged Mark and gave him the typical "guy slap/pat" on the back.

"Mark, thanks so much for everything, the condo hookup, the dinners, the wedding … there is no way I could've done it without you. I owe you big time, man."

Mark took a step back from us and lifted his glass in the air. He smiled a "Mark" smile, which is nothing more than disguised emotion behind a smart-ass grin. "To the Atwoods. May the years ahead be filled with crazy, fun times with your good old buddy, Mark! Cheers!"

Mark walked us out to our car, and after one last hug and wave, we drove off back toward Rainbow Row, our vacation retreat, my bronze mermaid, Buster, and our last evening in Charleston. It was time to bring to completion the most incredible, beautiful, exciting, eye-opening, life-changing two weeks of my life.

I woke up early Friday morning. Nick was still snoring lightly, one leg sticking out from underneath the sheet, one arm over his pillow-covered face. I closed the door quietly and made my way to the kitchen for some much-needed coffee, after which I made my way to the patio for one last conversation with the mermaid. I know it seems silly, but I was going to miss the bronze friend of mine. She had become my confidante, a listener of my stories, a secret keeper, and, most importantly, she kept her opinions to herself. We recapped all adventures of the fully experienced fourteen days, and we mentally promised to meet up again, after which I rose from the chaise and closed the patio doors to start the day.

Nick finally awoke, and we spent the next few hours grudgingly loading the car with all our belongings. I wrote a letter to the Morettis, thanking them for their hospitality, complimenting them on their beautiful home, and reminding them not to forget to contact us if they ever needed a house sitter. To be honest, I begged them to contact us if they needed a house sitter at any time! Nick and I took Buster for one last walk, during which time we both decided that one day, in the future, we wanted to add a dog to our little family.

The drive back to the airport was quiet, and Nick held my hand the entire time. It was a beautiful morning, and the sun was already shining as we pulled into the airport, making it even harder to leave the city that my heart now thought of as its second home. I had fallen in love with the history, the atmosphere, the new friends, and all the memories made. I knew there was a lifetime ahead for Nick and me, one of excitement, discovery, and memory-making, but that wasn't making it any easier for me.

The past two weeks were life-changing, and boarding the plane one hour later, I realized the Lacey who arrived in Charleston fourteen days ago, was not the same Lacey who would be departing the plane in Cleveland. I was full of confidence and peace that filled me from head to toe. I was a changed woman. I was Lacey Atwood.

CHAPTER 16

Whirlwind: an energetic process *or* something that involves many quickly changing events, feelings, etc. In the first few weeks after returning from Charleston, my life fit both of those descriptions. Moving my stuff and myself into Nick's loft, filling out a ton of paperwork for the legal name change, preparing for our first holidays together, and getting back into the work grind, turned the days into weeks very quickly. The sails on Lake Erie were no longer, and the sky became darker, so much earlier.

Leaving my place was a little harder than I thought it would be. I had enjoyed learning how to be comfortable with myself in that apartment, and the woman who moved in there three years ago was assuredly not the same woman who walked out the door for the last time. It was well worth the trade, though, and I loved sharing Nick's loft, which now represented both Mr. *and* Mrs. Atwood.

I initially had some concerns about living with someone twenty-four hours a day, seven days a week, but that thought dissipated very quickly after those first few days of coming home to Nick. He had made the transition from vacation to reality an easy one, and there was not one day, walking through the loft door, that some delicious aroma wasn't hitting me in the face.

That first Monday back was a tough one, though, and walking up the steps to the office took all the motivation and willpower I possessed. Yes, I loved the families I worked with, and most of them were thankful for the assistance I provided, but some of them, eh, not so much. The Turner family, less Jack Turner, was a perfect example of one of the thankful families, and on that first Monday back, a Monday returning from a vacation, mind you, Jennifer Turner was on the schedule, and I had no idea what awaited.

The key to the agency door turned too quickly, and a gnawing pit settled deep within my gut as I walked through it. Making my way over to my workstation, I plopped my stuff on the floor near my chair and sunk into well-worn seat familiarity. It was only a matter of moments before a group of coworkers gathered around my desk to welcome me back, and it was Abbie who noticed it first, of course.

"OH MY GOD! YOU GOT MARRIED? DID YOU GET MARRIED? IS THAT A WEDDING RING? DID YOU REALLY GET MARRIED?"

Laughing, I pulled the chair out next to mine and told Abbie to sit before she hyperventilated as I answered the barrage of questions. "Yes, it is a wedding ring. Yes, I did get married. Yes, I do have some pictures the photographer sent me."

I spent the next twenty minutes making sure Abbie didn't pass out, receiving congratulatory hugs and wishes, and flipping through the pictures on my phone, showing them all the adventures from Charleston. As I pulled up Sean's photos, the group gathered nearer as I swiped through the wedding day photos, resulting in the second round of hugs before the girls all left back to their respective workstations or offices — all of them except Abbie.

"Lacey Coleman, oops, I mean Lacey Atwood, I had a gut feeling this would happen." She reached over and brought my hand up to her face to better look at the large diamond. "Are you sure this is what you wanted? You okay with all of this?"

I looked at her and opened my mouth to reply, but she stopped me, chuckling. "You don't even have to answer that. I can see the love and happiness in your face, Lacey." I leaned over to hug her, after which she pulled back from me and scooted her chair a little closer to mine. "Now, tell me all about the hotel, your displays, and all the juicy news."

I gave Abbie a brief "R" rated version of the hotel, the LEDs, and all the titillating news before she finally returned to her desk, and I turned my attention to the day ahead. Even opening my planner and looking over the week's schedule seemed overwhelming. Nick was right. I needed to find a different career. Lying in bed last night, I told him I was thinking about starting my own business of some kind, and although I wasn't sure what yet,

I felt a new sense of energy and a need to change direction. Like Katt says at the beginning of her book, fantasy play can get lost in the obligations of real life," and now that I was married to Nick, who relentlessly supported my desire to discover and follow my dreams and passions, it seemed like a good time for a change. He had enthusiastically seconded the idea, although he wasn't too thrilled when I explained I wanted to stick it out until spring until I explained.

Families involved in social services are often left to deal with worker transitions more than would seem morally ethical or compassionately fair. Those struggling with mental health and addictions have it tough enough already. It can become very frustrating and often traumatic for clients when they tell the same story repeatedly to worker after worker, and I didn't want to be one of those workers, at least for Jennifer Turner and her children. I wanted to see it through to the end, and I felt strongly that she was heading for a successful outcome.

I told Nick I was determined to be the worker celebrating their graduation from the program, even if it killed me. Although I doubted Jack would be part of that celebration, Jennifer and her children deserved it. After graduation, I would gladly, and without looking back, put in my notice of resignation; however, the part of it "killing me" was undoubtedly the wrong choice of words.

Nick turned to face me that day, concern in his eyes. "And that, Mrs. Atwood, is what scares the shit out of me." He reached up and put his hand against my face, rubbing his thumb gently up and down. "I get it, Lacey. Your stubbornness is one of the things I love about you. That said, do what you need to do. I swear, though, if anyone ever threatens or hurts you or even sends you any more of those creepy messages, I'm going to stomp some ass, got it?"

I had laughed at the time Nick said that. In my mind, though, I had felt a touch of anxiety as I thought of the messages I received in Charleston and the decision not to tell him about it. I still thought Jack was behind it all, somehow, or in some way.

The phone ringing jolted me from my mental rewind of the previous night's conversation. Picking up the phone, I answered it without looking at the number or the name. I should have known; I had thought "them" into action. It was Jennifer Turner, and I could tell from the moment I heard her voice, Jack was back in the picture, and it was the reason for the phone call.

Although I was due to meet with Jennifer later this afternoon, she called to confirm the appointment; well, that's the reason she provided. She added that visitation with the kids was going smoothly, and that the caseworker also had a meeting with her today, which was good. I would be able to check in with the kids as well. Additionally, she had received a scheduled review hearing notice, and she was excited at the prospect of having the kids returned to her full-time.

All of that was good news, but I patiently waited for the mention of Jack. I had a feeling that he was another reason for the call, and, unfortunately, I was right. Jennifer stated there had been no appearance, nor any attempt at communication from Jack, until recently. Three days ago, while returning from the store, Jennifer had sensed an ominous rumbling of discontent, and looking around, she immediately discovered the source. A heavy cannonball of dread dropped in her gut as her eyes fell upon Jack, talking to some friends in a parking lot across the street ahead. He noticed her immediately, and despite her quickened steps, Jack Turner kept his sight on Jennifer until she passed.

Legally, he hadn't broken the law; Jack was outside the restricted legal perimeters and had not spoken to her. However, it was enough to trigger Jennifer, and for a brief moment after returning to her sister's home, she felt as if she would lose control of everything she had worked so hard to regain. I could hear the tinge of wavering courage in her voice as she spoke, and the work notes I had just typed became blurry. My eyes filled with tears as a wave of despair landed upon me. *Is this ever going to change?*

I hung up the phone and let out an audible sigh.

Abbie poked her head up over the partition. "Welcome back, Lacey."

It didn't take long to feel as if I had never been on vacation, and by two o'clock, I was back in the groove, popping in and out of houses, catching up with families. Sliding into my car seat after meeting with another family, I picked up my phone to enter Jennifer's temporary address into the navigator when a beep sounded, and, simultaneously, the blue envelope icon lit up.

Nick's incredible face popped up next to a message. **How's your first day back, Mrs. Atwood? I, your HUSBAND, miss you and hope you get your sweet little ass back home as soon as you can because, mmm, I'm going to take that body of yours and ...!**

Well, if I hadn't wanted to put an end to my workday before that message, now I desperately wanted to put the next two hours behind me. I turned the key and fastened my seat belt before replying to Nick's message. **You sexy, smooth-talking husband of mine... I, your WIFE, am counting on that!**

Twenty minutes later, I walked up the sidewalk leading to Jennifer Turner's sister's home. Every sense on high alert, I startled and froze in place at the shouting of my name; however, I quickly recognized the sweet young voices belonging to the Turner kids who were now running toward me. Jennifer Turner, her sister, and the Children's Service worker trailed behind and laughed as four little arms wrapped around my legs.

As they neared, I immediately detected a familiar weariness in Jennifer's eyes, and after exchanging greetings, I asked if I could speak to Jennifer alone for a few minutes. The kids were successfully un-pried by a challenge to race back to the picnic table, and two minutes later, we headed to the porch swing.

I watched Jennifer Turner's composure fall apart piece by piece with every step. It was as if by finally being back in the presence of her most significant ally, her emotions finally had a safe place to show up once again. Sitting down, I sat in silence, waiting until the tears had slowed, and she had regained her composure. I fully expected to hear and witness a complete return of "Codependent Jennifer," and I was pleasantly surprised to see that was not the case.

"Lacey, I really hate him, and although I know it's not healthy to hate anyone, I can't help it." I saw her bottom lip start to quiver again. "He's just never going to change, and I'm so tired of being treated so shittily! I don't think I'll ever be able to forgive him for what he's done to this family." A tear slid down her face, and she reached up to wipe it away with the end of the sleeve-covered arm.

I turned to face her. "Jennifer, look at me." She looked up with her tear-streaked face, a trail of black from her eyeliner snaking its way to her chin. "We've talked about this before. You're perfectly justified in feeling everything you're feeling about your husband right now. He has a lot of proving to do if he ever wants to win back the respect and trust that he destroyed."

Another tear slid down Jennifer's face, another wipe of the sleeve erased it. "But for now, I want you to concentrate on continuing your counseling and doing everything in your power to get the kids back. We have no idea how this is going to play out with Jack, but you have some decisions to make."

"Lacey, I want a divorce. I'm really ready to start a new life."

One more tear slid down her cheek, but this time, a smile reappeared. One more wipe of the sleeve to erase the liquid drop of sadness. If only a sleeve-covered swipe of an arm could delete years of sorrow.

"Well, then Jennifer Turner, you have some work to do!"

We rejoined the worker, Jennifer's sister, and two laughing, energetic children, spending the next thirty minutes discussing the upcoming review hearing as well as scheduling the next appointment. Jennifer didn't know it yet, but we would be looking to plan a program discharge date during the next meeting. The family, well, at least Jennifer and the children, were meeting most of the original goals, and this winter would mark almost a year since the start of services. It was me dragging my feet, as I felt the Turner's had needed that extra time to flourish and grow.

I walked back to my car with a smile on my face and a lightness to my step. *Now home to Nick!* Before pulling out of the driveway, I sent Nick a text. **On my way, babe, about twenty minutes away.**

By the time I was at the end of the driveway, a text popped back up. Technically, it wasn't a text. It was more of a Nick "selfie." My stud of a husband was bare-chested and teasing with unbuttoned jeans. He stood at the grill, steaks sitting nearby.

And how do you like your meat again, my sexy wife?

I had to put the car in park for a minute while I regained my senses before attempting to drive the two-ton torpedo back home. That would teach me to marry a photographer who knows exactly the response he's seeking from others. I brought the phone closer to my face and enlarged it, something I didn't really need to do, and detected a bulge behind the opened zipper. Perhaps the first course wouldn't be the steak at all; maybe it would end up being the dessert. I sent a text back. **Better be careful, Nick. We don't want anything grilled that isn't supposed to be.**

CHAPTER 17

Twenty minutes later, I pulled into my spot next to Nick's car and made my way to the front entrance. I poked my head into the gallery, said "hi" to dreadlocked Trevor, and headed to the elevator. My interest in what awaited behind our condo door was piqued, and I could not escape the mental erotic movie, now running on an endless loop inside my head; the anticipation was nearly palpable.

I heard the familiar pulsing of music playing as the elevator doors slid open, and upon reaching the loft door, I stood quietly outside, hoping for another duet, but, alas, no crooning duo. I opened the door to see Nick walking back inside from the balcony, and his smile triggered the same from me. He was still dressed exactly like the picture, and steak definitely wasn't what I was thinking about at that moment.

Nick walked to me, and after removing the purse from my shoulder and the computer bag from my hand, he pulled me close to him. Hands traveled up my waist to the back of my head, where fingers wove through my hair like a snake in a reedy marsh. Pulling my head to his, Nick's lips touched mine, and his tongue pushed through my slightly parted lips to find its familiar playmate. Our tongues played tag as Nick's hands made their way back down my neck, over my shoulders, down my back, and then rested on my ass before pulling me even closer to him. I followed suit and let my hands travel down Nick's body, down over his naked chest and back, and continued down to the top of his jeans, finally resting on his jean-covered backside.

The smell of the cooking steaks wafted between our bodies and disrupted our intensifying passion — a man and his steak, an unbreakable bond. Nick pulled back, arms still wrapped around me and smiled, winked, and kissed me on the forehead. "Smells like we're going to have to continue this later, wife."

He pulled me back to him, his hands sliding back down to the bottom of my dress and then sliding underneath, continuing their upward journey to the edge of my panties, where his thumb traced the lacey border. He leaned close. "Go shower, baby. I left something for you on the bed."

He didn't have to say it twice as I loved all of Nick's surprises, and I eagerly made my way into the bedroom where I saw a red and black, polka-dotted gift with a giant red bow on top, waiting on the bed. I sat and placed the box on my lap, after which I untied the bow, removed the lid, and pulled back the red tissue paper. I lifted out a button-down blouse made from a black silky material, and my fingers slid over the smoothness as I placed it on the bed next to me. I next removed a shiny, gold body-chain halter from the box; it was beautiful with twenty or so gold-colored chains hanging from the halter collar. *This man of mine definitely has a sense of style!* Setting the chained halter on top of the blouse, I reached in again, pulling out some gold and black panties, a black garter, and a pair of silky black stockings, and underneath those, a note beckoned. **There is another box under the bed.**

I hopped off the bed, knelt, and lifted the bedspread to see another identically wrapped box. Sitting back down on the bed, I repeated the undoing of this box, as I had the first box, and lifted the top. Inside was a pair of black, spiky, high-heeled, over-the-knee boots. *Ohh, boy, Nick!* Under the boots, another note teased — **one more box in the bathroom.**

Setting the boots on the floor next to the bed, I walked into the bathroom and saw a small box placed on the vanity countertop, and after repeating the unwrapping process, I removed the lid to see a beautiful set of gold tasseled-chain earrings. Lifting one from the small box, I held it up to my ear and looked in the mirror; the earrings matched the chained halter top perfectly. Nick, once again, had managed to pull off the perfect gift.

The searing steak's aroma infiltrated my nostrils and registered in my brain as a signal to "get my butt moving!" While I was excited to see how the outfit would look, I was even more excited to see what Nick's reaction was going to be, and I was anticipating the outfit's "after-effects" following dinner — *if* we made it that far.

Ten minutes later, I exited the bedroom feeling like a princess, an exotic dancer, a high-priced escort, and a red-carpet-walking actress, all in one. The chained halter top looked beautiful and sexy under the black, unbuttoned blouse that hit the upper thigh and left just enough of a compelling gap between the hem and the leather boots' top. The earrings hung as if they were strands of my hair and added the perfect touch to complete the outfit. Quite frankly, I turned-on myself after catching my reflection in the balcony window. *Maybe Lacey, this will be the next LED to adorn the Fantasy Play Hotel™.*

I walked, more like strutted, out into the big room to the beat of Massive Attack radio playing through the speakers, the intoxicating music making it easy to feel like a walking body of oozing sexuality. Nick was standing against the balcony railing, facing into the condo, and I strutted the invisible walkway toward him.

The sun was descending, and the gold shimmer reflecting off the water volleyed for attention with the flickering balcony candles. The cooler air, accompanying Cleveland's late fall evening, was balanced by the heat radiating from the candles and the recently used grill; however, a different kind of warmth permeated the evening air as well, the warmth from Nick's penetrating gaze as I neared him.

He hadn't moved, and I could have fooled myself into thinking his breath had ceased until I heard the short, deep, "mmm" sound from behind his closed lips as I walked the final steps toward him. I stopped a few feet away and turned so he could experience the glorious one hundred and eighty degrees "Lacey" view. Completing the turn, my legs weakened at the intensity radiating from Nick's piercing eyes.

"Woman, you are in danger tonight."

Nick reached out his hands and slid them under the gold chains, gently tugging me nearer for increased access to the skin he so craved. His hands followed a downward path to where the top of my boots hit my thighs, and then two fingers took over, lightly tracing around the inside of each boot top as he leaned forward, invading my mouth with his tongue. My hands traveled to the back of his head, where they encouraged him into an even deeper kiss. Leaving their boot top location, Nick's firm hands moved back up to my hips, my waist, and found my hard nipples, after which his fingers slid gently over each one, causing little gasps to escape from behind my lips.

Nick pulled back, and his mouth returned to near my ear. "I've been thinking all day about what I'm going to do to you tonight, Lacey. But, food first, because you're going to need all of the energy you can get."

I looked at him and laughed. "Tease! I cry unfair!"

Nick looked at me and smiled. "I'm sure I can figure out a way to make it up to you."

Taking my hand in his, Nick led the way toward the table, where he pulled the chair out for me to sit and then continued to stand behind it after gently pushing me forward. His hand grazed my hair on its way to my chin, which he gently lifted until my head was resting back against his bare abdomen. I looked up past the bare chest into his face as a lone finger glided over my cheek to my mouth, where it teasingly traced the outline of my lips. Nick's eyes never disconnected from mine, even as he sighed, bringing his hands back to my shoulders. He looked down into my face and smiled. "Food first."

Not only had Nick cooked the steaks that teased me from the earlier suggestive photos, grilled vegetables, and roasted sweet potato slices topped with melted butter and a sprinkle of brown sugar, now accompanied them on my plate. A fresh bottle of Nicholas's "best" was uncorked, and, soon enough, the heady sweetness added to the sensory delight. The sexual heat was rising to perfection, as well.

I ate every bite of food on my plate, which wasn't an easy task considering Nick was often running his hand over my thigh throughout the meal; however, I somehow managed and finally nudged my plate away. Nick pushed his chair back and grabbed up both of our dishes, took them into the kitchen, and helped me up from my chair after returning.

We danced body-to-body, candlelight flickering around us, to the rhythmic beats streaming out to the balcony. Now, what happened next, I'm blaming on the wine, the satisfaction of a full belly, and the empowering effects of the outfit I was wearing, as I have no other excuse for the brazen impulsiveness that overtook me. "Clint Eastwood" by Gorillaz began playing, and before I even had time to talk myself out of doing it, I gently pushed Nick back toward the chair, nodding for him to sit down. I took three steps away and stopped, standing with my back to him, and as the pulsating beat streamed around me, I allowed my inhibitions to fly free. My body joined in partnership with the music's rhythm, and I began to dance for my attentive audience of one.

Reaching up, I pulled off one sleeve and then the other, holding my shirt in my hand until I turned and tossed it on Nick's lap. The look on his face, still one of intensity, was now balanced by a satisfied grin, convincing me he was enjoying the show almost as much as I was.

Beckoning Nick to stand, I turned around, so my back was against him and reached back, bringing his hands around to the front of me after which I entwined my fingers with his and led them on a journey up under the chains to my breasts where we brushed united fingers over my nipples. I felt Nick's mouth and stubble against my neck as he began kissing my skin, progressing down to my shoulders as we continued to move to the music. A firm hand found my waist and nudged me to turn around. I found myself willingly hypnotized by the darkness of his eyes before his mouth returned to my neck and quickly traveled upward, his tongue entering me in a way not unlike how he invades me in other places.

To my surprise, Nick gently urged me backward until I was the one now sitting in the chair. It seemed the wine and heat of the moment were contagious, and it was now Nick's turn for some showcase dancing as he started moving to the music and finding his rhythm. His bare chest, the slightly unbuttoned jeans, the way he moved; the combination made it difficult to remain seated, and while keeping his eyes fixated on me, Nick began unzipping his jeans. Taking a step forward, he reached for my hands and placed them at the top of his jeans. I needed no extra invitation, and I quickly pulled the jeans down, leaving Nick standing in only the black boxer-briefs, now filled deliciously.

Of course, I should not have been surprised by Nick's enticing dance; I've danced with him several times, but *this* dance was a bit different. I usually danced *with* him; this time, I had a front-row seat. Nick took another step closer, and I reached up to pull down his briefs, but he quickly stepped back, stopping my move midair. Reaching out for my hand, Nick pulled me back up; however, instead of continuing the dance, he reached down and scooped me up, threw me over his shoulder, and walked inside through the balcony door.

I started laughing and continued laughing until he gave me a swift little smack on the butt, saying, "There will be none of that, little missy!" Nick continued with me into the bedroom, where he gently unpeeled me over his shoulder and laid me down on the bed, telling me to "stay right there, and *don't* move a muscle!" Leaving the room, he soon returned with seven items; a blindfold, a tube of lotion, a rather large-looking vibrator/dildo, and what looked like four leather straps.

Reaching the bed, Nick bent down, mouth near my ear. "My bad, Lacey. I took a spin at the fantasy play spinner earlier today when I was thinking of you." Nick took my ear lobe between his teeth before he continued speaking. "The spinner landed on vibrators and restraints. You game, Lacey?"

His hot breath and the huskiness of his words gave little doubt I would even think of saying, "no thanks." I looked up at him and nodded, which was really all I could do without the threat of drool running from my mouth.

Nick set the items on the bed, picked up the blindfold, and then lifted it over the back of my head. He spent a few seconds adjusting it, and I was soon sent into darkness, although I could still hear him moving around toward the top of the bed.

I jumped as I heard his voice, once again, near my ear. "I'm going to need you to roll over on your belly, baby."

I obliged and rolled over. Nick reached up, took the other pillow on the bed, and placed it underneath my hips, lifting my butt slightly. Making his way around the mattress, Nick secured each wrist to a bedpost, ensuring they were secure enough that I would not be moving around much at all.

The bed shifted with weight as he silently sat on the bed next to me, and I gasped as the squirt of cool lotion hit my back. Warm, strong hands began to rub the silky wetness into my thirsty skin for several seconds before the weight on the bed shifted again. I felt Nick place a leg on either side of me as he straddled my body while continuing to rub the lotion over my body.

His lips brushed against my ear. "Just relax."

Nick's firm hands created a warmth that turned the lotion into melted butter. I heard the vibrator turn on as his voice sounded next to my ear. "You aren't falling asleep, are you?"

I shook my head no, but truth be told, Nick's magical hands had me awfully close to meeting up with Mr. Sandman. Nick touched the tip of the vibrator against my clitoris, and all thoughts of a rendezvous with Mr. Sandman immediately disappeared. *That is one powerful vibrator.* He removed it almost immediately, leaving me wiggling my ass and craving more. Nick was in full-out tease mode, and he was enjoying every second of it.

I felt the shift in his body as he rose, and I heard him moving to the end of the bed, where he removed both of my boots and then proceeded to tie first one ankle and then the other to each of the bottom bedposts. I now laid spread-eagled with my ass in the air, but yet was comfortable enough as Nick had left enough room in the straps to have some room to move around.

I sensed as Nick returned to the bed and the vibrator; however, this time, he began to move it over my clitoris, then back a bit, where he gently pushed it inside of me. With the vibrations filling me internally, I felt him reach for something else, and a moment later, a cold squirt of lotion fell upon my ass. With his one hand continuing to grind the vibrator around inside of me slowly, Nick used his other hand to guide the cream over my body, squirting more as needed. It was difficult to remain still, and my bottom half was soon moving and squirming as I tried to find the perfect position to accomplish my goal of another orgasm, like, *soon!*

Nick urged me to the finish line, and as his finger traced my bottom seam, I found the perfect movement. I came again as Nick circled my asshole with his finger, making the second orgasm more intense. He pulled out the vibrator, and not even giving me a momentary break, replaced it against my clitoris as he entered me. I pressed back against him, and soon we were syncing ourselves in rhythm with his firm hand gripping my waist. It didn't take long at all, and as Nick's grip on my waist tightened, we climaxed as one.

I couldn't move, figuratively, as well as literally; I remained restrained, my energy spent with the last orgasm. Nick didn't move for a few seconds either, taking some deep breaths before removing himself and running into the bathroom to wash off before returning to the bed, where I laid as a willing captive.

He reached down, untied the blindfold, and unhooked all the leather straps, and once freed, I turned over with a smile on my face. Nick joined me on the bed, turning to his side so that we faced each other. "You, my dear, are intoxicating, and you make me feel fantastic."

I scooted closer to him and kissed his lips before jumping out of bed to shower. "You are pretty incredible yourself, Mr. Atwood, although I'm not so sure how you expect me to get up and go to work in the morning. I have a feeling I'm going to be really tired tomorrow!"

Nick laughed. "You and me both, babe."

The warm water felt good and restored some of my exhausted energy. Walking back into the bedroom, I giggled at the sight before me. Nick was already sound asleep, his head back, the pillow covering the top half of his head. I walked to the closet and slid on my robe before I quietly walked from the room, closing the door softly behind me. I commanded the music to be turned off as I walked to the kitchen, and the loft immediately filled with dense, dark silence. Nick had gone out of his way to create such a special evening, and I felt that I needed to do my share and clean up from dinner.

Fifteen minutes later, all dishes were quietly washed, dried, and put away. The problem? I was now wide awake, it was already 11:15 p.m., and I needed to get back into sleepy mode. I made myself a cup of chamomile tea and grabbed my phone before heading outside onto the balcony, snagging a blanket off the couch on the way. I continued through the balcony door, now wrapped cozily in the blanket, and sat down in the previously used exotic dance viewing chair.

Leaning back in the chair, I picked up my phone, scrolling to see the latest friend updates on that famous book of friend's site: new baby photos from new moms, cryptic memes that leave one wondering the story behind them, uplifting-quotes, and an invite to Abbie's holiday party. She had added a personal message to my invite: *You better be coming with that new husband of yours!* That would be fun. It would be our first holiday season together, and I was excited to start celebrating as a couple. Financially, Nick and I were sitting rather well, so plans for the holiday were already in motion. We wanted to host our first annual Atwood Christmas party and had already started the list of friends to invite. My favorite holiday, with my favorite guy; a win-win for me!

I set my phone down on the table so that I could finish the last sips of tea, which had succeeded in making me sleepy again, and I wanted to return to snuggling against my husband. The phone's beep resounded in the silence of the room. I felt the dreaded pit in my stomach before I even picked up the phone.

I still think I should be your lover because I know what you like.

My heart dropped, and I could taste everything I had eaten earlier as it threatened to crawl up my throat. Walking toward the sink, I filled a glass with water and drank it, hoping it would keep everything at peace, which it did, until the wave of panic hit. I turned and looked toward the balcony window.

I knew there were no other lofts that could provide any visual access to this one. My mind started turning, and a mental debate began. What were the odds that someone out on Lake Erie could peek in using a high-powered set of binoculars? *Not likely, and how would this person even know I was here, or where our loft was for that matter?* Was this person watching me? Was I being followed? *It was possible if they were willing to travel each day all over the county of Cuyahoga.* But why? And why me? Which brought me back full circle. Who had any reason to harass, cause me grief, or stalk me, for that matter? *Jack Turner.* Whether he was the one masterminding this ongoing harassment through another person, or he, himself, was the guilty one, Jack Turner was behind all of this.

I sighed and turned off the kitchen light. I felt terrible about keeping, from Nick, the text I received in Charleston, and I didn't want to continue to make matters worse. I decided to tell Nick about the messages after work tomorrow, and in the meantime, I would call Lt. Bob to see what he thought I should do about all of it. As much as Nick was going to want me to put in an immediate notice, I would not let someone scare me enough to have control over my decisions, especially Jack Turner!

I crawled back into bed, snuggled up close to Nick, and slept like a baby for the rest of the night.

When the alarm went off, I immediately set it to sleep two more times before swinging my feet off the bed and motivating my tired body to move. Nick was already in the kitchen and had toast and coffee, as well as a warm cozy hug and kiss on my forehead, waiting for me. He made it hard for me to want to be at work instead of spending time with him; however, Nick was going to be out the door sooner than I was today as he had a breakfast meeting with the gallery owner's downtown to discuss some new projects.

Nick took a shower while I finished my toast and poured myself a second cup of coffee. Fifteen minutes later, he entered the kitchen, looking and smelling delicious as usual. How a guy made jeans look exclusively molded, I would never know, but his buttoned-down black shirt, and those jeans, made me almost think about calling in a sick day and holding him hostage in the bedroom. I walked with him to the door and wrapped my arms around his neck, looking up into his face. His eyes scanned my face before locking with mine. That look! Enough to still cause my knees to feel a bit weakened!

"I love you, Lacey Atwood."

Leaning in, I gave him a little kiss on his lips before replying. "I love you back, Nick Atwood."

CHAPTER 18

It had been hard to leave Nick, but I dreaded more, having "the talk" with him after work, and I was hoping a busy day would keep my mind occupied. One hour later, I pulled into the parking lot across from my agency, this time with a more cautious eye on the individuals waiting at the bus stop and lining the sidewalk in front of the temp agency. *All these people see me, day in and day out, walking across the street, pressing the code to enter my building, and then returning to my car at some point.* I was never one to be paranoid, but now I found myself analyzing the men standing in line, blowing their cigarette smoke out into the air. The familiar scents of tobacco, as well as weed, hit my nose as I walked past. I scanned their faces, smiling and nodding to those saying hello, trying to notice if any of them were looking at me differently. *Get a grip, Lacey.* I entered the code and walked inside through the door.

Making the way to my desk, I looked over the partition tops, no Abbie yet. I wanted to process the whole text message incident with her before I made the call to Lt. Bob Chandler, but it looked like that wasn't going to happen. I had nearly two hours before I had to see my first client, and I wasn't going to allow myself any excuse-making. Grabbing my phone and the little, yellow, folded piece of paper with Bob's number on it, I headed outside into the back stairwell, removed from prying eyes or gossip-seeking ears. Part of me was hoping he wouldn't answer so that I would be able to delay the conversation a little longer. No such luck.

Bob answered on the second ring. "Lacey, nice to hear from you! Or should I say, Mrs. Atwood, nice to hear from you? I hear that congratulations are in order."

I laughed. "Boy, news travels fast around these parts, Lt. Chandler. Where did you hear this?"

The laughter returned through the phone. "Lacey, it's Bob to you, and most of Cleveland probably knew about the marriage before the minister said, "You may kiss the bride.""

I sighed. "That just goes to show you how antisocial I am. I hadn't a clue so many knew."

Bob chuckled before asking, "So to what do I owe the great pleasure of a phone call from you this morning?" He continued before I answered. "Please tell me our stalker isn't back in business."

I sighed again. "Unfortunately, yes, and I haven't told Nick about it yet. I intend to do that tonight." I continued, "I received one while we were in South Carolina, and last night, there was another one — same kind of deal, saying the same kind of things."

It was Bob's turn to sigh. "Not what I wanted to hear, Lacey. Do you have any spare time today to come down to the station so that I can look at the messages, and we can talk about options?"

I looked down at my planner and did some mental switching of appointments to free up some time around noon, which Bob said worked perfectly. Hanging up the phone, I leaned back in my chair. This day was going to be a long one, and for the first time since Nick entered my life, I found myself nervous about having a conversation with him.

I met with two new families, both new referrals and domestic violence cases, before I pulled into the police precinct parking lot. *I'm getting too old for this kind of drama!* The thought of coming to work for the last time was becoming something I relished, and I was becoming more and more excited about the prospect of new adventures. But first things first.

Pushing through the front door, I walked to the front desk, and after asking for Lt. Chandler, I turned and sat down on the wooden bench to wait. Leaning back against the seat, I rested my head against the wall and closed my eyes while breathing and exhaling several times deeply. I just wished the whole thing would disappear! Unfortunately, wishing doesn't work, hence the need for police officers like Bob, who was now shaking me out of my thoughts with his Boston accent.

"Lacey, come on back."

I mentally shook my thoughts away, rose from the bench, and followed Bob into the back room over to his desk, where I sat down across from him. I returned his smile with one of my own, albeit a weak one, and from nowhere, I felt an old familiar feeling. Tears would arrive soon. *Dammit!*

Bob looked at me as he saw the change in expression.

"You doing okay, Lacey?" Those are wrong words to say to a woman with tears on the verge of spilling over eyelids, but he didn't know that. I shook my head "no" and attempted one more smile, failing miserably, and allowed the tears to flow over and down my face slowly. Bob reached back to the desk behind him and grabbed a box of tissues, setting it in front of me.

"I'm sorry, Lacey. I know this isn't easy."

I nodded my head and lifted my finger in a "give-me-one-minute" gesture, took a deep breath, and regained my composure. Grabbing another tissue, I wiped my cheeks and dabbed under my eyes. I tried again and was somewhat successful in mustering up a feeble smile, but at least it was a smile.

We spent the next hour going back and forth between waiting while Bob made some phone calls to his "connections" in the investigative unit, writing out a police report, and discussing my options. I needed to change my phone number yet again, which was a pain in the ass, considering all the people I would have to contact with the updated information. Unfortunately, it was nearly impossible with modern technology to make myself invisible to the outside world, especially those with access to a computer and any kind of internet-savvy.

I hoped that Jack Turner, or whoever this guy/girl/person/creep was, would get tired of harassing me. I knew Nick would want me to quit immediately, but I just needed him to support my decision to wait a couple more months so I could finish on my terms, and maybe if I let him equip me with some mace and some hidden weapons, legal, of course, it would ease his mind a little. Bob promised to have some extra eyes out for me, and if I let him know in advance of the scheduled visits with Jennifer, he promised some extra patrols of the area when I was there.

Bob walked me out to my car and, once again, made me promise to call him if I were to receive any other text messages. I gave him my solemn word I would do so, and before getting into my car, we agreed to another double-date over the holidays. Pulling from the parking lot, I took another deep breath as I drove to the next stop, a team meeting at a partnership agency. Perhaps, the team meeting would last longer than usual, as I was not looking forward to this evening's conversation at all. Nick was *not* going to see it my way.

The rest of the day flew by; I knew it would. Any other day, time would have dragged, mocking me to the end. But, no, not this day! Before I knew it, I was getting off the elevator and walking down the hallway to our loft. Music streamed from behind the door, and as I opened it, a delicious aroma of something Italian-smelling wafted my way; behind the delightful aroma, a handsome husband peeked his head around the corner of the kitchen wall.

"Hi, beautiful."

Following the aroma into the kitchen, I set my purse and coat on one of the island stools and walked toward Nick. Upon reaching him, I wrapped my arms around him as he stood, stirring a big pot of spaghetti sauce, and peeked over his shoulders at the bubbling redness.

"Hi, handsome guy of mine. This smells delicious."

Nick set the spoon on the spoon rest and turned to face me, wrapping his arms around my waist. I could tell that he was reading my face. *Maintain normalcy, Lacey, normalcy.* His expression let me know I had failed at the poker face for which I was striving.

A look of concern replaced the smile that had, a moment before, been beaming from his face. "Lacey, what's wrong?"

Shit, Shit, Shit. The tears started immediately, and now Nick was really concerned.

"Lacey, what's going on? Are you okay?"

I swallowed and took a breath. "Nick, I need to tell you something."

The concern level skyrocketed; it showed all over his face. Nobody wants to hear those words, and Nick — Supermanish though he may be in my eyes — was no different. He turned halfway around, turned the stove knob on low, and, grabbing me by my hand, led me over to the couch. After sitting, I turned to face him and silently commanded the tears to stop as Nick reached over and picked up one of my hands, lacing his fingers through mine. He looked at me with a half-smile.

"I don't know what's wrong, Lacey, but unless it's you saying you changed your mind about wanting to be with me for the rest of your life or that you just found out you're dying, we can handle whatever has you so upset."

A short laugh escaped my mouth. "Okay, I'm going to hold you to that."

I breathed in deeply before I started spilling my guts, and for the next ten or fifteen minutes, I didn't stop talking. I told Nick about the text message I received in Charleston and the one from the previous night. I told him about today's visit with his buddy, Lt. Bob Chandler, my intent to change my number again, and Bob's reassurance that he would be watching over me if I needed him. I ended with a request, a request for his patience and understanding in my wanting to finish the next two and a half months. I promised him that, afterward, I would turn in my notice.

Nick hadn't let go of my hand until this moment, and as I scanned his face, I didn't see any hint of anger or disappointment. Releasing his hold, Nick brought both hands up to my face and leaned in, bringing his face closer to mine. He took a deep breath, and I could feel the lump starting in my throat as he began to speak.

"Lacey Atwood, I need to say a few things. First, you are a woman I respect and admire, and I would *never* second-guess any decision you have made or will ever make, and, no, I am not just saying that because you're my wife. You know how I feel about your job, but it's *your* job, and I respect that. Second, I never want you to feel you can't come to me with anything, and I do mean *anything*. I've got you, babe. We're in this together."

Tears began to trickle slowly down my cheeks, and with his thumbs, Nick met each tear and gently erased it. He continued, "Third, we're going to the store tomorrow and picking you up some mace, some pepper spray, some ninja knives, and some semi-automatic weapons."

I giggled. Nick reached over and pulled my face closer to his. "Okay, I'm kidding about the ninja knives and the semi-automatic weapons." He leaned forward and kissed my forehead. His eyes glistened a little bit. "Just promise me, Lacey, you're letting them know you're leaving in three months, tops."

I promised him exactly that. I didn't know what I would do after quitting my job, but I did know I needed something different. It was time for me to follow my passions, my heart, and my dreams. It was time.

CHAPTER 19

Winter hit Cleveland like the Tasmanian Devil on high octane fuel. The powers that be, well, at least the ones on the news, predicted a harsh winter, and they were not kidding. Even before Thanksgiving's arrival, temperatures hovered in the lower thirties, and a blanket of white covered the ground. Never a northeast girl at heart, especially during the winter months, the freezing temperatures had me questioning the decision to remain on the job. However, the plummeting temperatures remained outside; the temperature *inside* the loft remained toasty and warm, and not from the thermostat setting. With some red-hot chemistry and a fantasy play wheel, many a chilly evening provided the perfect excuse to remain indoors for some additional idea testing and some indoor sports.

The holidays descended as quickly as the cold weather had. I had introduced Nick to my mother prior to our Charleston vacation, and she was as warm and welcoming to him as I knew she would be. But then again, how could anybody be any other way in Nick's presence? She had been the first person I had telephoned after Nick proposed and was the first and only person I called after our wedding, so I was thrilled when Nick suggested we spend our first Thanksgiving together with my mom and her new husband.

It was a beautiful visit, and the four of us spent hours around the table, laughing and sharing stories, catching up with our lives, and basking in the sense of authentic Thanksgiving family togetherness. My mother and I maintained solely superficial bonding in the past; however, this Thanksgiving was different, and I experienced a closeness I hadn't felt in a long time. At one point during the evening, she had pulled me to the side, and with emotion-filled eyes, told me that she "was thrilled to see me so happy," and those words alone surpassed all expectations I had for the evening.

Driving back home that evening, Nick and I tuned into some Christmas music, and while holding hands, we serenaded each other with everything from Durante's "Frosty the Snowman" to Bing's "White Christmas." I was content. I was at peace. And I was engulfed in an encompassing love, both inside and out. I couldn't picture myself any happier than I was at that moment, and I felt life was finally on track, that I could finally relax into the rolling waves of life, knowing my partner would never allow me to fall off the ship that together we sailed.

Oh, Lacey. Always the optimist.

Alas, hindsight is something else, and I had no idea what the future held for me or us. At that moment, in the car with Christmas carols serenading the falling, fat snowflakes, nothing else mattered, as full-blown holiday "blissment" blanketed my little universe. I was ready for more magic, and as usual, Nick was more than prepared to make it happen for me.

One relaxing weekend morning with only fifteen days left until Christmas Eve, Nick looked at me across the kitchen island with a smile and little boy giddiness.

"Babe! Do you realize I didn't even know you this time last year?"

He had walked around the island and gently pulled me off my stool, pulling me close. "Tell me what you want for Christmas, Lacey, besides a live tree. I've already heard, over and over, how much you hate artificial trees." I laughed, and he continued. "Seriously, any specific clues, ideas, hints of what you want?" I opened my mouth to speak, but he cut me off. "You can't say "nothing," you can't say, "whatever you get me will be good; I need ideas, woman!"

I laughed and shook my head. "Boy, you know me too well." I looked at him, and as seriously as I could say it, I said, "Socks. Socks and a gift card for a spa day."

Nick looked at me and began laughing. "Socks? Did you just say socks?"

I joined him in laughter, nodding my head. "Yes, I said socks." Through my laughter, which by now had turned into that ridiculously uncontrollable "laugh until you cry" laughter, I nodded my head again and explained. "I like socks, and my feet are always cold."

Now Nick was laughing just as hard as I was, tears overflowing from his eyes, and, honestly, I really had no idea why it was all so amusing. And, while I had never heard of humor being an aphrodisiac, it played the role at that moment. Nick bent down, picked me up, and threw me over his shoulder, the laughter following us into the bedroom.

"I will give you socks *and* a spa day, woman."

True to his word, I walked into the condo from work the next week, and there, standing in front of the balcony windows, was a giant tree, a *live* Christmas tree! I didn't even want to know how he managed it, as the lease clearly stated the forbiddance of live trees, but there it stood, full of colored lights and smelling deliciously like Christmastime. Nick had walked over to where I stood. "We're going to go out and buy some ornaments together, but I wanted to get the hard work out of the way, so all you needed to do was just enjoy it."

We spent that evening with the lights off, Christmas lighted tree twinkling with colors, sharing some wine, and listening to Christmas music. I was brought to tears by the perfection of the moment and remained compliant with maintaining joy and peace as the carols ordered me to do. I needed no wrapped gifts, for I had all I needed, but there was a Christmas party to plan, presents to purchase, and a tree to decorate, all within the next couple weeks. For that moment in time, though, I was soaking in the real feeling of Christmas, the meaning and the importance, the blessings that surpassed wrapped presents and glittery trees.

And I had been right. The next few weeks were full of work, completing time-sensitive paperwork, gift-buying for Nick and my friends, and planning our First Annual Christmas party, all while trying to keep my sanity. I found the perfect watch for Nick and added a few more things: some shirts I saw him mentally drooling over, a set of shot glasses I knew he would like, and as a special surprise, a boudoir shoot portfolio. Yes, I know that seemed like it would be redundant, but I knew Nick would enjoy seeing me in little

Santa and elf costumes, red and green stockings, and with candy canes strategically placed across my body.

We had scheduled our Christmas party for the weekend before Christmas week, so the odds of having everyone attend would be much greater. And it worked! Thirty to fifty of the friends we held closest to our hearts RSVP'd they would be showing up during the open hours we had posted. I was excited to see them all; Nicholas, his wife, Mark Santauri, who would be bringing a "friend," Bob Chandler and his girlfriend, Abbie, her husband, and some other coworkers and their spouses or significant others. Nick's gallery buddies even RSVP'd in the affirmative. Speaking of the gallery, Nick also invited some of the individuals he had befriended during the Cleveland project. Hand-delivered invites went to ten of the attendees who were now employed, learning a new trade, or genuinely working to improve their situation.

I had finished up the last day of work, eight days before Christmas, and now eighteen work-free days delightfully stretched ahead. Jennifer had been my last scheduled client before the holiday break, and she had surprised me with a gifted painting, a symbolic representation of herself, a before and after. It was a tree with one half, dead and withered, barren, leaves and raindrops, falling. She had written words in each of these leaves; DESPAIR, HOPELESS, PAIN, SORROW, HATRED ... it went on. The other side of the tree, however, was full of life. Green leaves filled the treetop. The sun was shining; flowers were blooming with roots of HOPE, LOVE, POWER, EMPOWERMENT, THANKFULNESS, and STRENGTH.

It was beautiful, and as much as social workers are reprimanded and reminded not to become attached to clients, keeping that separation, that distance — not so easy. Tears crept down Jennifer's cheeks as I hugged her and told her how proud I was. Jack Turner had seemingly disappeared, and coincidently, all anonymous texts to me had ceased as well. A confident smile appeared on her face as she informed me she had filed divorce papers, and the court review hearing had gone well. It seemed the Christmas season was gifting everyone miraculous gifts this year!

Days passed quickly, and while I wanted to treasure each moment of our first Christmas together, the quickened pace of party preparation only seemed to shift my focus from the desired relaxation and peace. Two days before the party, Mark flew in, and Nick picked him up from the airport, bringing him back to our place for some shared wine before his new "girl of the moment" picked him up. It was great to see him again, and we spent several hours in front of the tree catching up on all the latest news from Charleston.

One bit of news was disheartening and came as a shock for both Nick and me. Joe Morgan had suffered a mild stroke the week after we returned home, and although it seemed that there was no significant damage, the tone in Katt Morgan's voice while talking to Mark seemed to have concerned him.

We had just finished talking about the Morgan's when a knock at the door interrupted any further conversation. Nick headed toward the door, at which time Mark turned his attention to me. "You look utterly stunning as usual, Lacey. Married life really agrees with you."

I would have felt more comfortable had he said that in Nick's presence; however, I reminded myself that this was Mark, and words Mark wants to speak, he speaks, especially to those of the female population. I smiled and nodded. "Thanks, Mark, and I have to agree. I love being married to Nick and have never been happier."

I raised my glass of wine in a toast, as from behind Mark, I could see Nick walking toward us with Mark's latest piece of eye candy in tow. She was gorgeous but, then again, so are all of Mark's women. It was just too bad the brains didn't always match up with the looks, yet I still held out hope that he would learn one day.

I nodded to Mark as he lifted his glass, and with a smile spreading over my face, I said, just loud enough, "To marriage!"

Trying hard to maintain composure as the blond beauty of a girlfriend almost squealed with delight as she entered the room, "Ohhh, I love marriage!" Mark grinned and nodded his head to me in defeat as he recognized my perfectly timed toast.

Nick came around the couch and settled next to me. "Who's getting married?"

I looked at him, giggled, and shook my head as Miss Blonde settled in next to Mark and planted a big kiss on his lips, wrapping her hands around his arm. Mark's face turned a shade of deep crimson, and I can honestly say it was the first time I witnessed him taken to that level of embarrassment. "Nick, Lacey, meet Becky."

Nick stood back up, apologizing, "I'm so sorry, Becky. Would you like a glass of wine?"

Receiving an affirmative answer, Nick disappeared back into the kitchen to pour the desired wine, as Becky began her chatter, and with each of her spoken words, I watched Mark visibly shrink into the couch. "So, getting back to the marriage topic. I actually have a one-year plan, and since Mark and I have been video-chatting for a few months now, I'm hoping, just maybe, there will be a special, small, wrapped package under the tree for Christmas."

I couldn't help it, and I began giggling as Mark almost spit out the sip of wine he had just consumed. He shot me a look of invisible daggers that I swear I could practically feel. I smiled at Becky as Nick walked back into the room. "Becky, Mark and I were just talking about how marriage just suits some people, others, maybe not so much."

Nick looked at me and smiled as I continued to giggle. "What am I missing?"

I shook my head, trying to keep the giggles from erupting into full-blown laughing, and looked over at Mark. If anyone could turn this around, Mr. "Melt them with my charm" could do it.

Looking at me, Mark shook his head and then looked back over at Becky with a smile creeping onto his face; he had regained his composure, and his level of cool was back in check. Attempting to avert a full-out disaster, Mark raised his glass in another toast, with Nick and me following suit. "To Nick and Lacey, who have obviously set the bar high on what a marriage should look like, and one which will be very difficult for others to attain." Mark winked over at me and grinned before taking a sip of wine. I admit, for being placed on the hot seat, it was a formidable recovery.

They stayed another hour, with Becky gifting us all the details of her exciting career as a blossoming "model" and aspiring "dancer." I provided her a tour of the loft after she kept remarking how beautiful it was, and as we reentered the big room, Mark was rising from the couch. "We need to get going. We still have some stops to make tonight, and I need to finish up some last-minute Christmas shopping tomorrow."

Walking them to the door, we helped them with their coats, following with cross-over hugs between the four of us. Mark smiled at me. "As usual, Lacey, always a fun time with you two."

I giggled. "Likewise, Mark."

Nick closed the door behind them and turned to me. "What in the world are you so giggly about tonight?"

I updated him on the missed exchange of conversation, and he nodded and chuckled in agreement. "That's Mark for you, always after the looks before anything else. But, I must hand it to you, wife of mine, that was well-played; very well-played indeed."

Nick reached for my hand and led me back toward the couch, where he pulled me down on top of him with my back against his. His face burrowed into the back of my head. "I'm one of the lucky ones, you know?"

I turned my head slightly, giving him a sideways glance. "How so?"

Nick wrapped his arms around my waist, and his voice sounded near my ear, sending chills up my arms as he spoke. "Because I found the one with the brains, the beauty, the sexiness, and the compassion. I found the whole package."

I reached down and unwrapped his arms from around my body and stood up, looking down at him. He looked up at me, puzzled as I stretched my hands out for his, a big smile spreading over my face. "Come on, Mr. Atwood, it's time you unwrapped your total package."

Nick smiled back and sprung off the couch. Like the perfect guy he is, he wrapped me up in his arms, and capturing my eyes with his, he spoke. "First a dance; then the bedroom." And, to the faint strands of a Christmas carol playing in the background and the twinkling, colored lights providing just enough light, Nick slow-danced me before taking me by my hand and leading me to the bedroom. Another perfect evening in the books for the Atwood Coleman couple.

CHAPTER 20

We were ready! The day of the party arrived with a visual serenade of soft, fat snowflakes filling up our balcony deck. The colored lights were shining, we had Christmas music playing, and the food we ordered teased us from the kitchen island and counter. On two end tables, baskets of small, festively wrapped, house party gifts waited to be gifted. Nick had been responsible for the "guy" gifts, and I was impressed with the shot glass and cigar combination he chose. For the ladies, I decided on peppermint lotion and mittens.

Nick and I stood back and scanned the set-up before everyone was due to arrive. Everything looked perfect, and I was beyond excited for the guests to arrive. Leaning in next to me, Nick pointed toward the tree. "Lacey, what is that?"

I followed his finger's directive but saw nothing out of the ordinary. "What in the world are you talking about? I see the lights and ornaments."

Nick extended his finger a bit more as if that would help me see what I was supposed to see. "Baby, right there, next to the snowman."

Looking closer, I spotted what looked like a small, wrapped box.

I turned around to look at him. "Nick, what is that?"

He shrugged and pointed back at the tree. "Not sure, but maybe you should go check."

I walked over to the tree, and sure enough, a silver, paper-wrapped little box with a deep blue bow sat atop the branch, right next to the snowman. I reached up and lifted the box. "What is this, Nick? It isn't even Christmas yet."

Having followed me to the tree, Nick now stood next to me as I looked at him with curious eyes. "Lacey, every day is like Christmas with you. Just open the present."

I untied the bow and unwrapped the box, handing the bow and paper to Nick. Lifting off the box top, I saw a smaller, burgundy-colored, jewelry box which I lifted out. I turned around and looked up at him again. "What have you done, babe?"

Again, he just shrugged his shoulders and continued to smile his shit-eating grin as I lifted open the hinged box. Inside were a pair of beautiful diamond earrings. From a small diamond heart at the top of the earring, three long strands of mini diamonds hung; these earrings were definitely expensive, and they were breathtaking!!

I smiled at Nick and reached up, placing my hands at the back of his head, pulling his face toward mine. "These are beautiful, Nick! Thank you so much!"

I plastered his lips with a delicious kiss, which I hoped showed, even just a little bit, the gratitude and pleasure I was feeling. I think it did because I felt him harden against me as we continued to kiss. There was no time for that, though. My eyes caught the clock; only one hour from guests pouring in, so we both made our way to the bedrooms to change. Nick donned a button-down black shirt with his jeans, while I topped my jeans with a silky, cream-colored, button-down blouse. The new earrings complemented the outfit perfectly.

The doorbell rang just as we exited the bedroom, and from that moment, it didn't stop until way into the wee hours of the next morning. Food, drinks, laughter, good conversation, and relaxing Christmas music filled the hours, with the evening passing as perfectly as I had hoped. Mark showed up sans Becky. I didn't ask any questions but suffice it to say, there was no mourning going on, and he was his normal charming self, even hitting on two of my single coworkers. Cleveland's finest, Lt. Bob Chandler, showed up with a new girlfriend, and he pulled me aside at one point during the evening to ask if I had received any further text messages. He was just as relieved as I was when I reported that I hadn't. My favorite Italian and his wife arrived with a bottle of wine and thick Italian laughter that filled the air. I introduced "my" Nick to Abbie and her boyfriend, and her cheeks reddened slightly when Nick said he had heard so much about her.

The stars of the evening arrived together in a group. The men and women Nick and his team befriended on the Cleveland streets walked in with smiles on their faces. They entered the party full of self-confidence, with new stories, and with an external joy and happiness that would have been enough of a Christmas present for both Nick and me. This was my family. This was *our* family. These were the people who had cheered us on, had supported our crazy decisions, and loved us unconditionally. Well, to be quite honest, they had *no* clue as to what some of those crazy decisions were, but I was positive their love would still be unwavering. There were several times over the evening that Nick and I, at opposite ends of the room, caught each other's glances, and without speaking a word, exchanged the deepest of conversation.

It was nearing 2 a.m. before the last of the guests, Mark and the gallery guys, made their way to the door, slightly intoxicated, and that's putting it mildly. Nick and I made sure Uber was available to provide safe rides home for anyone who needed it, and the five of them took us up on the offer. Closing the door for the last time, Nick and I both collapsed on the couch and decided all clean-up would take place the next day, many hours from that moment. With every good intention to make our way into the bedroom, we both fell fast asleep lying on the couch in the middle of a conversation about the party's success. The first hosted holiday party was under our belts and declared a raving victory!

The sunlight streaming through the window awakened me, and I picked up the phone from the nearby table, 8:17 a.m. Nick was still sleeping and didn't even move when I slipped out from underneath his arm. I headed toward the bathroom en-suite to shower and change before cleaning up, and he was still snoring when I walked back into the big room thirty minutes later. I tried to be as quiet as possible and not wake him; however, loading the dishes in the dishwasher can be done only so quietly. After making his way into the bedroom and then back out twenty minutes later, a freshly showered Nick helped with the very last bit of cleaning.

The rest of the day, we were just all-out lazy, and we laid in front of the TV watching a Christmas movie marathon. The remainder of the week was going to be full of last-minute shopping, some stop-ins at several Christmas parties, and an appearance at an invitation-only Christmas Ball hosted by some of the older-monied Cleveland elite. We needed this day of chill. The calm before the holiday storm!

I had been right, again, and just as I had thought it would, the week flew past. Parties, shopping, the Holiday Ball, and the get-togethers with friends filled our days and evenings. Christmas Eve appeared at our door before we even realized it was there. Nick and I promised each other that Christmas Eve and morning were ours only; it was our first one, and we wanted to make it our own.

That morning, I awakened to Nick, jostling me awake like a little boy realizing Santa had visited. He was so sweet, and all over again, I fell in love with his little boy eagerness. He had made hot chocolate and pancakes, but he would not let me eat until I made my way into the big room, and I laughed as I followed him, still sleepy-eyed, into the room. The space under the tree had been slowly filling up with presents over the past few days, but it was blatantly apparent that several more gifts had joined the others. Someone wasn't playing fair, but I wasn't going to complain about too many Christmas presents.

Nick had spent way too much money on me like I knew he would, and I felt somewhat guilty opening gift after gift: sweaters, a new purse, new boots, a new winter jacket, scarfs, books on my "to-read" list, gift cards for my favorite salon, and *socks*! Tons of socks! Thirty pairs of soft fuzzy socks, ankle socks for working out, and of course, knee socks, which I knew were just as much for Nick's delight. There were also a couple of new outfits from Leather and Lace.

Nick loved the shot glasses, the shirts, and the other small items I bought for him, and I saved the boudoir shot portfolio for the last present. I watched his expressions change from curiosity to enjoyment as he unwrapped and then opened the book to the first photo of me, dressed in a Santa outfit, stockings, garter, and push-up bra underneath an opened button-down red jacket. Instead of Santa pants, I wore a red mini skirt.

Nick looked at me. "Wow!"

That was all he could say. Each page he flipped, he looked at me and either sighed, said "*Wow*" again, or narrowed his eyes toward me. I could tell he was getting aroused by the flushing of his cheeks and the darkening of his eyes. Turning the last page, Nick set the book down on the table and pushed me gently back on the couch, climbing on top of me. He reached down and scooted his pajama bottoms off, and I quickly followed suit, pulling my silk pajama bottoms down past my ankles and then pushing them off the couch. He entered me, at once, intensely, and urgently, and we both climaxed immediately. Suffice to say, I would be scheduling another boudoir shoot shortly if it would result in more of what just happened.

Nick laid on top of me for a minute, breathing heavily, before opening his eyes. "Now *that* was a Christmas present that's unbeatable. When did you get that done without me knowing?"

I smiled up at his face. I confess. I faked a sick day a couple of weeks ago."

Nick kissed me. "That's my sneaky little woman, full of surprises."

And with that, the first Christmas Day of the new Atwood-Coleman union commenced. It ended twelve hours later as we crashed into bed, full of Christmas cookies and food. We had made several stops later in the afternoon to drop off some presents to friends, and at each visit, food was offered and, yes, willingly eaten. Gym days were a-coming.

Nick and I decided, last minute, to attend a New Year's Eve party at the newest dance club in downtown Cleveland. Tickets were $100 each, so although the place was crowded, it wasn't impossible to move. Adding to the fun, we even bumped into some of Nick's friends and spouses as we danced our way toward the countdown, and as the golden hour of midnight struck, with glitter showering us from above, Nick and I shared our first kiss as a married couple in the New Year.

We eventually Ubered our way home too many hours later, and as I laid in bed, nestled up to my husband, warm, happy, and cozy, I fell asleep, replaying all that the past year had presented to me. A lot had happened during this year: meeting Nick, the indescribable breathtaking speed our relationship progressed, his proposal, Katt Morgan's offer of a lifetime, our vacation down south, seeing *my* photos all lit up in LED on the walls of the Fantasy Play Hotel™, our wedding, and now our first holidays together. If the past months were indicative of the future, I had no complaints, and my only New Year resolution for the upcoming year was to keep Nick on his toes, loving on him as much as I could.

New Year, here we come!

CHAPTER 21

For all the excitement the holidays held for me, January always hit like a ton of bricks. No more vacation time for a while, the snow continuing to pile up, the temperatures continuing to plummet, families feeling cooped up and dealing with their after-holiday let down. Conflicts grew, tempers flared, and patience wore thin.

The first few days back to work consisted of catch-up phone calls, and it appeared that most families continued snail-progress following my return from the holidays, except for Jennifer Turner and her children, whose progress had sped-up. The holidays seemed to have strengthened a bond with her extended family as well, and she finally felt the needed emotional support from her parents, both sisters, and even an estranged aunt. The support had worked magic, and Jennifer had stepped forward to lead a women's self-empowerment group. A call to the Children's Service worker verified that the children were three weeks away from a full-time return, and both were thriving in school.

Jack Turner, Mr. POS himself, was supposedly still living with a couple of his friends on Cleveland's other side. My heart momentarily dropped during the phone call when Jennifer reported he had contacted her a couple times, begging for another chance, and letting her know he would stay sober. I had my doubts, and thankfully, she did as well. My only hope was that he was now a distant nightmare from the past. I knew he was behind all the anonymous creepy text messages. I just had no proof, and I hadn't received any since the last one I reported to Lt. Chandler. While at our holiday party, Bob reminded me to let him know if I needed any patrols during my visits.

However, since the creepy texts had ceased, and Jennifer was still at her sister's home, I felt rather confident there would be no need for that.

Two weeks had passed since the catch-up client phone calls, and as I turned the key in the ignition, shutting off the car, I briefly reconsidered that conversation as I scanned the neighborhood for any trace of Jack Turner. I momentarily considered calling for a drive-by patrol, but stubbornness prevailed, and I quickly departed my car and headed up the sidewalk before I could change my mind.

Before my lifted fist even made contact, Jennifer opened the door, greeting me with a beaming smile and a face appearing ten years younger. I couldn't recall ever seeing her so relaxed and healthy. The sounds of two, just as happy, children appeared behind her, and I immediately remembered it was a day off for them. Jennifer's sister, Karen, waved from the kitchen as the children, both holding a hand of mine, led me to the playroom to show what Santa had delivered. It wasn't until fifteen minutes later that I finally joined Jennifer and her sister at the dining room table for a meeting that I was somewhat dreading.

I knew what Jennifer's reaction would be, and I understood it completely. There is a safety net feeling when a caring social worker meets with a family, week after week, for a year. The dark hidden secrets, insecurities, and vulnerabilities seep out of the woodwork cracks. If a family feels a genuine commitment, trust develops. Having to walk away from a family, regardless of everyone knowing the certainty of that moment, is not an easy farewell for the worker and each family member involved.

I spent the first fifteen minutes talking about the holidays and catching up on Jennifer's involvement in her church and the support group. The divorce paperwork, now filed, seemed to have provided Jennifer with some added confidence. According to Karen — and verified by Jennifer's crimson cheeks — Jennifer had been talking to a "very nice" gentleman she had met at church. Jennifer shook her head, stating, "He's just a really good friend." But, again, the reddened cheeks made me believe it was more than that. The divorce was in process, and everyone seemed to be heading in a healthy direction, so I was happy for her.

I looked across the table and met Jennifer's eyes, and it was apparent that she recognized where I was heading with the conversation. I looked down at the plan of care I had on the table in front of me. I could feel the lump enlarging in my throat. *Don't cry, Lacey.* I continued. "Jennifer, you've met all the goals we developed way back a year ago." I looked up to see eyes welling up with tears and reached over, gently placing my hand over hers. "Jennifer, you are *so* ready for this."

Jennifer shook her head. "I don't know if I'm really ready to graduate from the program."

I spent the next thirty minutes reassuring, convincing, empowering, re-assuring some more, validating concerns, and reviewing all the natural supports the family now had. By the end of the thirty minutes, we were all in agreement, some unwillingly, that graduation for Jennifer and the children would happen the first week of March. Nick would not be thrilled as it put my departure date at three months, versus the two I had hoped for, but it was close enough. I would put in my four weeks' notice mid-February, four weeks away, so at least he would know I was serious. It would also allow me to transfer all my other clients and allow my agency some time to hire somebody new. I reassured Jennifer that the next eight weeks would involve preparing her for the transition.

The walk to the front door was a somber one, and I could tell Jennifer was struggling with the upcoming departure of our weekly visits. I turned to face her before opening the door. "Jennifer, here's the deal. There are a lot of clients that I work with that will never attain the degree of change you have. I wouldn't say this if I didn't mean it. You have a beautiful life ahead of you, as long as you believe in the power you own. You got this. I believe in you; now you have to believe in yourself."

Jennifer's eyes threatened to overflow again; however, this time, a smile graced her face, and after reminding her of the next scheduled appointment, I closed the door behind me.

The temperature had dropped over the last hour, or at least it *felt* like it had. My phone chimed, but with my thick mittens on, I would have to wait until I was in my car before I could read the newest loving message from

Nick. The chills Nick provided me with, I could handle, this twenty-degree stuff — not so much. Turning my key in the ignition, I flipped the heater switch to high and pulled off my mittens, spending the next two minutes rubbing my hands in front of the warm air before reaching into my purse for my phone. The blinking blue light immediately resulted in a quickly spreading smile in anticipation of Nick's words, or, better yet, a teasing photo.

I am sad that you won't be my girlfriend. Why is that, Lacey?

A chill traveled down my spine from the base of my neck to the bottom of my back. I felt sick. I looked around, yet nothing seemed out of place, and I didn't see any cars with stalking men. The warmed air, now filling the vehicle, failed to warm me as an icy chill seemed unable to leave my bones. *This* chill wasn't from the descending temperatures. *This* chill was from a place deep within my gut. *This* chill sent the butterflies, having taken flight moments ago, scurrying to shelter. *This* message truly scared me. How odd I hadn't been over to see Jennifer since my vacation, and *now* while here, I receive one. It knew it was Jack Turner, and I needed to see Lt. Bob Chandler.

Sitting across from Bob thirty minutes later, a warm cup of coffee cradled between my hands, I watched as he looked over the text message. He called at least three different phone numbers, telling them to "Get back to me as soon as possible. I need to figure this out!" Of course, as was the pattern, no sooner had the message been sent to me, the number it was coming from was no longer in service, was no longer linked to any specific name or location. None of this made any sense. Nobody had access to the new number after I changed it, and I was confused about how Jack Turner would have been able to get it. Bob suggested we take a different approach. After speaking to both my phone provider and the phone manufacturer, sternly telling them this was a police matter, we had a tracer and locator reestablished on my phone.

If I hadn't been creeped out enough already, the use of the word "girlfriend" in the message heightened everyone's attention, including my own. I did stay true to my promise and called Nick to let him know what was going on, and while he did listen and express his concerns, he did not pressure me to quit immediately. With the assurance and the added protection of the phone tracer, I left the police precinct with renewed confidence that this would soon be over. At least I hoped so.

CHAPTER 22

The rest of January passed uneventfully. Nick and I fell into the blissful routine of a married couple eternally in the honeymoon stage of their relationship. We used Fantasy Play Wheel often and had even dared to venture into the latter section of *Fantasy Play 101*, with one evening devoted solely to the Dominant/submissive list of ideas. I must say, I enjoyed Nick taking full control, verbally *and* physically, always respectfully, and at no time did I ever feel demeaned or taken advantage of. I'm sure that both Katt and Kitty would be thrilled to hear that we had daringly tipped our toes in the section of sizzle.

I continued to work bi-weekly with Jennifer, developing some new goals for her to strive for after I stepped out of the picture. She had made up her mind to register for some summer classes at the community college and applied to a salesclerk position at the college bookstore. Jennifer was like a flower bud, blooming beautifully in her new environment, and that just made it easier for me to walk away in a few weeks.

Financially, Nick and I were doing fantastic. He was currently working on the new project with his old partners and had started final negotiations with the gallery owner down in Charleston. Additionally, an editor had contacted Nick about creating a coffee-table book of his photographs, and, *no,* not my photos. I still wasn't sure what direction I wanted to pursue as far as a career move. Still, a coffee-table book model was not it, and Nick assured me I had plenty of time to figure it all out due to the healthy compensation we received for our visual contribution to the hotel's lure.

Speaking of the hotel and the Morgans, Joe had suffered some additional medical complications in mid-January, resulting in the need for a heart catheterization; however, the stubborn guy that he is, it didn't stop him from continuing to manage the hotel. From what the Morgans had said during the three-way conference call with Nick and me, Joe was one of *those* patients who kept the nursing staff on their toes, and I didn't doubt that one bit. He sounded good on the phone, and before we ended the call, they made us promise a return visit in late spring. Adding that we would have full access to any of the hotel rooms for our stay, they didn't need to twist our arms further.

February hit with a second whammy of snow. Although I was sick of the snow and cold, February offered Valentine's Day as a perk, and it was now only twenty-four hours away. Luckily, it landed on a Saturday this year, and I stopped at the mall earlier in the week to pick up something extra red and lacy with which to surprise Nick. We had dinner reservations at Nicholas's restaurant, and although Nicholas had told us numerous times, we *always* had a table waiting, we didn't want to take any chances on the day of romance. I just needed it to hurry up and arrive now!

Each day had passed by agonizingly slow, and Friday was no exception to the sluggish pace; however, it was some consolation that it had finally stopped snowing after relentlessly coming down the past couple of days. Not that it mattered at this point. At *least* two feet of snow piled up on the streets' sides, narrowing the drivable pathways to one car only. Just one more reason for career retirement!

I pushed back the chair from my desk and stood up, poking my head over the cubicle to let Abbie know I was getting ready to head out. Since the last creepy text message, she had been extra concerned and now insisted we walk to the parking lot together at day's end, and as we pushed through the outer agency door, the frigid air slapped us in the face like a frozen wet blanket. I looked up and noticed the sky beginning to darken and snow clouds starting to form once again. *Ugh.* I hated winter and the ever-present darkened sky.

Crossing the street, we talked about the plans we had for the weekend. Abbie hadn't been thrilled when I informed her of the submitted four weeks' notice, but she had gotten over it and was back to her talkative self. I walked with my head down, carefully watching where I was stepping, as ice removal didn't seem to be an agency concern. Abbie continued chattering about an upcoming vacation cruise. With my concentration focused on each potentially life-threatening step, I didn't notice when both her voice and her motion simultaneously stopped, and I continued to walk for several more seconds before realization struck. I turned around, prepared to question the sudden stop. Abbie pointed past me, and as I turned back around to look in the pointed finger's direction, I saw paper-wrapped stems tucked under the windshield wipers of my car, with the topping blood-red rose flowers leaning against the iciness on the window. A card stuck out next to the stems and lay tucked beneath the wipers as well.

I knew they weren't from Nick, and so did Abbie. With heavy feet, I walked toward the car, looking around the lot with every step. I recognized the few parked cars as belonging to coworkers, and I could see people huddled in the bus shelter, but besides those few people, there was no one else around. Abbie joining me at the car, I grabbed the card, unlocked the doors, and told her to get in. It was freezing, and I felt more protected inside my car rather than outside.

I carefully opened the envelope and pulled out a card with a red heart on the front. An additional scarlet, hand-drawn heart filled the opened card's left side; the printed words: FROM YOUR SECRET ADMIRER scrawled on the right side. Those were the only words, and there were no other clues.

My first call was to Nick. I wanted to make sure the flowers and the card weren't from him, although I already knew they weren't. He told me he was on his way even though I told him he didn't need to come, but I may as well have been talking to a brick wall at that point, and he *was* only fifteen minutes away. My next call was to Lt. Bob Chandler, who, fifteen minutes later, turned into the parking lot the same time Nick did. Nick walked up and wrapped me in his arms, and after assuring Abbie, I was now in good hands, I shooed her off.

Nick, Bob, and I stood outside, talking for a few minutes before Bob walked back to his patrol car and retrieved a plastic bag, in which he placed the flowers and the card. Nick and I agreed to meet him back at the station, and fifteen minutes later, we were all sitting around his desk where I had just been sitting a few weeks ago. Bob handed over the bag containing the flowers and the card to one of the other officers who promised to send them off to have them checked for fingerprints. There had been no threat, nor committed crime at this point, so for Bob to pull strings to have something checked for fingerprints was purely him calling in favors. Nick was frustrated and worried. I understood; so was I.

I reassured both Nick and Bob that I had put in my four-week notice. Additionally, I made a promise to have a coworker accompany me to the agency parking lot at the end of each day. To assist in alleviating Nick's concerns, Bob promised an extra patrolling officer whenever I requested one. There was nothing more to be done at this point. I just needed to make it through the next four weeks.

Driving my car back to the condo, I said silent prayers that all this new bullshit hadn't ruined Valentine's Day. Walking into the loft, both of us not saying anything, I was worried Nick was retaining a pending tirade, so my nerves were jangled as we walked through the door. I took off my coat and sat down to take off my boots. Nick did the same and then walked over and stood in front of me, reaching out with his hands and pulling me close to him. *Uh oh!*

"Lacey, I don't know what I would do if something happened to you. This shit has me worried."

I leaned in close to him, feeling his warmth. "Nick, I know. I'm pretty scared myself, but I have only four more weeks, and then I don't have to deal with this anymore." I looked up at him. "After that, my goal is to hibernate here in our place until Spring hits, so I'm not even going to be out there, out *anywhere*, without you playing my bodyguard, I promise."

It must have been enough to hear because Nick dropped the subject, although I knew he was still worried, still concerned, but, again, he was trusting my judgment, and I respected that. However, with that temporarily out of the way, I was now back to being excited for tomorrow, our first Valentine's Day as husband and wife.

It ended up being a memorable one, as perfect as I had hoped it would be. Nick and I enjoyed seeing Nicholas again, and I overate, drank a wee bit too much wine, and laughed way more than I had over the past few weeks. Nick had pulled out a beautifully wrapped, rectangle box as we sat in the "romantic corner" of the restaurant, and I opened it to see a stunning linked bracelet with a heart clasp, which Nick pulled out and hooked on my wrist.

After arriving home later, giddy and warm with wine, I changed into my newly purchased sexy items and walked into the living room to model for Nick. It wasn't until three hours later that we fell asleep, spent and gloriously tired, entangled in each other's arms and legs. So far, each of our first holidays together was everything I had hoped they would be, and even the recent events and worries were proving to be no match for the strength of the love we shared.

We would need that overpowering strength over the next few weeks; however, as the heat of our spent passion sent us off to sleep, I had no clue to what lay ahead, nor did I care at that moment.

CHAPTER 23

It had arrived! It was the Turner family graduation day. I awoke and smiled as I looked over at Nick, still sleeping, pillow laying over half of his face. I wanted to climb on top of him and take advantage of his sleepiness, to wake him in his favorite way. I looked over at the clock and immediately erased that thought from my mind. I had a *lot* to do, including the transfer of three family files to the new worker before noon, the purchase of a cake and pizza for the graduation, a stop at the office to pick up a discharge packet and to print a graduation certificate, and the submitting of paperwork for three other families. It all needed to be done before arriving at Jennifer's sister's house.

The sun was shining as I turned into the agency lot and pulled into a parking space, one that was visible to the office personnel on the second floor; they were all hyper-vigilant at this point. I admit I felt a little safer, knowing they were keeping a watchful eye on me. Abbie was on her cruise, so the office was empty of the usual cheer, and I was in and out within fifteen minutes, and yes, I had a coworker walk me back outside. Only a few more times of walking through that heavy agency door until I was a free woman, and I couldn't wait.

My busy schedule vacuumed up the hours, and soon enough, I was pulling from the pizza place with two mouth-watering cheese pizzas. I quickly stopped at the store down the street from the pizza shop to pick up a cake, chocolate with sprinkles in the frosting, per Jennifer's request, my stomach now signaling hunger due to the delightful mix of aroma.

Kendra, the family advocate, pulled into the driveway immediately after me, and together we walked to the front door. I juggled mixed feelings, with the one of bittersweetness, pushing for the lead, and I feared the possible bevy of emotions waiting behind the front door. To my delight, a family of smiling faces greeted us as the front door opened.

The mood was upbeat and immediately infectious. Jennifer Turner, her sister Karen, her other sister Kimberly, her mother Jill, and the two Turner children, had all joined together for the special event, and I quickly felt part of a joyous family reunion. I had front-row seating to a "real" *Lifetime* movie happening in my presence, and I would long hold the memory of Jennifer's laughter in my heart.

Forty-five minutes later, after Grandma Jill and Aunt Kimberly took the two young ones outside to play, I placed the hefty pile of closing paperwork on the table and watched as Jennifer penned her signature on every starred line. Last "r" inked, Jennifer put the pen down, held up a "wait a minute" finger, and disappeared through the kitchen doorway, returning one minute later with two wrapped boxes in hand. I looked at her, shaking my head.

"You know I can't accept anything from you."

Fully intent on ignoring me, Jennifer first placed one of the wrapped boxes in front of Kendra and then set the other one on the table in front of me.

"Lacey, what are they going to do? Are they going to fire you if they find out?"

Well, she had a point. I had no plan on remaining a social worker or renewing my license, and my acceptance of the gift seemed of vital importance to Jennifer. Kendra and I unwrapped the presents simultaneously; hers was a beautiful white soft scarf with matching gloves. After lifting the lid from my unwrapped gift, I removed the framed picture of Jennifer and her children as emotion began to make its way up my throat. Below the photo was writing.

Thank you for pointing me in the right direction, but allowing me to discover on my own.

I felt the lump travel upward, and my eyes started to water. Those seventeen words held more meaning than any precious stone, and Jennifer Turner didn't realize what she had just gifted me. I stood and walked over to her, after which we hugged, but before emotions overtook us entirely, I chuckled, telling her that I desperately needed some cake. Apparently, two hungry little bellies needed some, too, as evidenced by their noisy arrival back into the kitchen.

I *felt* it before I *heard* it; something wasn't right. The doorbell rang, and we all exchanged looks. I believe, at that moment, we all sensed who stood outside that door. Jennifer's sister, Karen, arose from the table to walk toward the front door as it opened without invitation. Jack Turner! Making a bad situation worse, Jack was drunk, or high, or something. He walked, or more like stumbled, down the hallway toward us where we stood immobile with disbelief; however, I was immobile only for a moment.

In less than ten seconds from Jack's entry through the front door, I was up from my chair and situated in front of the family before he made it to the table. Kendra had the phone held to her ear, already calling for help. Jennifer's mother was yelling at Jack to "get out of the house," but it was Jennifer's voice that succeeded in rising to the highest decibel.

The rage, the pent-up anger, the hurt and the frustration, spewed from her mouth like an active volcano, finally erupting after an extended period of dormancy. Jack Turner's smug smile only added fuel to the pending combustion. Everybody was on their feet now, and Jack turned his full attention to his "soon-to-be" ex-wife. One of Jennifer's sisters steered the children toward their bedroom, fearing what could occur.

Jill, Jennifer's mother, had been standing on the other side of the table; however, when Jack took another step toward Jennifer, she sprang into action and moved toward her daughter. Jennifer stopped her with the abrupt loudness of her voice.

"Mom, stop right there!"

Jack took another step toward Jennifer. "Well, well, well. How's the slut of the year?" I've been watching you, you stupid whore. Just letting you know, I'm going to take care of that new guy you've been talking to, bitch!"

Jennifer stood her ground. The stink, the heaviness of the alcohol Jack was emitting, filled the room, and my heart thumped heavily in my chest.

Jack took another step toward his ex-wife and then stopped, looking at each of us. "I've been watching *all* of you."

He stopped his gaze at me, and a grin appeared on his face. "Ah, Lacey Coleman." He put his hands over his mouth and laughed. "Oops, my bad, I mean, Lacey *Atwood*."

Jack turned and took a step toward me. I could see Jennifer *also* step toward me, and I reached my arm back to stop her as I heard sirens nearing in the distance.

Jack's breath hit me as he continued his alcoholic rant. "I've been watching *you* especially, Lacey, but I'm sure you're aware of this. You know everything, don't you? You're the bitch who ruined my family, the one who told my wife and kids to hate me."

Jack took another step toward me. Jennifer moved, and before I could stop her, she positioned herself in front of me at the exact moment that Jack lifted his arm, his balled fist at the end of it, and swung. It happened over a few seconds, but it seemed like it lasted longer, as everything suddenly changed to slow-motion. *This* time Jack Turner didn't stumble in his drunken stupor. I reached up as soon as I saw Jack's arm rising and pushed Jennifer back, right before his fist hit me in the face. When they say, "you see stars," they mean it! I vaguely remember the door bursting open and police officers rushing in, tackling Jack as I went down. Down and *out*.

According to everyone there, I was out for only several seconds; I don't know. I *do* know that when I opened my eyes again, I was still on the floor. I watched as two officers led Jack, still yelling, out in handcuffs. Jennifer, her mother, and her sister, Karen, were all crying. Kendra was attempting to bribe the Turner children outside with some cake. Lt. Bob Chandler stood talking on his radio, and I could hear more sirens in the distance, nearing. I tried to sit up, but Bob put out his hand for me to stay still.

"You're going to have one hell of a shiner there, Lacey."

I laid my head back down and looked at him. "I'm really okay. Can I please sit up?"

He shook his head. "Not till they check you out."

The siren stopped wailing, and two paramedics soon hovered over me, taking my vitals, checking me over for broken bones. I reassured them the only thing hurting at that moment was my eye where Jack's fist had connected. The front door opened again, and ten seconds later, Nick knelt next to me, just in time to help me up, and then back down as a wave of dizziness swept over. Bob and the paramedics all advised a trip to the hospital for x-rays, and I finally relented, but only if Nick was permitted to drive me there. The paramedics weren't thrilled; however, my stubbornness prevailed, and Bob assured us that he would have my car returned to our condo. I needed to talk to Jennifer first.

Jennifer was a wreck. What was supposed to be a memorable day for her had turned into a disaster. Sitting across from each other at the kitchen table, I noticed the tension filling her face. She looked drained.

I smiled. "Do I look that bad?"

She nodded her head. "Your eye is already swelling up, Lacey."

I reached across the table and took her hands in mine. "Jennifer, listen to me. Do *not* let this get in the way of anything. Jack won't be bothering you anymore. He'll probably be going away for quite some time, and I'm going to be okay." I squeezed her hands and smiled again. "I am so proud of how you handled this whole thing!" I reached up and wiped the tears streaming down her cheeks. "No more crying!"

She looked up at me and took a deep breath. "Will I see you again before your last day of work?"

Nodding, I promised I would stop by in a few days to check up on things.

Nick walked back into the kitchen and smiled at Jennifer. "I hear you were one heck of a brave lady."

She turned bright red. I looked up at Nick and then back at Jennifer.

"No, she's not brave, she's *fearless*, and I couldn't be prouder."

Besides the dizziness, I felt fine. Nick drove me to the hospital, where we sat for what seemed like hours. Well, it actually *was* hours before the doctor walked back into the room, proclaiming clear x-rays and no broken bones. A prescription for pain medication accompanied me home, as the redness around my eye had started turning a variety of colors, and the swelling continued to increase. Sitting in that emergency room, I concluded that the *only* way I would remain at work for two weeks longer was if I could stay office bound.

First, I didn't want clients asking me thousands of questions, and I knew that would happen. Secondly, I just didn't want to be out in the field anymore. While it was a relief knowing I was now out of danger, it had still been a highly traumatic week. I called my supervisor during the wait for the doctor's signature on the release paperwork, and she reassured me that no more home visits were in my future. Frankly, it wouldn't have mattered at that point if she hadn't agreed; I just wouldn't have returned.

There was now *no* doubt in my mind, or in anyone else's, that Jack Turner was behind the text messages, the flowers, and the card. He had said it right in the kitchen earlier, he had been "watching" all of us, especially me, and he blamed me for his loss of family. I was relieved that it was over, this time for real! Bob called Nick while we were in the hospital and assured him that Jack wouldn't be seeing anything but jail walls for quite some time. He had amassed several charges, including violating a restraining order, trespassing, breaking and entering, and assault.

I shared my decision to remain office-bound with Nick and watched as relief fell over his face. Quite frankly, I was just as relieved, and as we drove from the hospital, I reached over, grabbed his hand, and said a silent prayer that the day hadn't ended up any worse than it had. All bad behind us, now only "good" ahead!

Chapter 24

I intended to depart the agency and my career with an amassed unused vacation day payout, so I planned to use only two sick days to recuperate before returning to the office. Those forty-eight hours allowed Nick plenty of time to nurture and take care of me, and I couldn't have asked for a better caretaker. He had his hands full, switching me from the couch to the bed and then back again, meanwhile keeping me stocked with ice packs to keep the swelling down. Lt. Bob Chandler called to check on my recovery and let me know that Jennifer Turner had filed her Incident Report and added that he would let me know how they were doing.

I slept on and off those two days, and I had mixed feelings when I heard the alarm sound Thursday morning. It would have been *so* easy for me to turn off the alarm and return to sleep. We didn't need the money, and I had already finished my social work career in my mind. However, I *needed* to complete the two weeks to make a "clean" break. I *needed* a sense of finality. There was another reason I grudgingly left the bed that morning.

I'm very aware of the pressure that a replacement social worker experiences. If important matters are left a mess or unresolved, it's the families that suffer, and after reminding myself of that, I convinced myself I could last two more weeks. Nick was up and ready with a cup of coffee and a plate of bacon when I emerged from the bathroom, thirty-minutes later. I had spent ten minutes staring at the messed-up face reflected at me in the mirror. I could hardly believe it was me; makeup was *not* going to cover all those colors!

Finishing my coffee, Nick told me he was taking me out to dinner after my day was complete, black eye or not, and I was okay with it. As long as I was with Nick, it didn't matter how bad my eye looked.

I kissed him once more before walking into the hallway. "Thanks for putting up with me, Nick."

He pulled me nearer and shook his head. "*Somebody* has to do it."

I closed the door with a "smartass!" directed back at him over my shoulder and headed out for my last ten days as a social worker.

Everyone in the office was aware of what happened, and the workday morning seemed to be nothing less than a seemingly endless parade of people coming over to "check the damage" and dole out numerous hugs. Office management even treated everyone to pizza for lunch, and that alone, resulted in multiple "thanks for the pizza" comments jokingly directed my way.

Lt. Bob Chandler telephoned just as I returned to my desk from the lunchroom, where I had devoured two pieces of grease-laden, drippy-cheese pizza. He had just left the Turner home and wanted to let me know they were doing okay. He also informed me that he had my bracelet. I looked down at my wrist and gasped. I hadn't realized it had fallen off. I told Bob I would be leaving the office around 4 p.m., and if he wanted to, I could meet him in the agency parking lot. That "works for me," he said. I'm surprised Nick hadn't noticed the missing bracelet, but maybe he had and just didn't want to add any more stress.

The paperwork went quicker than I expected, and I finished early. It was only 3:30 p.m., and all that remained on the day's schedule was for the supervisor to approve my last assessments. I sat with Abbie for a few minutes, scrolling through her cruise photos. I would miss her more than anything else, and we had committed to scheduling monthly "catch-up" dates. Returning to my desk, I looked at the clock again; 3:45 p.m. I couldn't wait any longer. I just wanted to get back to Nick and preparations for our dinner date, so after sending Abbie the "peace out" sign over the partition, I headed down the steps.

It was still freezing, and flakes were, once again, starting to fall from the muted-gray sky. *Ugh.* I pulled my coat closer around me as I walked across the snow-covered street into the parking lot, watching my every step so I didn't go falling on my ass. The parking lot had been full this morning, so I had to park in one of the back spaces to which I now headed. At first, I attempted to ignore the uneasy feeling, chalking it up to some minor post-traumatic stress; however, the familiar twinge of "something isn't right" seemed relentless in its attachment. I breathed deeply and silently scolded myself. *No more boogieman, Lacey! Breathe! Everything is fine now!*

I stuck a mitten-covered hand into my coat pocket and pulled out my keys. Nearing the car and only five feet away, I lifted the remote and pointed it forward, my finger hovering above the unlock button when I felt a shift of air. I heard something, someone, and I froze in place as I *felt* the presence, and immediately after, *smelled* the presence behind me. The smell of skunky, cheap weed hit me as I first turned my head, and then my entire self, around.

A man stood facing me, clothed in worn baggy pants and a dirt-covered hoodie. His hair hung long and appeared to have not met a brush in some time. He stood with one hand deep in his pocket. Clenched tightly in his other hand, he held what appeared to be a piece of paper or a picture of some sort.

"Hi, Lacey."

His hand emerged from his pocket and, emerging with it, a small knife, which he now slightly lifted so I would see. He opened his mouth to speak, his breath reeking and his body odor almost succeeding in causing me to gag; I could smell *both* over the few feet of distance.

"Just don't yell or anything, and everything will be okay. I'm not going to hurt you." I could tell he was high on something. His words slurred, and his eyes were glassy.

"I just want to talk to you."

My stomach turned.

I recognized him as one of our friendly neighborhood "using" drug dealers. I didn't know his name, but I had often seen him hanging out at the edge of the parking lot, back by the trees in one of the druggie "hot spots." We had called the police, reporting him and the others several times, but it never worked. They would leave for a few weeks, just to return a few days later.

I mustered up a half-grin. *Keep it cool, Lacey.* Bob would be pulling into the lot any moment. I prayed he would, at least. The guy lifted his arm and turned the picture around, lifting it out toward me. It was one of the photos Nick had taken of me during one of our photoshoots. I was fully dressed and sticking my tongue out at Nick behind the camera. It was my favorite one, well, it had been my favorite one, until now. *How did he get that?* He stepped toward me, and I took another step back, not breaking eye contact.

He continued to speak and was undoubtedly high on something more potent than weed. "I was standing right over there a couple of months ago," He pointed toward the trees at the back of the parking lot. "You were walking to your car, and it was really windy, remember? I really think you wanted me to find the picture."

I remembered that day. My appointment book had flown open, and the photos Nick had snuck into my book had flown everywhere. I remember thinking I had picked them all up. Guess not. I looked around the parking lot and saw no one. *Come on, Bob!*

He took another step toward me.

I shook my head at him. "Listen, there's going to be a cop pulling into this place any second now."

He chuckled and then spent a few seconds in a coughing fit before shooting a wad of phlegm from between his lips to the pavement below. "I don't believe you."

I wrapped my fingers around my keys and felt for the little canister of mace hanging from the key ring. *Thank you, Nick!* I didn't move as he continued to talk, and my goal was now to keep him calm until Bob arrived.

He started to cry and began talking faster. "I actually think I love you, Lacey. I know you probably don't think you could ever be happy with someone like me, but I can take care of you. I tried to let you know how I felt by sending you messages. Hell, I even bought you flowers. Not even a thank you!"

My stomach flipped as another coughing bout ensued, followed by another slimy wad hitting the pavement at his feet. "The one day you walked past me, and I asked how you were doing, and you said you were doing good. You smiled at me, remember? And right then, I knew you were interested in me. I figured you knew it was me texting you all the time."

I had a difficult time processing everything he was saying. All I knew was that I finally saw Bob's patrol car pulling up to the corner light, and I also knew that he would have no way of knowing what was happening as the bus-stop shelter obscured any vision. I shook my head and again looked up at the man's face.

I spoke calmly. "Listen, I don't want anyone to get hurt, and you *will* get hurt if the police officer pulls in and sees you are holding a knife, so please just put it down."

He started to cry harder, shaking his head. "This is just a pocket-knife. I always carry it around with me. I love you, and I could never hurt you."

I saw the light turn green, and the squad car turned the corner. *Stall him, Lacey.*

"Listen, I know you're probably a really nice guy, and maybe I can help you figure things out."

The cruiser turned into the parking lot and went out of sight for a moment as it passed the other parked cars. The man's back was to the drivable path, so he didn't see the squad car as it came into view. I looked past his shoulder as inconspicuously as possible and continued to speak calmly. Bob had stopped driving and was assessing the situation. I lifted my hand to brush some hair from my face and slightly shook my head, maintaining eye contact with the man at every moment.

"Listen, I know this time of year can be difficult." I attempted a half-laugh and then continued speaking. "My black-eye is the perfect example of that."

I saw a brief second of clarity flit across his face, while in the near distance, I watched Bob open his car door and lift his gun in our direction.

The man's words came out blurred as the crying intensified. "Wow, Lacey. Who did that to you? Did that new husband of yours hurt you? Do you want me to …?"

A loud voice halted him mid-sentence. "DON'T MOVE!!"

The man turned his head toward Bob, and I prepared to hear shots fired or for him to lunge at Bob or me or something. Two more squad cars turned into the lot, sirens blazing. Looking back-and-forth between Bob, me, and the approaching officers, he appeared to be at a loss as to what was happening.

Their guns pointing, the officers simultaneously yelled, "PUT YOUR HANDS UP!"

Looking back at me, the man began to shake his head back and forth. "I'm sorry. I just really love you."

My heart raced as I nodded my head and lifted my hands. "Listen, please just hold up your hands, and we can get you some help."

And, he did. He lifted his hands just like I asked. Bob, and his fellow officers, rushed him, pushing him to the ground as he continued to cry, repeating the same mantra over and over. "I just love her. I just want to be her boyfriend."

Bob walked toward me, shaking his head while the other officers hand-cuffed and then escorted the man over to the cruiser. "Are you okay, Lacey?"

I'm pretty sure I was in shock, and I started laughing, shaking my head. "It wasn't Jack Turner, after all, Bob. It was *him*. He admitted to sending the text messages, the flowers, the card, all of it!"

Bob's eyes widened, and his mouth dropped open a bit. "He said he did all that?"

I shook my head and laughed again. "All of it!"

Bob had me sit in the back of the squad car while he wrote the report. He asked if I wanted him to call Nick. I asked him not to. I just wanted to go home.

The supervisor and director walked over to the parking lot, and I spoke with them before heading back to my car. I was done. I was done with the job. I was done with the career. I was done with pulling into that parking lot ever again, and that's exactly what I told them. They could keep my vacation pay if they had to, and I told them I would call any client they wanted me to call. I would walk through everything with the new social worker if need be, but I *was done!* They understood.

Everyone left the parking lot. The other squad cars left to deliver the man to the station, and my supervisor and director went back to the office. As Bob walked me back to my car, it all caught up to me, the entire fucked-up week, and as I turned to thank him for everything, the tears arrived.

Asking me if I needed a hug, Bob reached out his arms, and I willingly accepted.

"Bob, thank you so much. That is two times this week you've come to my rescue."

He looked up at me and smiled, holding out his hand. "Just doing my duty, ma'am."

My bracelet dangled from his fingers, and I reached up, taking it from him, clasping it tightly in my hand as I entered my car and rolled down my window.

"You sure you're okay to drive, Lacey?"

I nodded my head as I turned the key in the ignition. Nick and I owe you a dinner or two, or ten, so we'll be in touch with you, Bob."

He smiled and shook his head. "No need for that. Well, unless you are talking about a visit to Nicholas in Little Italy. You may be able to convince me to agree to that."

I laughed. "You got it!"

Pulling from the parking lot, I began to drive down the street but didn't make it too far before having to pull over. Adrenaline had set in, and I needed to do some deep breathing before continuing the drive back to the loft. I saw the blinking blue light of a text message from inside my purse. Panic filled every beat of my heart, and only after several minutes was I able to press the button. It was Nick. **Where are you??**

Needing to hear his voice immediately, I picked up the phone and ordered it to "dial Nick." His voice was like music to my ears.

"Lacey, where are you? You were supposed to be home an hour ago?"

I felt the tears begin to fall. "Nick, maybe we should just stay in tonight."

Concern laced his voice back through the phone. "Lacey, what's going on? Are you alright?"

I wiped the tears from my cheek and smiled, despite his ability to see it. "I am now, but *boy*, do I have a story to tell you."

Nick replied, "As long as you're okay, Lacey. I also have some news to tell you."

My heart and pulse eventually returned to a semi-normal rate, and after a couple more minutes of deep breathing, I turned the key and began the drive back home.

Twenty-five minutes later, I walked through the condo door where my handsome husband stood, clad in jeans and a t-shirt, barefoot, with a glass of wine in hand and a smile on his face. I dropped my purse on the floor, not even taking the time to remove my coat before rushing over to him. One look into my eyes was enough for him to know something serious had happened, and after placing the wine glass on the table, he led me over to the couch. Nick silently sat as I told him what happened. He was shocked, concerned, and thankful, and I patiently listened as he processed each of those emotions with me.

I turned to him after he had finished speaking. "Nick, I can't go back to work. I'm done. I told them they could keep all the vacation pay or earned time I had left. I hope you don't mind. I just can't do it, and if I have to, I'll just get another part-time job or something."

Nick put his hands on each side of my face and stared at me. "Are you crazy? There is no way you're getting another job anytime soon, Lacey!" He continued, "I have some news to tell *you*. Are you ready for it?" Not thinking there was anything left that could possibly shock me, I shook my head in the affirmative. *Oh, Lacey. One of these days, you will learn.*

"Katt Morgan called me earlier today. Joe had another heart attack two days ago, and they've had some pretty intense discussions, all resulting in the same conclusion; managing all the hotels is too much for him anymore. The Morgans have offered us a once-in-a-lifetime opportunity, Lacey. They have offered us a fifty-fifty partnership of the Fantasy Play Hotel™ in Charleston, provided we agree to be in-house managers. What do you think?"

CHAPTER 25

I went over and visited Jennifer Turner and her family, as I promised. Before leaving, I removed my silver, peace-sign necklace and draped it over Jennifer's neck, telling her to take care of it until I saw her again. She would be okay. The "friend" she had been talking to had magically turned into "boyfriend," and he had even talked Jennifer into co-leading the youth group at the church they attended.

Jack Turner received a two- to five-year sentence for the charges he had accumulated. My parking-lot stalker, drug dealer, Matt Denardo, was already on probation before the recent arrest. Lt. Bob Chandler informed me that he would serve one year before being ordered for psychiatric and drug treatment. The ensuing investigation led to the discovery that my former agency's janitor was Denardo's best friend, and a drug addict. In exchange for an endless supply from Denardo, the janitor was accessing my personal files and passing the information to him. He plea-bargained down to a twenty-four-month sentence.

Lt. Bob Chandler and his girlfriend enjoyed a no-holds-barred, order-anything-you-want dinner at Nicholas's restaurant a few weeks later. We sat around for hours, laughing, and sharing stories, surrounded by love and friendship.

Joe and Katt Morgan hired a couple of new consultants to help get the latest hotel up and running in California, as well as to take some of the hands-on business off their plates. Katt is currently working on a new book. Joe is "taking it easy" and enjoying days at the poolside, as well as doing some woodworking, something he said he always wanted to do. Nick and I had shared a laugh at the idea of Joe doing woodworking, but you know, they say you shouldn't judge a book by its cover. Joe and Katt sounded fantastic during the conference call when Nick and I telephoned them with our answer to their generous offer.

Yes, we took the offer. Nick will continue his photography but as a secondary career. Mark Santauri was ecstatic when he found out we were moving down there. As for me, well, I'm looking forward to learning the ropes of running a five-star "specialty" hotel. I've also been doing a lot of thinking about passion and what mine truly is, and I think I may have figured it out the other day while re-reading the introduction to *Fantasy Play 101*; it's writing. Spidey-sense, gut-feeling, or whatever you want to call it, I have a feeling that there will be plenty of fascinating "tales to tell" awaiting in the Fantasy Play Hotel™. Are you game? See "ya" all in Charleston!

The End

ABOUT THE AUTHOR

Jodie Jamison resides in a quaint little Northeast town where she enjoys creating characters and storylines that her readers can vicariously relate to. Jodie believes that romance and sexual play can be delightfully intertwined and intends for the reader to experience a relatable sense of adventurous curiosity when reading her novels.

I hope you enjoyed your time in
FANTASY PLAY HOTEL™ / ATWOOD.COLEMAN II
Please don't forget to leave a review.
Thank you.

Made in the USA
Las Vegas, NV
16 June 2022

50309508R10125